I0634648

RECALL

The Sigma Code Chronicles
BOOK ONE

JW BELL

INDIES UNITED PUBLISHING HOUSE, LLC

ISBN: 978-1-64456-480-6

Library of Congress Control Number: 2022938076

INDIES UNITED PUBLISHING HOUSE, LLC
P.O. BOX 3071
QUINCY, IL 62305-3071
indiesunited.net

Acknowledgements

*I would like to acknowledge Jayne Southern, my editor,
whose guidance was so professional and
knowledgeable, the best editor ever.*

Dedication

*I dedicate this work to my children, who put up with my
constant disappearance in order to write and endured
their dad's blank stares and dumb looks while he
figured plot twists in his head.*

This above all; to thine own self be true.

William Shakespeare

CHAPTER ONE

Exhausted from the workout, she had trouble thinking. Even her muscles betrayed her as those in her hands and arms continued to wave a combat knife that wasn't there, a stab, a slice with the imaginary edge. Everything was automatic. The woman shuffled into the room, collapsed onto her bed, and lay in the dark, too sore to move. She'd trained in secret for weeks and her progress astounded her. Her confidence now that of a killer, lethal with weapons of all kinds. Not like before.

The bright of day would shine in about an hour, and it was time to sleep would her body let her? Muscles screamed and cramped, arms and legs spasmed. She labored to breathe.

What kept her at it was blood: then and that yet to come.

They don't remember me – that was clear to her – and being brutally honest, I don't care if the one who raped me remembers.

A flash of that memory shot through her mind: pain, the humiliation of being taken from behind, not even seeing his face, the noise of slaughter around her. Something to be endured, she brushed it away as part of life.

She intended to kill him, even if she had to kill them both, even the one to whom she'd grown close. She'd do it too.

But, she reminded herself, his death would not be for the rape. But for what came afterward. The death. Benjamin. My little Benji.

She blinked quickly before her eyes betrayed her. My baby! Benjamin. My little Benji.

Benji. She had to think of something else. Quickly. My training, that will do, it will enable me to …

She grabbed the air above her as though it was her knife and sharpened the imaginary blade. She loved knife combat. Knives were so hard to master, but tonight things had turned.

Several times her knife ended up in the right place.

All I needed was a bit more force and I'd have killed … she held it up and stared down the edge, at the smooth gleam. They say it feels like stabbing an overripe watermelon, slightly resistant at first, then slides in.

She pantomimed a stab to someone's gut and repeated it several times, each action slow and deliberate, a twist of the wrist at the end of the thrust. The effect was electrifying each time.

Yes. I'll kill that son-of-a-bitch. I'll kill that son-of-a-bitch. I'll …

She dozed, the thought of sliding a knife into him a constant replay.

CHAPTER TWO

The flickerin' in the hearth did nothin' against the night, but I didn't need no help noway. This was my woman's place an' I knowed where everything was. Been sneakin' in here fer almost a year. We'd cozy up an' hump. I'd fall asleep after, an' then git up afore first light 'cause we din't want the Masta ta know.

The smell of Shannie's collards, greens an' neck bone hung all over the cabin, an' my mouth watered good. Maybe there'd be some leavins.

I tiptoed ovah ta the table an' took a gander. A extra plate was a layin' there. First, I thought maybe Shannie put it out fo me, but as I got closer, I see the food on it already been eat.

An' what else? That prime neck bone sat there, ne'er been touched. Now, who in hell would do that? Shannie's neck bone was the bes' part.

I stood there a scratchin' my head an' then another smell in the air tol' me what's goin' on – Masta's pipe smoke was a hangin' stale in the air.

My eyes eased my head up ta the loft, seein' if I had sight a him ruttin' up there, but nothin' come ta me 'cept flickerin' shadows.

"What you doin' here, boy?"

I jumped and turned. Masta stood 'hind me, an' I almost losed it in my drawers.

"This ain't yer shack. Now you better git on away, Fox Boy." His laughter cut the room like a old knife aguttin' a fish. "That piece of ass up theah," he nodded to the loft, "Shannie, she's prime, but only foah her Masta. She's even light 'nough ta pass fer white." He pointed the stem of his clay pipe at me. "Ain't nothin' here foah ya, boy." Masta walked ta the fire and lit a taper.

"An' you keep from my missus too."

At mention of the Mistress, I seen her face afloatin' in my mind, plain as if afore me, curly red hair, the pale skin white like 'baster an' strange eyes, one blue, one green.

"Young buck. You stay far from my women. Don't come 'round 'em at all."

The light from the wick-stick shined off his deep, black eyes as he sucked that fire inta his pipe. Pale-blue smoke billowed 'round his silver-white hair so much, I had trouble tellin' 'xactly where his beard ended an' the smoke cloud took over. But the cloud never cover his eyes.

He stare at me with the calm face of uncaring death.

"Ya ain't gone yet, boy? You smarter than that. You cunnin' like a fox, always have been, even as a young buck. S'why I named you Fox Boy." He puffed a coupla times, smoke arollin' from his mouth like he was chewin' on a cloud. "You go on now."

Holdin' his pipe with his teeth he screamed, "Git!" Then he run over an' slapped me. My ears rang so bad I heerd nothin'. Then another slap. "I tol' ya."

I wanted to git away, but Shannie. I din' wanna jus' leave her. She mah woman. My eyes shot ta the loft an' seen Shannie's eyes a shinin' in the light, starin' at me, seein' Masta beat me.

I tried ta bust free, ta run, but ta do that I'd have ta hit him. An' if'n I hit Masta ...

Mah eyes jiggled at the next slap. His boot found my leg, an' I fell. It was hard ta breathe. He'd kicked my tally-whacker an' balls. Two more kicks, one in mah ribs, an' t'other in mah whacker makin' me puke. I tried ta roll an' keep from the kicks, but his knee dropped onta mah neck, trappin' the puke halfway up, burnin'. Then somethin' pop.

"Awrw! My scream come out wrong. My fingers grabbed at mah throat, tryin' ta breathe, but …. "Awrw." It was a whimper.

His hands push mine ta the side, grab mah neck, an' I think he squeezed, but I don't 'member.

'Cause that's when I died.

CHAPTER THREE

I sat in the cab, my stare straight through the window at the traffic, complete with a jack-hammer construction crew and the occasional honk of impatient assholes. I'd caught the cab outside the hospital when they released me. The cabby insisted that the air conditioning was on full blast, but my shirt was soaked and sweat drew lines down my temples.

I scratched my head like a goofball and pondered the glaring question in my mind – why? Why did this memory have to be one in which I died? Lord knows, out of all the lives that drifted through me, wanted or not, surely there was something better than that. I mean, if I have to recall a murder, why couldn't it be one in which I was the killer, instead of the victim? Surely there were some back there tucked in the ether.

For that matter, why do I remember any of them at all? Especially since my memory doesn't stretch far enough to include anything that's happened to me this time around. Well, okay, I hedged a little there. There should be but a few things rolling around inside the noodle since I woke up a few months ago. Evidently, I remembered how to speak English. I remembered how to eat, and dress, and all of those little handy things we all do every day. I'm handicapped in recall, along the lines of what happened to me before the day I woke up last September.

I pulled out my ID card and glanced at it again. The name on it was Stanton, Wilburn B. Stanton. My brain agreed with the name. It floats around in the foggiest of memories, and I gave that name to the hospital for a temporary ID card. It had floated in and out of my memory like a ghost for days before I visited the office of the people who make it official.

I still don't know what the B. stands for, Beaufort maybe, but naw ... didn't feel right. The last cop I worked for said it was probably Buttwipe. Didn't sound right at the time. Still doesn't. Nothing sounded right, except plain B.

The sweat on my forehead really poured, so I wiped it with my arm while I rubbernecked, wondering how much time I had before everything busted loose. Something was about to get my attention, and there was only one way to know what it would be. That was the pattern.

First, a memory comes slogging through my mind letting me know to be on the alert, like today. Then came the mystery. Usually, the memory gives me something of a clue, but somehow, I don't think there's any slave murders that need investigating. Not in the middle of the Bronx anyway.

I caught my reflection in the cab window, and it still wasn't right. The tough guy in my head, Hank, the man I was during World War II, a Brit commando in the Special Service Brigade, describes me as a pencil-necked little prick with small, ratty eyes, and lips that belong on a whore. The last cop I worked with said my lips were too big, eyes too small, and my body in general, although trim and somewhat toned, made everyone I met want to kick the shit out of me.

Personally, I didn't much care for my appearance either, but what the hell. We can't all be six feet tall with dark hair and a dimple in our chin. I'd've preferred to be well hung too, but life didn't agree. Average, short hair, no dimple, and well, average.

This life has been crazy as shit. Most are about priorities. The big priority I've been working on has been figuring out why I can't remember the things from this time around, but I can remember things from other turns around the block, so to speak.

Crazy, huh?

My eyes switched focus, no longer using the window a mirror, but to see things beyond the glass. I watched the working girls lining the street as they did their usual thing, plied their trade: showing underwear, stockings and garters, jiggling and shaking everything they had.

The parade of pros hitting the street didn't titillate me,

though. It reminded me of the late hour.

Sweat dribbled into my eye and stung like a bitch. After a rub on my damp sleeve, I glanced up. The freeway traffic overhead was the usual mob free-for-all, but by the burned orange color of the sky, sunlight would be gone before most of these girls would make a buck on their backs.

The cab muffled the screams, but I heard them anyway. I turned back to the whores. Two were in a fight that had top billing for the rest, except one.

The girl who stood in front of round one ignored them, but she did appear to be for hire, well almost. A couple of things didn't fit. She dressed too nicely – not enough skin, costume not tarty enough, her make-up too tasteful. Oh, she had the stuff on her face with jarring colors, but not thick enough for the street. Way too fancy, too expensive, and she was too old, not used-up enough. There she was though, walking right in front of me, hooking.

Then it made sense. I beat on the Plexiglas divider, "Stop the cab!"

The screech of the tires gave me no warning at all before the plastic safety divider smacked me in the face, almost busting my skinny-assed nose. It was there for his safety, not mine. A couple more hits like that and my face would be rugged as hell. I fumbled at the door handle as my eyes watered like a four-year-old's after a spanking but finally, the door opened.

The shot came as I stepped out, and right in front of me, I saw the girl drop, her head mangled and bloody.

Holy shit.

In two steps, I stood over her, my bowels about to go loose on me. Holy shit! I hadn't known she would be shot.

There was a whole lot I didn't know. In fact, the only thing I did know about this whole mess made my legs shake and my bladder want to let go: her face. Before the bullet mangled it, she was the image of Shannie.

I stood there with a mess at my feet. Everyone ran away or

dropped to the ground, and my mind whirred. By then, the 'holy shit' thought had stopped its ricochet through my skull, and my mind had taken up another mantra – now what?

"Stop! Hands where I can see 'em, and don't move." The voice pierced my ears like a mutt's howl through a foggy night. Somebody grabbed me, spun me around, and slammed me down onto the ground. I was dizzy as shit, not to mention the magnificent thump that happened as he so nicely laid me down on the concrete. The voice repeated its demand, "Don't move."

Of course, now that I understood, I did as asked. Silly of me not to realize the voice might have belonged to the police. Besides, now that I'd run out of the cab faster than a teenager about to pop his cherry, I remembered the bullet. Before it killed ol' girl here, it had to have come out of somebody's gun.

I ran my hand over my buzz cut: Wilburn B. you are a stupid, stupid, dumbass.

Everyone who hid a few minutes earlier now stepped cautiously forward, vying for a better glimpse at the mess. Sirens filled the air, the sounds attack me from all directions, like the red, blue, and white strobe lights that hurt my eyes.

Yup. A dumbass, old chap.

Thanks.

I heard snatches of conversation from the growing crowd making the same assessment as good old Hank, plus they stared at me.

This is definitely shaping up to whatever the Fox Boy and Shannie memory had been prepping me for.

"Aw, crap." This voice sailed over all the caterwauling, and of course, I recognized the voice as different from the one that demanded I stretch skyward and lie down at the same time. I didn't need to view the speaker to know to whom the new voice belonged. That strong Brooklyn accent … I mean a dog knows the smell of another dog's butt. The high regard this officer had for me showed in the disgust that dripped from his next phrase, "It's Buttwipe." The last cop that

I'd worked with.

"Officer, uh, uh—" I'd forgotten the name, and started to stammer.

"Detective," the new voice corrected, "Nancy."

That's the name! How the hell did I forget that?

Hank, the tough guy, always had a ball with the name: Nancy man, Nancy prance, Nancy the wanker, a bunch of mean things. Things I was always glad only my ears heard. Otherwise,

I'd get beat up or sued. Hank was a prick. Hell, he was a prick when he was alive, even more so now.

I ignored the buttwipe name and turned and calmly asked, "What's going on?"

"What the hell do you mean, what's ... get, get up. No. Put your hands on your head and—"

"Can I move out of all this mess first?"

"Hell, yeah. Move outta that mess, and get your buttwipe self over here, away from her.

That's right. Now turn 'round."

Nancy spent about twenty seconds shaking me around like a dish towel, I guess to rattle some sense into me. Then he led me off to the side, out of the way of what was about to become a circus.

The whore's faces all showed disgust, not so much at the violence, more at the loss of wages because of all the police activity. This would cut into their prime-time evening trade. Oh, they'd probably talk one or more of the officers into dallying a little later on, and then there'd be the creepy johns (those turned on by the violence), but for a while, business would be flaccid.

"So," says Nancy the Dick, "After the last case, I was hoping I'd never see ya' again." With a pull on my elbow, he turned me around. The first sight of his face convinced me he wanted to punch my nose hard enough to move it from where it was, to somewhere on my right cheek. "I came off like an asshole."

"Well, Nancy, that may have been my fault, I mean if I hadn't screamed ... but we can't change that now. Maybe you can admire it this way. You're an asshole, and I'm a buttwipe. Kind of poetic, huh? Maybe we're related." I opened my beady little eyes as wide as possible (probably only succeeded in making their bearing more like small, steely marbles) and stared at him, pretending I was Hank.

It didn't work. Sometimes I can do it, sometimes not.

Nancy's eyes dripped loathing, and he clenched his teeth so hard that it manifested as though he was in the middle of a really rough bowel movement. "Okay, we're both a couple of jerks."

He dropped his head in thought, and I saw through his thinning hair to his scalp. I caught a chuckle before anything came out.

The sight reminded me of my life in the fourteen hundreds as Brother Mick, a monk with a shaved pate. If you discounted the self-flagellation, the horribly uncomfortable gonads (after a few years, I grew used to that part) and the extreme mood swings of the Abbot, that life had been wonderful. The mental focus I achieved had been spectacular.

Did Nancy have a focus like that? I rubbed my head. "Hey, Nancy?"

"Yeah."

"You get laid much?"

His laugh was a slow, purposeful rumble through his chest, almost a growl. "Naw," he answered. "And I know damned well you don't either. A couple of horny little detectives." He nodded, his teeth shining.

Why did it remind me of a growling wolf?

"Only one problem with that," I retorted, and he raised an eyebrow. "Only one of us is a detective, Nancy."

His face threatened to explode through his eyeballs; before it did, I added, "All I do is remember what I'm not supposed to know and forget everything I should be able to know."

After a couple of seconds of him chewing the air while his mind deciphered what I'd said, Nancy calmed down. Well, enough so that his eyes sank back into their usual position. He draped an arm around my shoulders and guided me back to the crime scene. On the way, I caught the drift of a delicate perfume, but then a bus rumbled by and the diesel exhaust it farted out prevented any whiffs of anything – perfume, blood, or carnage. At least I didn't feel like puking.

I focused down on her. Grisly as it was, the smell didn't accent the visual and I controlled myself. Poor old, faceless Shannie look-a-like.

"You know her, Buttw— ah, Wilburn?"

I shrugged and squinched up my face, "Call me Stan. Wilburn sounds even more wrong than Buttwipe."

Nancy shrugged. "Yes or no?"

"Not her. Someone who had the same appearance … years ago."

Nancy chewed on that. "Thought you were incapable of remembering more than a few months."

"Different kind of memory."

He teased something off his tongue, studied it for a second, and then flipped it away.

"Different or not, you got a clue."

Something with the girl did have my attention, but I didn't know what, and it wasn't her facial features. "Listen," I walked around to the other side of her. "All I know is, someone who had the same face as ol' girl here witnessed a murder years ago."

I leaned in for a closer inspection. Although dressed like a high-priced call-girl, she wore a ring on the third finger of her right hand.

Get in closer, mon ami, Jacques, my former existence as a jeweler, whispered to me.

Bend down and inspect the thing at closer range.

I did. Not a wedding set, pretty good diamond though. Jacques spoke up, *Couple of carats, emerald cut. Expensive.*

"Hey, Detective? How come a streetwalker wears an expensive ring like that?"

"Huh?" He took a knee beside me. His eyes locked onto the

ring, opened in surprise, and his face paled. "Don't know." His fingernails scraped over the stubble on his cheek, as if he was checking his shave. "You're right."

His eyes jumped around, as if stewing over something. Without warning, he stood, grabbed my arm, and tugged me to his car. "Time to let the photo guys have their turn." He stuffed me into the auto like a criminal, complete with pushing me into the back seat while holding his hand on my head to ensure I didn't hit it on the roof.

A familiar action: the last case we'd worked, he'd done the same thing when he arrested me. I chuckled a bit and tried to make some small talk, "Seems like I remember doing this before." We both knew the arrest was one of the reasons he'd looked an asshole.

CHAPTER FOUR

The only sound I heard until we'd traveled a block or two was the hum of the engine. About then, Nancy eyeballed me via the rearview. "What about the bullshit claim, living several times.

Isn't that supposed to be about all you can remember?"

"Only the lives I've lived. Can't rem—"

"Remember this one." He finished the sentence for me. "Right now, I don't care about this one." He paused. "Except for the shootin' back there. No, I want to talk to you about what you can remember, and I mean the important life."

There was nothing to do but stare at him in the rearview.

"Yeah," he chuckled. "Go ahead. Use those beady peepers on me like you don't know what the hell I'm sayin'."

I knew what he meant all right. I knew. Sybil.

Clever and perceptive, Sybil was always the key. She'd been a holy woman in some ancient village somewhere in the British Isles, able to solve difficult problems with huge leaps of intuition. Sybil didn't even need obvious clues.

More than clever, she was brilliant.

Her advice was priceless. I'd acted upon her conclusion last time to solve the case, the one which made ol' Nancy here appear such a stalwart citizen. The fact that she swooped to the fore at the very moment his mouth flapped about her was really spooky, though.

"Before you deny anything," continued Nancy, "remember also, I'm a detective. I went to your shrink." As he turned a corner, a half-growl-half-laugh belched from him, "'Course she wouldn't tell me much, but it was what she didn't say that interested me. It was something simple, something I already knew. The strange part of our conversation was, she wouldn't have broken privacy laws at all to talk about it. But she didn't mention it."

He gave me a huge smile in the rearview. "You have these sudden leaps of insight." His grin was so big his teeth filled up the mirror. "So why didn't she say anything about it?"

A loud honk pulled him back to the road, but he carried on driving as if he wanted to kill somebody. He whipped around a corner and screeched to a stop at his headquarters. The car still rocked while he climbed out. "C'mon." He talked over his shoulder, slammed the door behind

him, and headed to his office without even a glance to see if I followed.

All the odors of the place closed around me as I rounded the staircase after him. I'd particularly depended on my sense of smell when I was Ahn, a primitive hunter, the trait stuck with me. The fragrance of the building enfolded us, and the bouquet definitely didn't cost much.

An appropriate name for the base fragrance might be 'Ladies Room Stale Trash Can.'

Quite the toilet water. A faint whiff of unwashed people drifted through too. Oh, and don't let me forget about the cheap hooker perfumes used mainly to cover up other funky aromas that lingered. Mixing them all together, you had 'Eau de Old Government Building.' Jacques was appalled, Ahn intrigued.

As I finished analyzing the air, something else drifted to my nose, very faint, and much more expensive, an extremely light scent.

Tastefully so, oui? commented Jacques.

It was good to have him with me, but I blocked him out and concentrated on searching out this new smell myself.

The exercise so engrossed Ahn and me, Sybil had to yell to get my attention: *smelled this before!*

Nancy started in again, "Your shrink's omission made me think. Coffee?"

I nodded and felt a grudging new respect for him as he walked into his office. Maybe he's not a real moron. He figured

Sybil out, maybe he can figure out something else too.

He grabbed a couple of mugs and wiped them with his hands. Seeing that, I tried to gauge where his hands might have been. Pouring, he nodded to the only chair in the room apart from his.

After he handed me a cup, he perched his butt on the corner of his desk. "Why did she omit such an obvious detail? The answer was simple, confidentiality. That meant your insights were important. Now, I already knew about your memory quirks, so the logical assumption was these insights came from one of your stupid past lives."

I thought he gave unnecessary emphasis to the word stupid. *Asshole.*

Shut up, Hank. I agreed with Hank, but I still thought it best to keep my own, internal, ass quiet; didn't need the confusion.

Pasting that gigantic grin on his face, Nancy proudly leaned back and laced fingers around his knee.

Yes, I'd underestimated him. It had been quite a jump in logic, more than I thought the guy capable of, certainly more than Hank knew him to have, again, more burgeoning respect from me. Also, I felt sorry for Nancy. Hank never felt sorry for anyone.

To be fair to the guy, I'd missed a few details in the last case myself. It had been Sybil who'd put everything together, but as I peered back at everything, all of the clues had been obvious, so obvious it was no wonder Nancy had come out the way he did. After all, he's the detective. He should've caught it.

I shrugged with a chuckle. I'm a mental patient.

"What's so funny, Stan?"

"Thinking about the last case."

While the words were still dribbling out, his face darkened, and I checked for a place to hide. His sucker punches hurt like hell. Then the clouds disappeared from his visage.

"It's okay." Nancy's eyes skewered me. "I think maybe we can work on this one together." He leaned on the word together.

Mixed with the Brooklyn accent, it drew the word out for almost a whole second. "All I need, is for you to let me know when what's-his-name gives you any information, so I don't seem dumb."

That was a tall order. He had the appearance of someone's fat uncle trying to decide what to eat, a piece of apple pie, or the waitress. I thought he'd drool all over himself.

Disgusting.

"It doesn't work like that." I tossed him a wad of tissues from his desk and motioned for him to wipe his chin. "Insights don't have a schedule. I never know in advance. Whenever Sybil knows something, she blurts it out and it comes on through. That's what happened the last time, and how you came off like an ass.

"Believe me. I didn't plan on identifying the killer in front of the lieutenant. I certainly didn't know you were about to walk in on the killer while she slept with your wife. I'm really sorry about her, too. If I'd have known everything, I might have been able to stifle Sybil, at least long enough to give you a heads up, but I didn't."

"You had to bring it all up again?" Nancy skewered me again. "At least the lieutenant fixed things."

I nodded, rubbernecking for a safe haven. "I didn't know she was a lesbian!"

Wilburn, whispered John, old band-director self, *the vein on Nancy's forehead is beating time to 'The Stars and Stripes Forever.'*

Hank woke at the mention of lesbian. He loved even the thought of two women making love. He sent pictures rolling through my mind along with detailed descriptions. I didn't mind the visual show and commentary, but I needed to ignore him. That was hard to do.

"Listen, Nancy—"

"I know. You're sorry. You're a sorry son-of-a-bitch."

Sybil's voice chatted away and together the whole thing was

confusing. Something about Shannie, but it wasn't clear. I supposed it had something to do with the look-alike's murder, but I didn't understand her. Sybil is rather close-lipped, not that she has any lips, other than mine. Listen, Sybil, you are welcome to my/our memories anytime you wish, but—

Sybil?

She was gone. I turned back to Nancy, "I'm sorry?"

"I've gone past that, Stan. You had that I'm-a-fucking-idiot expression on your face and woolgathering, so I waited. Now. I have some ideas about the hooker who was shot."

"I don't think I want to get involved. I mean, remember what happened the last time." I

had a hell of a stomach cramp. What with Sybil nosing around in my head, and ol' Nancy trying to make all of us a junior partner ... I ran my hand over my buzz cut and took a deep breath.

Nancy drummed his fingers loudly on his desk. "All right, what do you think."

"I need to go in the other room." The words jumped from my mouth; of course, it was

Sybil who'd said it, just as it was she who jumped out of my chair.

Opening the door, we walked through while I wondered what Sybil was up to.

Go in the next room. The smell came from there.

Oh, crap! We're on the smell thing again. Sybil!

Striding over to a desk in the middle of the room, we stopped and nosed the air like a dog hunting for a crotch to sniff. A small cloud of that expensive perfume hung there, growing stronger as we neared the adjacent chair. I felt like a red-dick dog searching for ... well, searching. But Sybil needed information, so I continued.

A particularly fragrant whiff drifted by me, and I recognized the perfume.

Sybil, you are quick.

It was the killer's favored perfume on the last case that Nancy and I had worked on, his wife's lover.

My eyes shot to Nancy. He had that stupid, hopeful stare that screamed, "We've got a lead!"

How do I tell him that he is about to be embarrassed again?

"Yes!" he yelled. "She was sitting there, wasn't she?"

Everyone in the room stopped what they were doing and stared at us, so I ignored the smell in the air and stood up straight.

"How did you know that?" He stopped moving too. His eyes bulged as he surveyed the room, and the other officers. His gaze settled. I followed it to the inevitable.

His boss had entered the room from the hallway, and Nancy hunched himself over like a rhino trying to hide, and he whispered, "She was here, wasn't she? Whoever it was, she was here. Only the woman wasn't a hooker then. Right?" Nancy stopped, realization creeping over his face.

His eyes darted back to the lieutenant for a second, and then dragged their way back to me with a certain appearance of doom in his eyes, "You're gonna do it again, ain't you?" He started to back into his office, but before he got very far, Sybil reached out and grabbed his arm to stop him. She needed to go in another direction. With a deep breath, I wiped my brow. Nancy wasn't going to like this at all.

Nodding upwards like a conspirator, I gave him a smile to coax him back toward me. I didn't do it well. My lips trembles, but I tried. Nancy and I drifted across the room pretending to be befuddled and confused, as if we'd inexplicably gone wangy in the head.

Well, I pretended: Nancy did an uncanny job that seemed as natural as it was. All the while, Sybil and Ahn, the hunter boy, sniffed the air. I didn't know what Sybil had in mind, but there was a germ of an idea rummaging around in my head, like the way an oyster must feel while it's making a pearl, or maybe a baby a couple of seconds before soiling its diaper. Hard to tell which.

I pulled Nancy behind me as I wandered through the room, visiting a desk and chair, then over to the coffee machine before we stumbled into the lieutenant. Maybe stumbled wasn't the right word. The man actually bounced back into the door of his office. The combined weight of the three of us banged the door open, and the way the lieutenant fell to the floor would have made a vaudevillian proud. I mean, few pratfalls have the style and panache of a bull gorilla getting his ass kicked, but this one did.

I didn't bother to cringe; Nancy did enough for us both.

"Hey, Boss!" said Nancy. "I'm sorry."

"Get in here and shut that damn door." The lieutenant's voice had a guttural sound to it that I didn't remember. Sybil didn't seem surprised, though.

I don't think anything ever surprises her, not even the stench that hung in the room. This smell was a stronger version of Eau de Government plus the few whiffy odors the lieutenant added all by himself, and probably the reason he stepped into the other room in the first place.

Who would have thought that a police lieutenant would do that in his office?

God, what did he have for lunch?

"What the hell is this, Detective?" The gravelly voice almost covered up the squeak of the chair as the police supervisor sat down.

"It's okay." Nancy moved the rest of the way into the office, shut the door, and took a seat in the chair in front of the desk.

I need to give ol' Nancy applause here. I mean, after all, he had no idea what was unfolding with me, Sybil, or his investigation, yet he was still gutsy enough to sit in front of his boss and lie. The signs of it radiated from him. Hank's interrogator days gave him great insight:

That bastard's posture is absolutely wrong. And he swallows too much. And he's developed a nervous tick on his left middle finger.

I had trouble holding in my giggle. That finger tapped the air as if coding Morse, or secretly sending a lewd message to an invisible best friend across the room.

"Stan here is simply following up the leads we have in the hooker killing." His eyes flicked to me, and I saw the immediate plea hidden there. I really did. It's just that I couldn't help him out. I also knew that dawn would crack soon for him, and he'd understand that he was SOL. I mean, when you push somebody out of the door into the Siberian winter, it doesn't take long before that someone figures out that the weather is cold. Especially if they don't even have a coat.

Sybil controlled everything now, and she stopped reacting to his pleading.

He stomped over to me so quickly I was unable to duck, grabbed me by my shoulders and gave me a shake, an easy one, not the dirty dish towel thing like before. "C'mon, Stan. Help me out here!"

Our eyes locked for a second and the smell of fear oozed from him. Ahn said it permeated the room. At least it covered up the marsh gasses looming in the office.

I pulled my eyes to the lieutenant. A rough smile crawled across my face, and Sybil let tough guy Hank do the talking, "Nancy cop here don't have the gonads to do what needs doin'."

It was as if the room melted away and the only things left were me, Hank, and the supervisor. "You pieces of crap always got your little political machine. Right now, it's more important ta say things the right way than ta get things done. That's bullshit."

"Stan! What're you doing?" Another shake and it took a bit for the room to refocus around me. But Hank still had control.

"Sit down, Nancy man."

I never understood Hank's obsession with Nancy's name. I mean, Hank's name is more American than English. The Brit version is Harry. Maybe he wrote his own name off to the fact his mother was American. She'd gone overseas back in World

War I, war bride, or war nurse who stayed and gave birth to him. Poor woman.

Anyway, the lieutenant's bearing was as if he'd been locked in a roomful of lunatics. Sybil chuckled loudly, and it echoed maddeningly through my head. It faded and her quiet little voice remained: *There's more people in the room than he'll ever know.*

My lips curled. Hank had liked her words. The lieutenant and I locked gazes and Hank spoke again, "Get that captain in here."

Clearly, the lieutenant was struggling to figure me out. "I don't care if you were instrumental in solving Detective Nancy's last case. You are not a member of this department, no standing here. While I'm at it, drop the tough guy act."

My smile showed my teeth, and, except for one blink when Hank let me have some control, I maintained eye contact. "Whatever. Do you want to know what's going on, or not?" Our eyes played chicken.

Inhaling deeply, he scooted closer to his desk, reached out, and buzzed his boss. "Sir, can you come down here for a minute? I'll explain when you get here."

Hank took back control of the eyes, and he and the lieutenant stabbed each other with fire while we waited. Nancy, fidgeted, like a three-year-old with dried crap in his pants, wiggling around, changing position every four seconds. He even leaned onto one hip to pick at his butt crack once, and I had a fleeting memory of him wiping the coffee cup.

My gag reflex threatened, but the antique doorknob squeaked, and Nancy's behavior bordered on apoplexy. Then ol' Nancy changed. It was like the sun rising on a vista of the Great Plains, heralding a bright summer's day. He sat back calmly as if he'd somehow become prescient.

"Thanks for coming, Captain," the lieutenant started in. Clearly, he didn't want to give me a chance to throw any bullshit. As he leaned back into his chair, his eyes darted at me, endeavoring to sling pig shit at me with his eyes. "Mister Stanton, the little pissant over there, was about to explain." Then he gave me the nod, "He cordially requested your presence. Said you were needed."

Sybil laughed at that. Her loud giggling was all I heard, and as I glanced around the room, everyone stared at me, but I ignored them.

Hank chose that moment to disappear, so my eyes skewered Nancy's. "Tell everyone that you know who killed the hooker." But his eyes made it clear he didn't have a clue. If they could produce feces, they would have. I had to do something. "Tell them about our secret."

At my words, Nancy blinked rapid-fire, like a naked co-ed staring at sailors disembarking on Fleet Day. Then, he whispered, "They're about to think we're both crazy as batshit!"

The words circumnavigated the quiet room to find their way into everyone's ears. I willed him to do it, but with all of Sybil's laughing, my concentration lacked focus.

Nancy took a deep breath, shrugged, and sighed slowly. "Stan here doesn't think the way most people do. He can't remember—"

"Not that," Hank interrupted but I pushed him aside. "They don't want to be bored with all that. What I mean is for you to tell them the hooker wasn't a genuine streetwalker."

He blinked again, obviously churning everything around, but he continued with my thought as best his meager talent enabled him, and he spoke cautiously. "She was a very highpriced lady of the evening."

I waved at him with a half-opened hand. "Tell them the rest. Go on," I said, touching my ring finger with my thumb. "Yeah. That part was simple. Why would a streetwalker have a ring like that?"

I rubbed my nose as grandly as possible for him to see, without being too obvious, and then I unobtrusively sniffed at the air. Clearly, the nitwit didn't understand, so I had to help him out again. "Don't forget the expensive perfume." Nancy barely nodded. Sybil grabbed control,

"Curiously, a friend of mine thought the scent was familiar."

At least she gave him a howdy-do this time before buggering him.

Not now, Hank.

Nancy's head trembled. His eyes gave up the shitting himself idea but appeared ready to overflow with piss. "Don't, Stan."

"It was the same scent that Nancy's last killer preferred, and it started the detective here thinking. What did the two women have in common? Maybe we didn't figure things right before.

Was it possible that there were," I leaned toward Nancy for emphasis, "*are*, several high-priced hookers? Maybe a whole stable of them? Is it possible that the woman we thought committed the last killing, was framed, and there are more running around?"

After it was out, a glimmer of recognition shone in Nancy's eyes. A subtle bob of his head told me he understood Sybil's lead. He sat back, cleared his throat and sipped his coffee. Even his color flowed again. His cup tilted, he saw me clearly, and I sniffed the air again and then rubbed my nose, pointing outside the door.

With a slight lift of his brows, he swallowed and stood. "You see, lieutenant," Nancy swaggered to the door, "that same odor was here in the precinct house when we came back today. In there. One of the damn hooker's been here." With a tip of his head, he inhaled deeply, his eyes darted to his boss, but once there, they had a target lock.

Sybil chuckled.

"Someone here knew," said Nancy, staring at the lieutenant as if he had a *High Noon* showdown. He'd finally put everything together. Although I did observe calculation behind

Nancy's eyes, his overall expression seemed ready to cry too. He'd put everything together.

Hank pushed me to the side, and we copied ol' Nancy's swagger, "You ran them all like your own little army, except in this particular army you demanded freebies. Swinging your little willie everywhere. But then you found out about the affair. That was bad enough, but it was a lesbian thing, and that was too much. You went stupid. You killed. Then you framed your girl. It was pure luck that Detective Nancy arrested your little betraying lover." One more step.

"Tell me, lieutenant," I queried while making a grand show of picking something off my tongue. Sybil had taken charge, but I thought that tongue thing was a good touch, dramatic. I liked it when Nancy did it. "Have you been to the firing range today?"

The man's eyes flashed. "What business is that of yours?"

"Because Detective Nancy here mentioned that you smelled faintly of cordite, gunpowder. Tell us, where and when did you last fire a gun? I'm sure it wasn't your service revolver. Was it?"

The lieutenant licked his lips. Otherwise, he sat without moving, mute as Helen Keller.

The room now stifling, sweat soaked his shirt, dripped down my back, too.

After a couple of very long minutes, the captain walked forward, the floorboards creaked as he did, and as he passed, I had a new whiff of Eau de Old Government Building.

"This is ridiculous." His rumbling voice always sounded as if he was chewing on something. "Larry, tell them where you've been practicing, and we'll toss this kid. Nancy, get out of here." He gaped at the lieutenant again. "Tell 'em, Larry."

The lieutenant scrutinized everyone in the room, eyes slowly moving from one person to the next, stopping at the captain. He shook his head. Then he eased open his desk drawer, the screech irritated even the air, and he ran his finger over a .44 lying all by itself.

My hand shot forward and slapped the lieutenant. I stared at him.

What the hell! Hank? Was that you, or Sybil?

It was my turn to almost shit myself.

Everybody in the room lurched forward. I stared at the man before me. "He was reachin' for that piec—"

The lieutenant grabbed my throat, choked off my words, clearly determined to kill me. While he held my pencil neck and dragged me around, Sybil whispered to me, and that bastard Hank was gone like a rabbit on fire.

Now my problem was how to breathe again, because I had to let everyone else know the solution.

Pandemonium filled the room, people shouted and shoved. I ended up on the ground with him squeezing my neck. Hell, someone fired a gun. That's when everything stopped, and the lieutenant let go. My ears hurt and rang like Big Ben in a small room. I rolled away.

CHAPTER FIVE

Chicken shit! Hank was back, yelling at me.

Me, chicken shit? You're the piece of chicken squirt that ran when he grabbed my throat.

Stand up, growled Hank, *you beady-eyed little prick*!

Jacques ignored the whole thing and commented on the smell of cordite. Fox Boy yelled something too! It sailed right by me.

I'd had enough and snarled, "Everyone shut the hell up!"

What d'you know? Not only my own inner voices quieted but so too did everyone in the room.

Then for the first time, I saw what had happened. The lieutenant lay on the floor, eyes open, and unfocused, his blood all over the floor, the window, and half of the people in the room, including me. Everyone else stood so still they might've been those stupid living statues.

The door slammed open and in bounced several protectors, each yelling and blustering, all of them aiming their handguns around the room.

"Stand down!" bellowed the captain. Even when he yells, it's as though his mouth's full of raw eggs. "Damn it. Everybody stand still." His hand rubbed over his mouth and chin like he was trying to catch the dribble of a cracked egg. Then he walked to the nearest chair and plopped down like manure falling out of a cow.

Sybil laughed. *Go ahead*, she whispered. My eyes stinging from the sweat dripping into them, I glanced over to Nancy. Poor bastard hadn't a clue.

Piss on this. Hank, back in charge again.

While he stared at the captain, I continued, "So there we have it. The lieutenant grabbed me and his pistol. If that's not an admission of guilt, then what is?"

25

Hank sauntered over to the captain. "Captain, if you had not jumped in to subdue him, he would have killed me. Couldn't help that he shot himself." Sybil laughed harder at that.

The captain waved at everyone. "For God's sake, put those damn pop guns up." With a malignant glower at Nancy, he said, "Clean up this mess. Nicos, take Nancy's friend here and get a statement." His eyes bored into me, "A complete statement. And Paterinsky, you guard the door until CSI takes over. Everyone else, get the hell out." With that he stood, shot a venomous glare at the dead lieutenant, and walked out, pushing all the rest of the bystanders before him. The only ones left were Nancy and me. Nicos waited impatiently next to Paterinsky at the doorway.

"Shit!" Nancy peered down at his pants. "I pissed myself."

I hadn't thought about it, but ... no. I still had a full bladder and dry pants.

"It was the lieutenant all along," Nancy leaned back into his chair, relief plastered sickeningly all over him, pissed pants and all.

Sybil laughed aloud this time, and I waded in. "No, Detective. That was a charade. This is only the beginning. The lieutenant was not the man in charge, simply an overseer. You are close enough to close things here for now, unless you want to open festering wounds."

Nancy's face drained.

"I thought so." I stepped out to follow Nicos. After traveling through the bullpen, we took the stairs, and instead of heading down, we climbed. In the stairwell, the Eau de Government clouded everything.

The exquisite perfume is this way, urged Jacques. Even my nose followed it, and Ahn was in his element, sniffing the trail like a bloodhound. On the next floor, we walked a short way as

Sybil hummed and chuckled. She knew something she wasn't sharing.

CHAPTER SIX

The barefoot giant dressed in a yellow shirt and loose-fitting gray pants stared at her. "Mu'izz," he yelled. "I will not spar with a woman. A woman!" The words echoed in the large room. "I only know one way to fight and will not back off."

"You will not hurt me." The woman, dressed in form-fitting black, walked out from among the others gathered to spar.

He snorted and brought himself to his full height. "I don't worry about hurting anyone. I just do it." The giant turned around and pulled his shirt over his head, revealing his overly hairy back and arms. He turned around again, and she saw the scars. Several stretched from his neck across his torso. Clearly, he'd been attacked with a blade and survived.

Sporting a menacing grin, he waved her closer. Bent at the waist, and his arms hung almost to the floor as he circled to his right.

She, too, readied herself, bouncing closer. Balanced and ready, she exploded on him. Her knee crashed into his face, hitting his cheek, dropping him to all fours.

"That was a mistake, girl." Her smile was her answer.

She came at him again, but he was ready and blocked her attack. He snatched her arm and pulled. He didn't let go, his musky smell pinching her nose.

She wrestled hard, but all that did was force his smell into her throat, burning it. She stomped on his instep.

"Bitch," he growled. "Come on, bitch." He locked his eyes on her and circled.

She bounced to him on the balls of her feet, ready to spring wherever she needed. He stood ready, and realization slapped her – this would be rough.

He circled closer, menacing and deadly.

She hopped away until she noticed his right knee leaned at

27

the perfect angle. If she ... her left leg shot out, driving toward the thigh – but it wasn't there.

He attacked. A palm strike and he popped her jaw. She sprawled back onto her bum and bit into her tongue, blood filled her mouth. Then he pounced, knee on her solar plexus.

Her air. Gone! She tried to breathe. Oh God, I'm paralyzed. She balled up her fist and drove it into his scrotum, hard.

Now it was his turn to turn blue.

She would've laughed if she could breathe. She rolled to her knees, keeping her head down and dragging in breath while she spat blood.

He recovered first, seized her, and pushed her face into the concrete floor.

His hold unbreakable, a hard yank on her hair moved her across the floor and flipped her over. Her first sight was his massive fist rocketing to her face. She turned into it, taking it with her forehead. It hurt but did little damage. He pulled his arm back again, and she gave the signal for surrender.

Ignoring it, his fist crashed down again. This time he aimed for her throat – a kill strike.

She signaled again. The official shouted for the fight to stop and gripped the giant's arm.

The giant shook off the official and drew back again but stopped. He leaned down to her.

"I told you I don't fight women, but that was only half of what I wanted to say. I only kill them." He reached his arm back again.

She saw his mistake. He'd leaned in too close. She threw her arm around his head, dug in with her fingernails and held tight like a leech. As he rose to fight, she pulled him in tighter, jabbing her right thumbnail deep into his eye.

The eerie howl filled the warehouse as the giant stood to his full height. The woman refused to let go, fiercely thumbing his eye into his skull.

Roaring in pain, the man shook her body away, unable to

dislodge her. His eye! He dropped to his knees, then down further as he signaled defeat.

"Stop."

She dug one more telling time, and while digging, she turned to the official. He nodded. She let go, and the big man dropped, holding his bloody face, gelatinous goo running down his cheek.

She left without a glance back. She'd honed her skills enough for one night.

Nicos used the night shadows to scan the area without being seen himself. The Brooklyn buildings, occasional piles of trash and garbage, and the broken streetlight ahead made the neighborhood appear exactly what it was – an inner-city slum.

Every city in the world had this same scene. Every city had an emotional mirror of the hopelessness that blanketed the area.

Not every city had the reason Nicos was here.

He ducked down the alleyway unfazed by the sour stink from dumpster after dumpster along the wall where the meandering homeless built their cardboard shelters. He walked right past. His ears didn't even register the glass whiskey bottle shattering on the concrete, carelessly

tossed there by the woman who had sucked it dry.

Constantly scanning for anything out of place, he peered around the corner where his short alleyway t-boned into the larger one. The new one was deserted, although the conditions were better. The people Nicos had come to see preferred it that way.

Nicos strolled calmly down the center of the darker alley, well away from anything that might offer concealment; any appearance of stealth would invite severe opposition. A third of the way down the alleyway, a spot, although not obvious, was better lit than the rest. Nicos stopped there and turned around as if searching for something on the walls of the abandoned warehouses.

His hands lay casually by his sides: anyone who cared to look would see they were empty.

After one complete circle, he stopped, shrugged and moved forward again. Two paces later, a half-whisper filtered through the darkness to his right. "Stop."

"Name?" continued the voice.

"Nicos."

"Your real name."

"Any name that a man is called by is his real name." His clipped words had a slight

indiscernible accent. Nicos took his time and turned to face the man in the deep shadows.

"Step toward me."

A faint sliver of light illuminated the shadows enough for Nicos to see a 9mm handgun aimed at his forehead. With a small shake of the gun, the man in the shadows indicated Nicos should back through the door behind him.

The door closed with a heavy clunk, and although lighter inside than out, the room was still dark. Nicos continued backing until he hit a wall. But the armed man advanced, still pointing the weapon. It touched his skin, and Nicos burst into a smile and held out his arms, "Brother!"

"You are a fool!"

"Why? Because I came with news?"

"Because you came." The new voice echoed through the building, and something about it, sharp and surprisingly high pitched, irritated both men, who turned to see a third man step from the shadows. "Why?"

Nicos bit his lip, an unconscious habit. When he realized what he was doing, forced himself to stop. "Sir, I came to let you know that the woman ha—"

"Has been killed. Yes, I know. There are more eyes on the street than yours." The man with the grating voice leveled his eyes at Nicos for two full seconds. Neatly dressed and groomed, the man motioned Nicos to follow. Turning, he walked back into the shadows, pausing at a nearby door, and entered the room beyond.

The brightness there made Nicos squint, but he strode to where he knew he should stand.

The man in charge made himself comfortable on an overstuffed couch against the wall.

"You knew we already had that information." The man was well aware his voice irritated people and he used that knowledge, especially in this kind of situation. He honed the edge to his voice. "I'm tired of this, Nicos. Tell me why you came? You know better."

Nicos swallowed, and his eyes shifted around the room. His hand itched for his service weapon, but that way led to trouble, especially here. "Mr. Mu'izz … I, uh, I wanted to know if you knew who that woman was." He took in the fine features, the fierce, almond eyes, and the delicately trimmed hair and beard of the man sitting before him. "I also needed to let you know that the lieutenant is dead too. He shot himself."

The guard who had let him into the warehouse silently stepped up beside him.

Nicos's eyes shifted quickly to identify him then back to the lounging man; he spoke more hastily. "They don't know anything. They think it's all about hookers."

"It is about hookers." The man called Mu'izz picked up a cup of tea from a nearby table, sipped, and put it back down. "We do hookers. That is one of the things that makes us money."

"But the woman wasn't a hooke—"

"I will worry about what she was."

"But …"

The lounging man stared Nicos down. After a long minute of a penetrating stare, Mu'izz inclined his head infinitesimally to the man beside Nicos. Less than a heartbeat later, Nicos felt the man's 9mm against his temple.

"Say the word, Abdul. From Allah's will to your lips."

Again Mu'izz watched Nicos's reaction. "Let me explain

something, Nicos. It has been a nightmare to put you where you are. Making you Alexandre Nicos, instead of a little urchin from the streets begging for alms. We put you in the police force, even gave you a wife."

"Yes, I agree. But you need to know about Stanton."

At an almost imperceptible nod from the man before him, Nicos said, "The man is cockeyed crazy. I had charge of him to take his statement … he babbled about voices in his head and how everything is connected to the hookers. Then he blurted out that there was a whole lot more than the whores."

The lounging man held up his hand for Nicos to stop while the man sipped from his cup again, but Nicos continued, "We need to—"

"I do not tolerate anyone who doesn't follow directions." With a quick glance and an infinitesimal nod, he put down his tea.

The gun exploded and Nicos dropped.

Mu'izz continued lounging and waved his hand, and the gunman bent down, hefted the body, and dragged it into the other room.

The ringing in his ear was loud and hurt. He rolled over, reached for his aching ear, and with no idea how long he'd been out, tried to stand.

Hands from the dark helped him to rise. Nicos turned to see the guard bending close – his friend who had let him into the warehouse and fired the gun. The man held Nicos at arm's length and shook him. As soon as their eyes connected, the guard said, "That was the last lesson. He let me shoot close and not kill you. Don't ever disobey." He nodded toward the doorway.

Nicos wobbled toward the exit, and said, "I am truly a fool." Behind him, the man muttered the very same thing, unheard by the deaf Nicos. Nicos put his hand to his ear and rubbed, raised his voice to hear, "I said I am truly—"

The hand slapped him enough to gain Nicos's attention, then again with more force. He held Nicos by the sides of his head, leaned in, and stared, his teeth gleaming in the night. "Yes." He nodded. "You are, foolish like a dung beetle that rolls shit wherever it goes. Now be quiet
and leave. Do not bring any more balls of dung."

CHAPTER SEVEN

It came as no surprise that I was to be reprocessed through Bellevue. The pompous expression on the captain's face gave it away. Besides, Sybil alerted me before we even arrived at Nicos's desk to give our statement. Not as bad as the last time though, probably because I had a memory of the last visit.

They did all of their poking, prodding, and in general, acted as if I were a robot on which to practice – several pokes and then one big goose.

Still don't understand that big prodding, and they didn't even ask me to cough. What are they, aliens?

Thankfully my stay didn't last long, because my *pro bono* doc, Doctor Sally MacPherson M.D.D. PsyD, and very pretty, pulled a few strings. She collected me as soon as I made a call and walked me to her office.

Hank was positively ribald, and I had to keep telling him to shut it. A couple of times, he kept at it until Sybil told him he should shut it.

Anyway, Doc's office is a much better place to spend time than Bellevue. Those guys in that place are crazy.

I gawked around her office – as classy as she was, with all the pictures on the wall, the interview area (I would have preferred a couch like those in stories and movies) and her neat, tidy desk.

May I trouble you for some coffee, mon ami? Jacques was always partial to coffee, although I really don't care for the stuff myself.

I sauntered over for a cup to satisfy him, but when I did, Hank protested. He wanted tea and then changed his mind when he saw the wet bar tucked away in the corner. He cajoled and finagled me to pour a small gin, but there wasn't any; there was Irish whiskey, Maker's Mark, a little Sky, well used Grey Goose, and a half-empty bottle of Captain Morgan.

Ahn didn't care about any of it at all. He was engrossed in the smell of the coffee.

As I wrestled with the inner storm, a movement caught my eye: Lacy, a mousey young lady who worked for Doc, a bizarre piece of work. In my opinion, she deserved a place here more than me. But she needed to be nearer the front of the line for some treatments. She was a nurse or something, I don't know, but she was always hanging around, and weird as hell.

Cute, with reddish hair cut in a raggedy way that, despite how unkempt it appeared, had a pleasing effect. Her tip-tilted nose added the impression that its pugness held her glasses in place. On the skinny side, with inconspicuous breasts, her overall appearance was she'd never outgrown her tomboy phase.

Something about her bugged the shit out of me. It was a deep-seated dislike.

Ahn said she moved like a clumsy cat.

I wouldn't say that, Ahn. But you lot need to listen to old Hank now, because I know trouble, and she's it.

Sybil was remarkably quiet on the subject.

"What are you doing back here?" Lacy's voice had a nagging quality, not really abrasive, edgy. She swaggered into the office as if she were the doctor. I like Doc, don't like her.

She ran her finger around her ear to place some of her red hair behind it. If she was trying to be cute, the gesture didn't work.

"Thought you were gone for good."

"So did I but …" How to explain the complicated mess of everything? "Certainly wasn't to see you."

Her pose made me think she wanted to display herself for me – leaning on one hip, hand on the other, humping the air with her pelvis. The pose piqued Ahn, but there was an air about it which reminded me of the time I brushed my teeth and felt a hair stuck under the toothpaste.

I think it showed on my face, because hers darkened several

shades, and she collected stray magazines. "Well, I didn't wish you here. Now get away from the doctor's coffee and sit down over there. She'll be here in a moment."

"Lacy?" Doc's soft contralto voice interrupted. "Would you please see to those things we talked about? I need to talk to Wilburn." Doc waited for Lacy to leave and shut the door. I watched the lettering of "Doctor MacPherson" on the door, as it closed. It always mesmerized me.

Doc's easy smile beamed at me as she grabbed a cup of coffee and walked to the other chair. "Well, Wilburn, I'm flabbergasted to have you in my office again so soon. I discharged you yesterday and now you're back."

Hank hooted when she sat down and crossed her legs. I think he would really have been outrageous had she chosen to wear a skirt or dress instead of comfortable slacks. I ignored him.

"I know, Doc. Hadn't planned on being here so soon."

She sipped her coffee and set it down on the nearby end table. "You're drinking coffee today. Didn't you say that Hank preferred tea?" I nodded.

"Then, Wilburn, why the coffee?"

"Honestly, Doc, I really don't like the name Wilburn. I know it was the name I came up with, but it doesn't feel like my name at all. Can't you call me Stan?"

"Yes, of course." She smiled knowingly. "I forgot that's what you prefer. But let's go back to the coffee. Why coffee?"

I stood up and meandered around the office, sniffing the coffee as I did. "Yes, Hank prefers tea, but one of the others likes the smell of coffee."

"Which other?"

"Ahn," I answered over my shoulder as I studied a photograph on the wall. It had a bunch of people clumped together, as though making sure they'd be in the picture, everyone smiling, and I think Doc was one of them; much younger though. Maybe it was her family. Whoever they were, they looked happy.

"I don't remember Ahn, Stan. Can you tell me about Ahn? Is it a man or woman?"

I answered absently, staring at the picture, "Man. He was a hunter, primitive guy. His senses catch more than most. Hey, Doc? What's this picture about?"

Her face darkened, "It's a picture of my family when I was younger." I heard her move behind me and Ahn smelled her approaching. Jacques approved of her taste in bodywash; the freshness of it like a meadow in early spring. "Do you like it?"

"Don't know. Gives me a funny feeling. Reminds me of something. Can't place what, though."

She went to her desk and thumbed through some notes there. "Stan?"

"Huh?"

"Says in the notes that you were present when Lieutenant Monroe shot himself."

I stood still, not wanting to breathe. "Yes, but I didn't see much. I was busy being choked at the time." I chanced a quick glance to see her reaction. Her mouth teased upward.

Hank hooted, *Let me tell you, mate, she'd love the feel of what I—*

Shut up, Hank.

Wank off, pencil neck.

Ignoring his suggestion, I turned fully toward Doc.

She sat down, still engrossed in the notes. "Why did you try to grab the pistol?"

"What?"

"Why grab the gun?" Her voice was very clinical in tone. "It says here that you grabbed for the handgun to keep Monroe from getting it. Is that true?"

I nodded slowly, unable to see where she was leading, nudged by Sybil's rising wariness.

"That doesn't fit with the way you have been reacting. Normally you try to escape violence. Yet this time … this time you didn't."

My other selves erupted and the resultant cacophony almost deafened me.

"—an? Stan!"

I wasn't sure how many times she tried to get my attention, but eventually, things settled down enough for me to hear her better. "Yes, Doc?"

"What happened? Your voices?"

"Yeah, the voices went crazy."

"Stan, look at me." She waved toward her face.

Her eyes were intense, the dark brown irises grabbing me and pulling me into them. Hank loved it, but Sybil told him to hold his tongue, and for once he said nothing.

"Stan, sit down. Good." She leaned slightly forward, and her contralto became richer with concern. "The voices interest me. I thought we had a handle on them."

"We do. They belong to my past lives."

She took a deep breath, sat back in her chair, and nodded. "We have talked about it before. There are several reasons for them, and how we proceed depends on that reason."

"I've told you before they are my past lives."

"Yes, I know that's what you think. But the problem lies in the low probability of that premise. More commonly, voices accompany mental illness. Schizophrenia. Sometimes they present because they are separate parts of your personality. Now, I discharged you because you didn't appear to be a danger to anyone, not even yourself. Besides, current thought says that simply hearing voices doesn't mean you are ill.

"Another explanation is Dissociative Identity Disorder, commonly thought of as split personalities, and believe me, that is rare. What you describe is unique and cannot really be proven. It borders on religion and reincarnation."

It was my turn to sigh, which I did while telling everyone inside to shut up. "Doc. I don't care what it's called. I know who these voices are, when they lived, and what they did."

A noise, a popping of sorts, outside the office startled me, and I stood up to investigate, but she waved me back down. "Regardless, Stan, I have to know what is happening so I can come up with a treatment, or at least a recommendation."

"Okay. For what it's worth, reincarnation is the wrong word. John, the band director." *Musician.*

"Okay, John, musician. Anyway, he seems to think it's more to do with harmony. Has to do with vibrations and ...."

More popping in the hallway, and the place exploded. The door blew in, followed by flames. Hank yanked me out of the chair in an instant. He dove over the desk, tackled Doc, and held her down with his hand over her mouth.

We were still there when from my vantage point under the desk, I saw two goons' feet come into the room. They chattered in a strange language. Automatic gunfire sprayed the two chairs, and a pair of boots shifted direction toward us. I pulled Doc with everything I had, while Hank scolded me for being a weak little pussy. She got the idea and we lurched to the side.

More automatic spray. Wood, smoke, fire, everywhere. Hank expropriated me. I watched in horror as we bounced up and over the desk, landing on the goon firing at us. With a deft thrust, my hand struck his throat hard and followed through to seize the automatic, a micro Uzi.

Once in our hands, it made us deadly. Hank turned it on the second man, sprayed him with a few rounds, and then we were out of ammo.

Hank dropped the weapon, grabbed the one from the dead guy, felt around for another magazine, found two, and we were off.

Unfortunately, by the time we raced through the doorway and dodged the flames dancing from the walls, all I saw was a third man disappearing through the doorway.

The bad news was that he carried Lacy on his shoulder. The last thing I saw was anger flashing in her eyes before she disappeared.

That's her, the Mistress, screamed Fox Boy. *She got the*

Mistress's eyes. She got them two-colored eyes!

CHAPTER EIGHT

After all the excitement at Doc's, here I sit in the squad room, or bullpen, again, a large room full of detectives' desks outside the captain's office at the precinct. I'm so bored.

I am the only one in the room. Everyone else is in the captain's office, arguing about what to do with me. Man, is the captain pissed!

The argument sounds like any everyday event inside my head which, by the way, is surprisingly quiet. There's a television a couple of desks away, which is kept on for a little background babble in the room. Unnecessary of course, with the squabble Olympics stoking up.

I made a conscious effort to tune out the live show and instead focus on what was making noise on the TV. Some old boy yelling about how we had to take control, or Isis would behead and swallow us. Checking the bottom of the screen, I saw a name – Senator John P. Stonegate.

Something about this old bastard exuded familiarity, and I wouldn't trust him to empty my bedpan.

Oh, he was smooth enough, and I'd bet women liked him if they thought the over-fifty crowd was sexy. His snow-white hair combed back, he had enough wrinkles across his forehead and around the eyes to appear trustworthy. It was a good touch. It made his message powerful, and while what he said made sense, something wasn't right.

Something in his eyes reminded me of a televangelist. A sadness about them, in the way of evangelists occasionally, even when they are supposedly filled with joy. Maybe like a jaded entertainer working the crowd. Yeah, that's the word – jaded. Well, he was a politician after all, so I quit thinking about it. I was in enough trouble right now without wondering why a senator was sad. But he reminded me of someone.

41

The captain's door opened and Detective Nicos's index finger beckoned me forward. Hank wanted to signal him back with another finger, but I walked forward with both hands firmly clasped behind my back, like a man on the way to the firing squad.

Shoulders back, head forward, dignity et al, *my boy.*

Good old Jacques.

I passed through the door and walked to the empty spot near Doc. The Eau de Government building was gone. I guess it's true. You can get used to even the foulest smells.

The freshness of a spring meadow replaced it.

Scoot closer to her, Wanker.

Ahn agreed, but for different reasons – Hank to gander down her blouse, and Ahn for the smell.

I scooted closer.

Doc cast her gaze at me as I moved in. Her chocolate irises had an almost pleading quality to them, and I felt guilty, but not enough to move away.

"Mister Stanton?"

Reluctantly I glanced up and met with the direct regard of the captain. "Sir?"

Nancy sidled up to me then, punched my arm, and dragged me to the side, and whispered,

"Quit dickin' around."

I focused on him, puzzled.

"For the second time," said the captain. "What happened today, Mister Stanton?" Oh! He'd been talking while Hank and I had been screwing around.

"What happened was while the doctor and I were talking," I peered toward Doc. She nodded. "It was our usual kind of talk abou—"

"They don't need to know what we talked about, Stan."

Nicos scratched his head near his ear. Then he leaned over and asked her to repeat what she'd said, but she ignored him.

"Okay," I said. "We were talking and these guys blew open

the door and tried to kill us."

"Like that."

"Yup."

The captain scrutinized me. Hell, everybody did.

"Go on."

"It was scarier than seeing a priest moon someone, so I grabbed Doc, found a gun, and we waited for the police."

Like hell! screamed Hank. *You didn't do shit. I jumped the desk, chopped the guy's*

throat, and killed the other asshole. Then I— Shut up, Hank. I know you did. Let me speak.

I turned back to the captain, "They snatched Lacy. I saw them take Lacy."

Nicos jumped in, "I'm sorry. I'm having trouble hearing things today. Was he talking about your assistant, Dr. MacPherson?"

"Yes. Lacy Dallrop. She's been working for me for a few months. Does filing, medical transcriptions, things like that."

Nicos had a puzzled demeanor for a second and then jotted something down on his notepad.

"Thought she was a nurse."

"No, Girl Friday."

"So, Mister Stanton, how did you acquire the skills to fire that weapon and kill those men?"

Of course, the short answer was Hank did all the killing, but they weren't ready to believe that. Hell, Doc might buy it, but she would still say it was part of my psyche. And Nancy would laugh.

I regarded the captain dead in the eye and said, "I have no idea." And, right then, it was the truth. What I remembered most about that attack was Lacy's eyes as she was whisked away.

They blazed with fury. Scary.

The captain scowled and moved things absently around on his desk for about thirty seconds. Then he checked to see if he needed a shave, stopping halfway through the exercise and held his chin. "Clearly something's happening that doesn't make sense."

"Excuse me, Captain," Doc raised her hand politely, in school fashion. The captain, hoisted his eyebrows. "Do you have another name on file for Mister Stanton? You see Stan here can't remember anything."

The phone rang while the captain, unblinking, regarded Doc. It rang a couple more times before he reached for it. "Captain Beaufort." The man listened intently to whoever chattered in his ear.

Sybil launched into a chant, which set our body hairs to doing a jig. I don't know how she does this to me, but as with every woman I ever met, she can climb right inside and kick the living shit out of me, and all of it without physically touching me.

I think all women can do this inherently. It's as though they reach down through the mouth of a man, grab his testicles and clang them together as they pull them out. And the topper is they do it with their minds. They don't even get their hands dirty.

The captain's face paled, and he pursed his lips tight enough that even an experienced bar whore couldn't have pried it open with her tongue. His eyes danced over me and then did a once over with Doc. He pointed to Nancy and drew his finger back to me, using his eyes to push him toward me. After a short chew on the inside of his cheek, he mumbled and hung up.

He focused directly on Nancy, "Cuff him."

"Cuff who?" Nancy was as puzzled as a bum on skid row presented with a bar of soap.

"Who? Stanton there. Now!"

Nancy reluctantly pulled out the hardware while the captain fell back into his chair and blubbered, "Word's come down that the hooker who was shot was the wife of Senator John P. Stonegate."

"So why am I cuffing Stan?" The left cuff zipped tight.

"Because he is officially a suspect." He threw down a pencil on his desk hard enough that it ricocheted almost back into his eye. But he didn't even flinch as it zoomed by. "Seems that someone called asking who he really was, like the doctor here did a moment ago, and guess what? There ain't no one named Wilburn B. Stanton. The name is nonsense. And that makes him the number one suspect."

Zip went the other cuff, but Nancy was so befuddled, he closed it on nothing, air, the same air in which I did a terrific dance to out-maneuver everyone else in the room. Well, everyone but Doc. She watched us as if we'd imitated the Keystone Cops, which I suppose was exactly how it appeared.

Oi! Wanker, pick up a chair and toss it through the window, and then duck behind another chair, bet they'll think you jumped.

Good idea, Hank. Worth a try.

In the aftermath of the crashing-window technique, I shut my mouth and walked quickly to the doorway while everyone clambered to see me go splat.

Then Fox Boy came through with a little input. He told me to stroll through the detectives' room and down the stairs, pretend I was the mayor out for a walk.

Fox Boy is a devious guy.

45

CHAPTER NINE

The captain leaned back inside from gawking out of the window, his eyes ready to explode from the pressure. From experience, he knew everyone saw the vein stand out on his forehead as he turned around to survey the room. Stanton hadn't jumped. That meant he was still here, unless
the little bastard had already disappeared.

"Nancy, ferret around out there and see if you can find your buddy. Nicos, get back in the window and help me find the little asshole. Nicos! Out of the window and—" He grabbed Nicos's collar and pulled.

"Damn, Captain. What the hell is the matter with you?" Nicos caught sight of his boss's face and froze. "Yes, sir."

Nancy came back into the office with a shrug and a head shake.

The captain glanced once and raised his voice for emphasis. "Get out there and find him.

Both of you. Damn it, Nicos." He threw a pencil, barely missing his detective. "What the hell is the matter with you? Your ears not working or what?

"And take everyone standing around out there with you!" He grumbled, returned to his desk, sat down, and cradled his face in his hands. Halfway through rubbing his face, he noticed
Doctor MacPherson still sitting in her chair.

"What do you need?"

He liked the pleasant way she smiled; at least something was pleasant.

"You did not answer my question, Captain."

"What?"

"My question about another name for him."

"Lady, you have to be somewhat intelligent. You're a doctor." He observed her complexion darken by several shades as he spoke.

With her notepad tucked under one arm, she approached his desk. Her tone of voice sickly sweet,

"I have long believed that one should make the first move in the politest way possible. And I have come to realize also that if that fails, then other options become warranted. Do not talk down to me, ever, you little man. I gave you a chance."

With that, she stalked back to the door, opened it, and stepped through. Outside, and in full view of all the detectives, lawyers, and everyone else in the other room, she whirled around and screamed, "Don't you ever stare at my breasts again! Look at my face when talking to me." The door slammed, and she stomped out of the room and down the hall.

Not until she had exited the building did she allow the tiniest of smiles to grace her face.

"How do you like that, you bastard? Bet you won't talk down to me again."

With gazes both up and down the street, she wondered where Stan had gotten to, and then concluded it didn't matter. With a mental shrug, she took a taxi back to her office. She needed to survey the damage there and call the insurance people to start a claim. Maybe by the time she'd finished, she might have an idea of where Stan might be.

Captain Beaufort sat, incredulous, staring after the doctor yelled and had her fit. Perfect. Now, what the hell did I do to deserve that?

He reached for the phone, stopped, and tapped the desk for a few seconds, and reached again. After dialing purposefully, he sat back all the way into his chair and waited for someone to pick up.

"Yes." The voice on the other end was direct, loaded with

confidence.

"Need to keep you abreast."

The silence on the other end was, by default, permission to continue, but the captain hesitated. "Word came down. The woman who was killed was important."

"How?"

"She was married to Senator Stonegate." He talked rapidly now. "I don't know why she was there, or what she was doing acting like a whore."

"I'll take care of it."

"But he's not anyone I'd want—"

"I said I've got it. I'll take care of the senator. You do what you're told."

"All right. You need to know we've put Stanton down as the primary suspect."

The merest of pauses, and then, "Make it stick. He's the reason why. Make it stick!" A split second later the phone went dead in the captain's hand.

CHAPTER TEN

Outside, Hank reminded me that the entire police force would soon be pouring out from the same doorway that I lately exited, and they would be turning this place upside down to find good old *moi*. So I upped my pace to match everyone else out and about. I purposely did not raise my head when I detoured the broken chair and all of the glass shards that littered the sidewalk. At the alley, I ducked in and squirreled in behind the nearest dumpster.

Of course, everyone was all a-twitter inside my head, so I spared a second to ask for some quiet while I figured out a plan. Actually, I would have been happy to follow Sybil's lead,

but her voice was strangely absent.

Hank worked to jimmy the cuffs while I turned my mind elsewhere.

The name on my hospital ID wasn't the real thing. I knew that. It was the reason why nothing seemed to fit the middle name except plain B. Then why did the B thing still bug me, needle me to dwell on it, and wouldn't let go? Surely, I had an inkling about whether I made up the name to begin with? Bruno was out. Brendan? Bob? Nothing felt right. It rolled around in the back of my mind. Had to be there with all of the other people I used to be.

Ahn interrupted my thoughts to say he heard Doc yelling at someone then slammed the door. He heard the pattern of her footsteps heading this way.

Got to hide! yelled Hank. *The bitch tried to turn you in. I thought her information was supposed to be confidential. Damn bitch.*

I swiveled my head around to find a place, but it just made me dizzy. About to run down the street, Fox Boy yelled for me to stop. *The place ta hide is theah. Nobody sees somebody aworkin'. Go 'head. Pick up a coupla boxes theah on the side a that thing we hidin''hind. Bigger the betta. They'll glance right at us an' neva see us.*

In one swoop, a nearby rancid-smelling jacket found its way over my shoulders. Jacques gagged, but it had to be done.

Shut up, Jacques, or the noise will come out of our mouth.

Ahn yelled, *She comin' out!*

I picked up the boxes, turned around, and walked straight toward the precinct entrance.

Be Damned. Fox Boy's right. Doc turned right toward me and walked on past, didn't bat an eye. Too busy gawking for me in every direction except right in front of her.

Then she ran out and hailed a taxi. I dropped the boxes and ran after her, not quite close enough to hear her destination.

A loud screech and I was hit in the ass, the impact slamming me onto the back window of the cab. Total darkness followed.

My nose, pushed across my face, now resided somewhere on my left cheek when I woke.

Hank reached up and pushed it back, which hurt more than I could ever have imagined.

Quit being a pussy and shut up, growled Hank. *Think of something worse, mate, and the pain'll pass.*

Had trouble doing it, although gang rape by a troop of male gorillas came close.

Several people stood by, and from their expressions, dancing wasn't in my immediate future.

Damn.

Police appeared from everywhere, along with several whining sirens.

Nicos's smirky little face appeared above mine. The EMTs were on the scene in seconds, and as soon as they had me in the ambulance, he crawled in, smiling like the Cheshire Cat, and zip-tied my wrists to the metal bars of the bed.

The traveling time to the nearest medical facility gave my inner horde the opportunity to blame everyone else for getting caught. Well, not everybody on the inner roster. The most curious thing was that Sybil didn't join in the blamefest. I think she stood above that kind of shit.

I was still stewing over Sybil when I arrived at Outpatients. One doctor examined my nose while I cringed, remembering aroused gorillas, when he stopped and eagle-eyed me for a second. "Did you set your own nose?"

I grunted with a slight nod. He gritted his teeth and smiled, "Tougher than you appear." He presented his fist for a bump, and off he strolled.

The entire time in the ER, Nicos chuckled and made a general ass of himself, sniffing around and standing in the wrong place. He even made the nurses walk all the way around him. Eventually, a huge guy dressed in scrubs strolled out, identified himself as one of the nurses, and spouted a lot of legal crap about not letting Nicos stand where he was because of privacy. Nicos pretended he didn't understand, said something about not hearing very well, and flashed his badge.

Mister Nurse pretended in kind not to understand about his badge and gently walked forward with a great imitation of Nicos's smirk as he displaced the detective. As I tried to keep from guffawing, I saw that the nurse had some time in the past had his nose reside on his cheek too. Hank should have been around to help set it.

Five minutes later, Nancy showed up, polite and all.

Nicos stayed outside. I caught him peeking from behind the curtain and when Mister

Nurse turned his head, he faded out of view.

Nancy's countenance wasn't as bad as the day he found out about his wife, but he did have a constipated aura about him, and although he hadn't said anything, he was red in the face. "What're you doing, Stan?" He stood directly over me. "Your run is over, and now they're about to find out why."

I visually fenced with him while the nurses worked. An occasional glance toward the busy people all around served me as an unspoken excuse for not talking. Meanwhile, the voices were crazy – Hank had a grand plan of how to take everyone out, Fox Boy was telling me to lie low and wait for a way to escape again, Jacques wasn't concerned. He was busy admiring the magnificent upper body of one of the nurses. I had to admit it was worth a gander.

Nancy leaned down and whispered, "C'mon, Stan. What does your mystery lady say?"

"Does that mean you believe me? My story was true, ya know."

He pulled up a chair, with a gesture at one of the nurses for permission first. The hopeful cast on his face almost made me laugh and cry simultaneously. I checked the squawking inside, but Sybil wasn't anywhere.

"Listen, Nancy," I shook my head, "I don't know what the hell is happening. I swear that story I told you is true. No double-crosses like in the last case, besides that wasn't my fault anyway. It was Sybil."

"I know, your little lady fortuneteller." He glowered for a second. "All right, I'll take what you said as truth."

The medical people disappeared, and the silence in the exam room was deafening. Even my head had settled down. I studied Nancy.

Why do I find it difficult to talk to him? He knows more about me than anyone else outside my head. Well, there's Doc, but for reasons I can't come to terms with, she doesn't count.

I had to stop thinking for a second to have Hank shut up again.

"Listen, Nancy, I'm as confused as anyone about all of this crap. Hell, I'm probably more confused." I ran my tongue around my teeth, swallowed a gob of spit, and chewed on the inside of my mouth. "All I know is that people keep coming after me, and I can't get that girl from Doc's office out of my mind. Why the hell did they take her anyway? And what's the deal with this senator?"

"Stonegate?"

"Yeah. Does he figure, or simply his wife? For that matter does she even figure? God, my head hurts." I tried to move my hand to rub my head, but it was zipped to the bed. "C'mon, Nancy. I can't even rub my head."

Ahn was trying to tell me something, but I pushed him aside while I pleaded with my eyes for Nancy to take off the zip tie.

I smell flowers. Ahn's voice was louder than usual.

"Nancy? Let's go. Get me out of here." He took out his knife and snicked it open.

I smell springtime! Doc.

Then I smelled it too. It dawned on me what Ahn had been trying to say. She'd help to

bury me back in the precinct. And now she's here.

"Nancy, get me out of here. Now. Doc is in the building an—"

"In the building? How the hell do you know?"

"Nancy! Cut the damn ties and …" I glanced out of the door and there was Nicos, talking to Doc.

Shit!

I yanked my arms, the plastic ties cutting into my wrists. Nancy peered over his shoulder, did a double-take, and bent down to cut them. After he sliced hard, there was a pop, and my arm was free. I grabbed his knife and freed the other arm.

A quick glimpse over his shoulder revealed Doc talking, animated, to Nicos. Her hand pointed to my room and then back to him. She jabbed the air in the direction, I assume, of the precinct.

I ran to hide behind the wall of the room, "I gotta get outta here, Nancy, and she's standing in the doorway."

Nancy nodded. "They'll take my job if I do this." I shrugged.

He took a hefty breath and let it out. After ten seconds later, he headed out of the doorway. Loud, indiscriminate talking broke out between the three of them, and as I peeked around the door jamb, Nancy talked with wild gesticulations as he walked toward the waiting room. He even pantomimed someone climbing through a window. The male nurse didn't take his eyes off him.

As quietly as possible, I squeezed my way around the other way. Then, before I was out of the door, I heard Doc's voice. "Stan! There he goes, everyone. Stan, don't go!"

CHAPTER ELEVEN

The lamp on the corner of his desk illuminated only the immediate area, and except for the soft flickering from the television in the next room, the rest of the senator's office remained as dark as the night outside. He sat head in hands, elbows on the desk amidst papers. The day had been very trying, and his aide, Johnson, had run interference to keep the press and generally obnoxious people from bothering him.

The speech was done, now all he wanted was quiet. The day had been critical. Without it, they were stymied, could not move forward, and it all would have been in vain.

Why was she walking the street like a whore? The thought would not leave him alone.

"Sir?"

The senator raised his head. Johnson stood half in the shadows before the desk. It was always hard to see him in the shadows; his skin was the color of dark brown sugar, and he wore a dark gray suit, too.

"Sir, would you care to go home? I think we can leave now. The limo is ready, and I think most of the reporters have decided to go with the press release."

The senator leaned back in his chair, the weary lines on his face deeper than usual, his breathing slow. His sonorous voice was perfect for political speeches. "Thank you, Johnson.

Give me a few moments to tidy up, and we can move on down to the garage." Rick had always been a great aide, even when he'd first started fresh out of law school.

Johnson slipped into the darkness of the other room without a word.

The old politician buttoned his shirt collar, straightened his tie, and ran his hands through his silvery-white hair. He bent over, drew in a deep breath, and opened the second drawer on his right, revealing a lockbox built into the drawer. With his other hand, he fished around in his pocket for the key and opened the box. Several deft moments later, he pulled out a file and placed it in the briefcase next to the desk.

Pressing the intercom button, he leaned downward, "Johnson?"

"Yes, sir?" The voice gave no hint that it came from a speaker.

"Let the driver know we're heading that way." He picked up the case, snicked out the light and strode through the darkness toward the door to the suite. Johnson fell in beside him, and the senator addressed his aide over his shoulder, "How's Amy? She weathering the storm, or is she needling you to come home?"

"She's not even in town, sir. Remember, I sent her off on vacation. The election was rough, and she needed rest."

The senator nodded. "Yes, I forgot." They walked the rest of the way in silence, the aide taking his cue from the senator. During the ride, there was a lot to think about.

Johnson watched the senator step inside the mansion. The aide missed the window curtain parting as they drove off. He ordered the driver to take him back to the apartment, not the house.

It was tough when Amy was gone, but he distracted himself. From habit, he spent several nights a week in the private flat his wife knew nothing about.

The talent had discovered him when he was still in high school, but he had perfected it while in law school at Stanford. The name his parents had given him helped – Richard Jung Johnson. His mother had always liked Jung for a name, thought the eminent psychiatrist fascinating, and pushed her son toward that field until the day she'd been told in no uncertain terms that he fancied politics.

During high school, when the guys saw him in the showers,

someone had yelled his full name, and when that happened, they all guffawed uncontrollably. It was quite a pun, sounding like he was really hung – Jung Johnson. From there he was off and running, well, humping. And as time passed, he imagined himself as quite a cocksman, all because it was so large. Simply displaying the thing gave him pleasure.

He absently rubbed it as he gazed out of the window watching the neighborhoods slide by.

By the light from the occasional streetlamp moving through the limo, Johnson made himself a quick drink using the cheaper spirits. He left the Irish whiskey and Makers Mark alone and didn't even think about taking Scotch. He liked all that stuff, aged, single malt, shit like that, but the senator wouldn't tolerate any of his good stuff disappearing. So he used only the bottles

he'd seen the senator pour for not-so-important people.

The top-of-the-line spirits tasted much better, but at least these drinks put him in the mood for the evening.

Sipping from his glass, he sat back to watch the dramatic transformation when they changed subdivisions; the quality of the buildings morphed a little slower. He nursed his drink and closed his eyes as they drove. Before he knew it, the entire feel of the area was that of a different city.

The smells changed too. Instead of fresh grass cuttings and aromatic chlorophyll with hints of pine, the air fully boiled with exhaust, garbage, and aromas from the different street corner vendors – tacos, hot dogs with sauerkraut, and the occasional bagel.

After they stopped, he leaned toward the driver, "Another warning. The senator is never to know where you drop me." Then as an afterthought, "I know it's his limo, but remember.

Deniability. Deniability is key." The driver nodded.

Rick stepped out of the limo, his eyes lingered over the women who clumped together while they flirted for their livelihood, enticing him into a little pleasure. He wondered which slut it would be tonight.

The limo sped away.

The young man released some energy by grabbing a nearby drunk as he staggered by and pushed the bum headfirst into the building. The hollow sound of the man's head hitting the brick made him chuckle, and the way he slumped to the ground added to his pleasure. Johnson stepped over him into the entryway. There, he turned around to measure up the working women around him again. Yup. More excitement in his crotch than the night he'd married Amy.

Taking the stairs two at a time, the excitement of his imminent entertainment was almost too much. Walking by a couple rutting in the darkened hallway, he never even gave them a glance as he fished around in his pocket for the key to his little dive.

His secret place. This was where he did what he wanted, to whomever he felt like doing it. The sex here was so much better. The available earthiness compounded the experience. Even the proximity of the whores helped. Nasty enough to be forbidden.

Slamming the door behind him, he walked to the mirror. His hair was nappy. That wouldn't do so he grabbed his brush. It had to be right. He didn't like his receding hairline at all, but even as he brushed, he resigned himself to that. Satisfied, he gave the mirror a devilish little smirk, turned to his closet, and changed his clothes; the whole time the question of what sort of doxy would be his pleasure tonight consumed him.

A knock on the door as he pulled up his pants. A quiet tap.

The opening door revealed the woman in the hallway. He loved the way women glanced at his package, and it made his blood flow even more. He let her gawk, even rubbed himself brazenly and used the time to appreciate the elegance of the woman before him.

This will be fun.

All the women who knocked on his door wore the same perfume. On most, the aroma was too delicate and gave off only a subliminal odor, too refined for garish use. But not so on this lady.

She strolled in as though she owned everything in the world, especially him, and for the first time, he recognized the scent clouding her as the favored perfume of the senator's wife.

CHAPTER TWELVE

Doc's voice made me jump. The sound of it filled the air and pushed its way throughout the hospital, like the feces that almost squirted into my pants. Her volume came near to covering the ruckus I made trying to run away. Now, it didn't matter how much noise I made.

I pushed and shoved everyone out of my way, the people around me cussed and yelled, calling me everything from asshole to colorful words that described unlikely events involving my parents. A veritable cornucopia of obscenities. One little lady of about seventy-five flipped me off while screaming like a jaded porn star.

Damn, what a foul-mouthed bitch.

With no time to get upset, or even find ways to trip up the people chasing me, alligators chomping on my ass came to mind as I ran.

I slipped out of a side door and stumbled as fast as I was able to, sporting a limp, a sore wrist, and a gorilla-raped nose. I turned down the street as another door to the hospital slammed open behind me. I didn't bother to take a look-see. I needed to be far from here, as quick as

Seabiscuit heading toward a string of fillies shaking their tails at him.

The traffic was terrible. Every single person and couple in the city, all fighting their way home, out to eat, or searching for a bar, were packed into this very block doing those things. About to dart into a crowded eatery, Hank yelled at me to keep on down the street. I turned down the next street. I hoped to thin out and fade into the air like beaming away in Star Trek, but Hank kept yelling at me like a drill sergeant on crack.

The next corner came up, I turned. Behind me, I heard a ruckus, but the noise spurred me on.

Find a bar.

Tried that, Hank, but you didn't like it.

A rough one.

I stopped in a rundown entryway and gulped some air, studying the broken door to the bar. No way was I ever walking into that bar. I checked to see if there were shit-scrapers for cowboy boots, but I didn't see any.

This is it, mate. Go.

Hank stole my legs when I hesitated, and it didn't matter how much I objected. The door opened and in we walked. After a few steps I twisted to keep the door behind me in sight, but

Hank growled at me.

S*imply walk forward, Pencil Neck.*

Jacques thought the alley back there smelled unsavory, so he wasn't prepared for the stale beer, spilled whiskey, with shades of vomit and a light urine bouquet. He was appalled, and not only with the smell. He thought the overall ambiance quite lacking. Shitty wasn't the word he used. I believe it was diarrheal.

Truthfully, it was the kind of place where the guy next to you would as soon punch you in the face as buy you a drink. The place was dark, almost lit by three weak-assed bulbs that hung from pigtails in the ceiling. And cracks between the floorboards were big enough to see through.

My hand slid up to cover my nose, but Hank stopped it.

Let them see the blood, mate.

"Give me a beer, will ya, dark and heavy," again Hank, and this time he pointed down to the darker end of the bar. I'd have asked for a glass of water and stood there like a flipping idiot.

The television babbled loudly behind the bar, but I paid it no mind at all as I walked to the beer.

They need to see you limp.

Let it go, Hank.

I sidled up to end of the bar, sipped, and squinted sideways at the obnoxious television.

The face across the screen caught my eye. It was a news channel and the reporter yakked about

Senator Stonegate and some speech he gave. The station inserted Stonegate's voice for emphasis.

"This heinous act of killing, the murder of my wife, is a deliberate example of what I've been talking about. The world of violence is reaching deep within our society. It is one more way the world is terrorized. Need I remind you of the dramatic hijacking today?"

The news anchor came back, and the senator's face slid to the side to share the screen with several hooded figures, carrying assault rifles on the airfield in Boston, ready to open fire for their jihad, and martyr themselves to gain access to a jetliner.

I took stock of the bar, unable to see much, too dark. Ahn, however, did see through the gloom of the bar. Several patrons sported badly healed broken noses, some had cuts and bruises on their faces, and one had several teeth missing and a swollen lip.

The door burst open, and in walked Nicos and Nancy. One of the guys sitting at a nearby table glanced up and snorted to himself. The others at the table laughed uproariously.

The two detectives strode to the bar and showed the bartender their shields. He barely glanced at them and continued washing glasses. Everyone in the room pretended not to watch, but Hank told me they were all intent on the barkeep and the cops. Two men walked up to the bar not far from me and ordered a couple more brews.

I watched the palaver from the shadows: I was trapped if they gave me away. I eased deeper into the shadows.

Stop, Stan.

They're about to give us away.

Stop moving.

I itched to run, but Hank's calm nerves, determination, and grip on my arms and legs kept me from inching away. I'd have run like a rabbit with a firecracker up his ass if Hank's hold hadn't been so tight.

A second later, two other rough sons-of-bitches came to the bar with their hands raised.

They were all going to turn me in!

Damn it, Hank! Let me go.

That bastard wouldn't let me move at all.

A couple more minutes and, the detectives nodded and then turned away. After they'd gone, the bartender made his way down the bar refilling drinks, keeping his eye on the door. The closer he came, the faster he moved. "Man! Don't know what you did, but those shitheads want you bad. I got rid of them." He tapped his fingers on the bar once. "Stay put. Nicos may be back, but he's okay, part of the Caucus."

"Terrorism is the number one enemy today!" The senator's voice screamed from the television. The barkeep's lips curled and he reached under the bar for the control. As he was about to click the button, Ahn yelled, "Stop!" His eyes had caught something. "Uh, sorry, pal. I need ta see something on the screen there. Mind?"

"Naw. What you need to see that damn senator for?"

"Not him. I'm searchin' the film behind him. Hold on a sec."

I let Ahn study the file film.

"Hey, can you pause that thing?"

The bartender shrugged, "Sure."

"Okay … now."

It was a close-up of the hooded Isis terrorist. Someone had gotten close enough to pan across several of them as they took up defensive positions. A woman dressed in that featureless thing they call a chador, with a veil over her face and everything. That didn't happen often, but that wasn't what Ahn had seen.

On closer examination, I found it. Her eyes. They were heterochromatic – one blue and one green. Fox Boy was going batshit crazy inside at the memory, the memory of the slave owner's wife. In the background were the hostages, and right in the middle was … Lacy?

What the hell is this?

No one answered me.

Somehow, I had to find that terrorist.

Sybil? How do I?

She didn't answer, but I had a buzz in my gut. "Where was that? Did that happen today?"

The bartender nodded, his eyes shifting around the room, "This morning in Boston. Why, you like what you see?"

Hank spoke before I could. "Yeah. That's the kind of shit that really speaks." Damn it, Hank. Shut up!

If I could have choked the living dog shit out of him, I would have.

He kept yapping. "I need to find an outfit like that!" The men in the bar surrounded me.

CHAPTER THIRTEEN

Abdul Mu'izz sat on his couch, dressed khaki pants with a crisp Oxford shirt the color of a sunset, hot tea in front of him while he talked on his cell phone. Before him and to the side of the tea, was a lite snack of untouched herring and crackers.

The hour was late, and Mu'izz's patience was raw. "It's been more than a day." He spoke into the cell phone in his hand. "The senator warned against losing him. He is very vocal." A forced chuckle came from his mouth, and then he took a sip of tea.

"And as much as he talks, nobody listens," the voice on the other end observed. "This is why."

Mu'izz sat up straight, the muscles in his jaw tight, hidden but unseen beneath his beard.

The deep breath he took before replying was the only thing that tamed the deadliness in his eyes.

"I will have our men attack as planned, but don't ever talk to me in that fashion. You are not in

the top tier. You take orders as much as I do, so do not think I will bow to your any whim."

He inhaled again.

"The infidel women continue to bring us money that we need. I think there is another enterprise we can use to bring even more. Drugs. Meth—"

Again, his jaw clenched as he listened.

The door opened and two men entered. Careful not to make any sound, they stood at a respectful distance. Then Mu'izz put his hand over the phone and turned their way. One of them stepped forward and whispered into his ear.

"Excuse me," he exhaled and sat quietly for about five seconds and then spoke into the phone. "I will have to go. They have found the man. He was in one of our bars." He stood up, pointed at the door, and the two men left.

"We are not through yet. Believe me, we are not finished. I will talk to you at a later time." Without waiting for a reply, he hung up and put the cell phone in his pocket.

Exiting the building, he was only in the bright sunlight for a few seconds, ducking directly into the back seat of a car that appeared to have been put together from spare parts from a salvage yard. The mismatched paint on the body functioned like camouflage and fitted right into the urban scene. The choice was this vehicle or a very fancy ride that marked him as a gangbanger or pimp. This man was much too smart to be taken for either.

Dark, tinted windows were rife in the area, concealing all the amenities he wanted:

comfortable leather seats and a well-stocked bar; he refrained from imbibing while his subordinates might see. As far as his crew was concerned, Allah was the reason for everything, and spirits were forbidden. They all knew about the bar, but they also understood it helped seduce the infidels into Allah's cause.

The soothing music had barely calmed him on the short uneventful drive; even the tension in his shoulders hadn't eased before the car slowed to a stop.

Stepping out, his driver and guard had taken up their positions, and he strode straight into the bar. Ignoring the obnoxious smells, he stood in the doorway and visually inspected it. The

'tender flicked his eyes up and gave a slight nod to Abdul; several other men populated the room, some at tables, some standing at the bar. The man for whom he searched was nowhere to be seen.

The bartender pointed at Mu'izz and muttered to Nicos. The detective turned around; after only the slightest hesitation, he joined Abdul.

Mu'izz stared, giving away nothing about his mood. Nicos licked his lips several times during the short distance that separated them. Mu'izz said nothing as the detective stood before him, waiting instead for his underling to report.

Nicos rubbed his chin and swallowed, his eyes darting to an empty glass still on the table from the last patron there.

Mu'izz caught the glance, and his lip curled.

"He was here." Nicos turned around and pointed at the far end of the bar. "The boys sent us away when we came in. I, uh, I didn't see the signal they gave until I was almost out of the door. It took me a while to ditch my partner."

Nicos appeared in pain as a smile spread across his face. He wiped his forehead with his arm; a broken chuckle escaped him. "That stupid shrink of his cornered Nancy. If it hadn't been for that, I would still be working on getting away."

Mu'izz grabbed a chair and sat. His eyes remained fixed on Nicos as he absently moved his arm through the air, signaling to clear the table. The two bodyguards attending him quickly took the empties and the bartender tripped over a chair to help. He ended up wiping the table.

"The level of your incompetence is growing exponentially, Nicos. What was the order I gave concerning—"

"I didn't see the Sig—"

Mu'izz had held up his hand to shut him up. Before Nicos could speak again, the elevated hand changed from four fingers pointing skyward to an index finger, the meaning clear. "What else do we know?"

Nicos's eyes flicked over the room. "The bartender here thought Sigm— uh, Stan, was a fugitive and he sent him to one of the camps. Said he had the bearing of being tough enough to handle it. Tough enough? That makes no sense. The guy's a wimp. I mean a real puss—"

The barrel of the .38 Special touched the detective's head at the same time as the round took the inside of Nicos's head to the outside. Two nearby men sprinted to the door, where the dispassionate bodyguards shot them without a single flinch well before they reached it. The smell of the carnage, the iron-tinged blood and the burned sulfur of the cordite, filled the room.

Thick lines of blue-gray smoke stratified the air.

The epitome of calm, Mu'izz stood while passing the handgun back to his bodyguard, who somehow made it disappear. He motioned to the bartender, "Which camp?"

No one moved – the bartender stood rooted to the floor, stupefied. The eyes of every man showed indecision. They wanted to do something, but it was clear no one knew exactly what.

The barkeep recruited them all, and now he gave deference to this executioner.

"You will make me repeat myself?" The irritating quality in Mu'izz's voice magnified the situation. He held out his hand, and the .38 reappeared in it.

At the sight, the bartender sprang to life. He put down the glass he'd been wiping and placed one hand on the bar. The other he slipped under it. "Sent him to the one in Wyoming."

Mu'izz walked forward, pistol held hip-high but leveled at the man. "You will put both hands on the bar. Did you think I wouldn't know about the weapon under there?" He motioned with the handgun for the man to move down the bar.

The guards pulled their weapons and covered the entire bar.

"I want him diverted to the Amsterdam Corridor." He held up his free hand to stop the bartender from speaking, "If you wish to continue working for the Caucus, you will do it now.

No discussion. No debate." Abdul stood close to the bar and simply looked, deadpan, into the man's eyes and waited.

The barman nodded, and Mu'izz turned and strode out. At the door, he stopped and spoke over his shoulder, "Half." Then he left.

The two bodyguards each shot twice, dropping four men. The guards strolled to the bodies and put one more shot into each head. Then they backed out, weapons ready and aimed at the remaining four in the room.

Mu'izz stood between the two bodyguards. "Punishment for thinking about killing me."

Again, he focused on the barkeep. "Clean up the mess and

switch the man to the Amsterdam
   Corridor."

   At a purposeful yet unhurried pace, he strode to his waiting vehicle. He raised the tinted glass that separated the back seat from the front; halfway up, he said, "Take me back, and find the doctor." A wicked grimace flowed over his face. "She grasps everything."

CHAPTER FOURTEEN

Doctor Sally MacPherson scanned the small bar through the window. It was one of those drinking establishments that has a mix of clientele – several local drinkers escaping from their spouses, taxi drivers from the garage down the street, and a few couples out for a drink.

The music was loud but not obnoxious. The blue lights around the booths were low enough to encourage relaxation, maybe a degree of intimacy, but bright enough to be respectable. The red and white lights over the bar were comfortable, both for the middle-agedbut-sexy bartender in her ultra-tight pants to see what she was doing, and the customers to see the snacks of beer nuts and pretzels scattered within arm's reach.

Barely had she stepped in the door when Sally turned to Nancy, "You have to run his—"

Nancy held up a finger and pointed to an open booth in one of the darker spots of the room, out of view from the windows, but a person sitting in it could still see the entryway.

Sally sat down and bounced over to the middle of the table. She drummed her fingers on the small table and watched Nancy sit on the other side. It took forever for his eyes to meet hers. He scanned the bar as he checked to see who came in before them. Not until a satisfied expression covered his face did he focus on her. "Now what was it you wanted me to do for you?"

"You have to run Stan's fingerprints again."

With a slight inclination of his head, he held up his hand, "You said that out there. And why would I run them again? He's, uh, kind of my friend."

"That's why! He needs you to help him."

"And being his friend means that I run his prints." With a shake of his head, "Doesn't make sense. By the way, why did we have to ditch Nicos? He's my partner and I don—"

"I told you." Her hands fluttered around as she searched for what she wanted to say until she folded them together and forced them onto the table.

"What can I get you two?" The bar girl, bored, stood next to the table.

Nancy rubbed his forehead, "Coffee for me. Doc?"

Sally took in a breath and rubbed the bridge of her nose. She shook her head, "Nothing for – no wait. Irish whiskey, please. Neat." The waitress sped off.

Nancy's eyes opened a bit wider for a second. "That's quite a change from nothing to straight whiskey."

"I know it's expensive. I'll get it."

Nancy shrugged without an argument. "So, what?"

Now Sally had to check around her. "I can't really explain why Stan needs to discover his real name. It's …"

"Privileged?"

She fixed her gaze on him. "Oh, no. That's not it. I'm not really concerned about privilege now." She chewed her lip for a couple of seconds. "If he can remember something, then more things might come."

"You want me to run them so he can remember things?" His expression of bafflement almost made her laugh. "What the hell are you doing?" He stilled.

Sally turned to find out what he'd seen, but nothing caught her eye. The waitress brought their drinks and Sally slipped her a twenty. The bar girl fumbled around for change, and Sally waved her away and beamed a smile at her.

After the waitress left, the doctor leaned forward, "What was it? You saw something.

What?"

Nancy shrugged and sipped his coffee; she studied him as he attempted to convey calm and failing. He slurped from his cup, "Saw a bartender who belongs down the street."

"So?"

"So he should be pouring drinks right now. Added to that, he was searching for someone. Plus, that was one rough bar. So, why is a bartender of a really rough bar loose, turning the town upside down for someone in the middle of the night?"

She picked up her drink. Her eyes narrowed and shifted from Nancy to the window, and back. "This guy's demeanor violent?"

Another shrug from Nancy. "It was a really rough bar."

She noticed he continued monitoring the window while he drank his coffee. She put her drink back on the table, half gone, and had to control her hands to keep them from fluttering.

"Listen, Detective. They're searching for Stan."

His eyes studied her. "Who?"

"I don't know their names, but they have an organization that does … things."

He put his coffee down and grabbed her hands to prevent them from bouncing around.

"Okay, you better tell me what's going on, because right now, there's a man out on the street

nosing around. I saw him, and I too think they want Stan."

She scooted around on her bottom to get a better view of the window, but Nancy grabbed her, "No, don't. Damn!" He grabbed her and pushed her to slide out of the booth. "We gotta go." Then he took off toward the back of the bar.

She had to run to keep up. He'd disappeared toward the restrooms, but before she ducked down that hallway, a noise broke out behind her, and she turned around to see.

A crazy man pushed people everywhere. Their eyes connected. "Hey! I got her. She's in here!"

More men poured through the door behind him.

Sally ran. Her eyes darted all around. Where the hell is Nancy?

She ran toward the back exit, and as she passed the men's room, Nancy peeked out. He waved her on, whispering, "Go, go. Out the door, into the alley. Go, stay in the shadows, and I'll catch up. Damn it! Go!"

She crashed through the door and traded the dimly lit

hallway for the deadly dark alley.

Stay in the shadows. He'll come.

Rancid garbage assailed her nose as other gross things made her shiver – her hand slid over something slimy on the side of the dumpster, a furry animal scurried over her foot, and a dark shadow urinated against a wall.

She stumbled down the alley, kicking through trash and slipping on the occasional slick piece of garbage. Several gunshots echoed off the buildings as she dropped behind the nearest dumpster. The shots had come from the door behind her.

Nancy!

A shadow stumbled into the alley and collapsed. It presented like the detective. He had to grab the dumpster to stay upright.

Her heart pounded, although she wasn't sure who it was, and her eyes bounced everywhere, staring into the night. Like before – as soon as the thought rang through her head, and she trembled with both anger and fear. Then she remembered: her reason to fear was gone.

Someone burst through the door. Another followed. Both carried handguns, and they kicked, cursed, and crashed around searching for something. One paused over the collapsed person for a second, raised their head again and turned down the alley away from her. The other headed in her direction.

She crept further into darkness, as she did a low growl came from deeper in the shadow and she clenched.

The nearest man paused, cocked his head.

He stepped closer and not knowing what to do, she squatted, afraid to go deeper because of the growling, cornered.

"Back here," the man yelled over his shoulder.

The other man was out of sight, but her imagination saw him stalking in her direction, weapon pointed at her. She crouched lower yet, her whole body tense.

"Behind the dumpster?"

"Yeah."

A pistol came into view. Trash moved against her butt. Her

breathing grew ragged.

She bolted and ran, into the dark away from the two men. But someone grabbed her, forcing her to the ground, into the filth. Rolling in the slime, she kicked at the form, hard, as she'd been taught, but only caught a leg. Then again, this time hitting something soft, she heard a grunt.

The explosion from the gun made her stop dead still, and the other man scooted forward. Hands grabbed her from behind, lifting her up to stand, squeezing her breasts roughly. Garbage covered her; the shadow of a man pointed a pistol at her; the other gunman, the one she'd kicked,

rose from the ground.

"That bitch kneed me. Tried to kick my balls!" With a vicious backhand, he slapped her face, stunning her. "Don't ever do that again."

"Don't try to force me to do anything then."

She felt the ferocious sting of another slap; dazed, she tasted blood. One of them grabbed her hair, yanked her forward, then thrust her deeper into the alley.

Gun. Get a gun! She wanted Nancy's, but it was too far away.

A feral cat hissed and lunged from behind the dumpster, startling the man holding her. He let her go to defend himself from the cat and fell to the ground.

A gunshot from behind her rang out.

She ran, but the man lunged, grabbing her ankle with an unbelievable grip and yanked her to the asphalt.

The alley was silent.

Not one varmint made a noise as he pulled her to her feet, placed his pistol to her head, and pulled her back to him so he could inspect his partner.

Dead. She knew from the odd position of the body, and the far-off streetlight glinting in unseeing eyes.

They slogged through the trash a little further to view the shooter. Even in the darkness, she identified Nancy. His condition was grave. Dark stains covered the body, which did not move.

At least he gave a good fight.

After gawking for long seconds, her captive yanked her hair and forced her away.

CHAPTER FIFTEEN

Carbonella brushed her hair, freshening herself, completing her morning routine to get ready for work. She stopped brushing and slipped the bra strap back onto her left shoulder.

Leaning close to the mirror, she acknowledged the beginnings of age lines and rubbed them lightly. Yep, damn things are there all right.

The door opened behind her. The reflection of Tom, her boss, confirmed he was checking out her ass. She chuckled to herself; she didn't care. Her butt was full and well-rounded, and it had an athletic flair, not saggy. Besides, Tom saw a lot more than panties last night. She laughed and wiggled her tush.

They'd done the dirty again – broken the fraternization rule. Even though they'd promised to call it off, they'd relapsed. It wasn't as if they were having an affair; both were single and enjoyed the other's company. No emotion involved at all; it was physical, a fuckbuddy thing. How was that hurting anyone else?

A stupid rule. No sexual relationships within the chain of command, and this was definitely in the chain.

He slipped in the rest of the way, stood in his boxers while she did her eyebrows.

"What?" Her husky voice demanded attention.

He was tight, firm with a growing stomach, and the most piercing blue eyes she had ever seen under his thinning blond hair that he kept perpetually in a brush cut. The picture of an active man caught in a middle-age drop in muscle tone. "They found Sigma."

Ten years his junior, she frowned and pointed him to the door. His expression was that of undeniable 'Are you crazy?' as he held his hands in the air. She did another definition stroke on her eyebrow while her mind took off, and she turned toward him. "Okay. It's against my rules."

"Against your rules! We've been bof—"

"I know what we've been doing." The huskiness gave her words more emphasis. "That's why I rescinded my personal rule." Her mouth spread in a sultry grin, and she turned back to the mirror. "Where did they find him?"

"Right here in New York." He bounced right into the conversation, barely containing his

excitement.

"He's been in New York?"

"He was already here." He snorted, "They had him in Bellevue when he escaped."

"Didn't escape. The damn doctor let him go."

"She's always been key, but too unpredictable."

She sighed. "We've been through that."

"He left." He stared with his hands slightly raised.

She took a deep breath, expelled more exasperation, unconsciously pulled up her bra strap again, grabbed her top, and pulled it on. "Okay. How did he surface?"

"He's connected to Gillian Stonegate's killing. Prime suspect. Wouldn't even have known, except they ran his prints again for some reason. Had a hell of a time blocking the result."

Carbonella took down the hanger with her jeans on them from the door and poured herself in, dancing around to pull them up, amply fleshed to fill them out. "Why?" She shook her hair to make it fall better. "We've been hunti—"

"I didn't want anyone to know who he was. Command decision. I'm still the commander here, by the way." He stood, moved his hands for her to twirl around, which she did with nary a blush. "Office." He pointed to the door.

She stood stock-still for a second gazing at him. Then she shrugged, "Yes, sir." She marched through her apartment, stopping long enough to grab her jacket and weapon, then did another turn and blocked the doorway. "If you show up at the office like that, you'll blow our covers."

His eyes followed the direction of her finger, and with a

blush, tucked himself back into his boxers. "Okay. Come on back in and let me get ready. Then we'll go to the office."

He disappeared into the bedroom and raised his voice for her to hear. "Anyway, Sigma's in Bellevue again. Maybe this time we can keep him there and talk to him. The whole damn thing is messed up."

He tucked in his shirt as he walked from the bedroom toward the door. Slipping on his shoes, he grabbed his tie and tossed it around until he'd tied it the way he liked it.

"Let's go." He shrugged into his jacket, adjusted it to cover his hip-holstered sidearm, and walked into the hallway.

They took the same taxi but carefully avoided talking about sensitive things, which cut down considerably on the conversation. Most of the ride passed in silence. Neither noticed the normal traffic, the driver's incessant chattering in a language that almost qualified as English, nor did they see crowds of people milling about on the sidewalk.

By long-standing habit, they stopped the cab about two blocks from the command post and she climbed out. Normally, he would have jumped out there because he lived down the road, and it wasn't unusual for him to walk. Today, though, he needed to arrive first; he needed to crank a fire under everybody.

Carbonella watched the taxi speed away and as she walked, the traffic noises filled the air, but her pensiveness shielded her from them. In front of the Chinese Restaurant, the aroma broke through her moodiness, making it hard to ignore.

Heavy with garlic and laced with whatever it was that the restaurant cooked early in the morning, probably soy sauce, maybe ginger, a little horseradish? Whatever, it made her stomach growl, and she patted it lightly and promised herself she would have Chinese for lunch.

Three shots fired from two, maybe three hundred yards away, pulled Carbonella's head back and refocused her. People scattered, clearing the street with remarkable alacrity, and Carbonella had a visual. A woman dressed like a streetwalker fired a couple of rounds from a handgun as she ran across the street.

Carbonella grabbed her weapon and took off, shouting while she ran. "Down. Drop.

Now. Get the hell out of the way!" She ran into the street. A car screeched to a stop, clipping her leg at the thigh, almost bending her knee the wrong way, but she continued.

"Move!" She limped to a stop, assumed a good firing base, her weapon extended ready to fire, exhaling all the way to help steady herself. A split second later, she lowered her sidearm. The hooker was too far away, and there were still too many bystanders. Sam and John were in pursuit. She let them take the chase.

Bystanders screamed that someone was down, and her attention changed. Tom!

Forgetting about her knee, she ran to the downed man. As she feared, it was Tom. Blood soaked the sidewalk, but he was moving.

She dropped to her knees next to him. His glazed eyes roamed aimlessly, and he tried to sit. She pulled off her shirt and wadded enough to push into the spurting wound and force him back down. "Lie still, you dumb bastard."

Carbonella checked his skin and eyes, maintaining pressure, and listening to Alice, the IT person on the task force, talking to 911. Sam and John came back from their chase, both gasping; John bent over, hands on his knees trying to get air; Sam stood straight, hands on his hips and panted out the SITREP, Situation Report, "Streetwalker walked up and fired. She's been here all day."

"You dumbasses." She focused on Tom. "A streetwalker in the morning? Nobody thought that was strange?" Her eyes dragged her face up to them, flaming the entire way.

John was still bent over, his breathing easier, "Easy Carbonella, I don't like it, either."

The ambulance pulled up and the EMTs took over. Tom was

alive but needed to go pronto.

Carbonella watched as they loaded him, and once he was inside the ambulance, she pulled all three of her people, Alice, Sam, and John to the side. She threw her bloody shirt to the ground and turned to Sam, "Give me your shirt." He stripped it off.

Carbonella grabbed the shirt and threw it on. "Okay. This location is blown. Alice, get me another one, and I want it today. Sam, what did this whore look like?" She buttoned up while Sam answered.

"Young, late twenties maybe, ratted red hair, classic hooker clothes showing a lot of skin. And tight little titties."

"Not the time to make jokes, Sam," her husky voice giving more emphasis again.

"He's not joking," ventured John. "Who the hell looks at a hooker's face?"

Carbonella skewered him with a dick-shriveling glance. "A federal agent is who, John."

Her eyes flicked over to Sam and withered him too, for emphasis. "Get me a description, and

Alice, I want that new command post now."

Carbonella stomped off, buttoning the shirt and fishing her cell from her back pocket. She had to call Control to let them know a man was down.

Sam and John stared at each other.

Alice punched numbers into her phone. Waiting for an answer, she whispered to the men,

"Her titties were small."

CHAPTER SIXTEEN

The senator faced the camera, took a sip from the glass near his hand, and disciplined himself to keep from wiping away the sweat beading on his lip as they signed off. The consensus of his advisers was to let things like that stand. The gleam there spoke of how concerned he was for the subject of his speech, and the thunderous applause confirmed it.

The oration had gone exactly as planned. Initially subdued as he talked about the death of his wife. he gradually built both volume and intensity as he segued into the true subject – terrorism.

The sympathy of his constituents dovetailed so well with the voters' outrage and contrasted the administration's apparent failure to protect the country's interests. They shared the same party, but his ability to predict was clear.

The president came off like a buffoon after rolling over for the terrorist last night, totally inept at being Commander and Chief. Stonegate chuckled, he had not had to say, 'I told you so.' It had been self-evident. Predicting the highjacking of two nights ago, with its subsequent resolution last night, had catapulted the senator into the national focus. His private polls had him at a commanding zenith in popularity right now. The president's fiasco had ended exactly the way he, the senator in charge of the committee on terrorism, had predicted. He hadn't had to gloat; during the news conference, he'd warned the world that the jihadists would crash that aircraft, and that was exactly what had happened.

He strode through the Capitol Building, toward the tunnel that connected the Senate offices to the Capitol. Waving the golf cart closer, he sat before the cart was under him. His driver arrived barely in time.

The senator turned around and spoke briskly to Rick who sat

at the ready in the back.

"I'm taking the rest of the day off. Let the press stew on what I said, and I don't want any clarification sent to anyone. All a clarification will do is diminish the lead I now command. In fact," he pointed at his aide. "I want you to take a day off, too. Amy back in town?"

"Not yet, sir. Said she'd be back sometime early next week."

The senator turned to the page who drove and signaled for her to speed up. That sort of thing was strictly controlled in the tunnel, but he didn't think anyone would snivel about it today. Not after that speech. "Well, see if you can find something to do without getting in the spotlight."

"Yes, sir."

"I want my limo out front in about a half-hour. I'm driving to the fishing lodge, and that is strictly need-to-know. If anyone shows up to bother me, I'll have your ass. Understand?"

The cart approached the offices and they slowed. Stonegate slid out of his jacket, tossed it to Rick, and rolled his sleeves to his elbows. The air was cool, especially with the breeze created by the speed of the cart, but a sweat stain covered the back of his shirt. He loosened his tie.

"Rick, I don't want to see you for twenty-four hours. In fact, no one for that time. Got it?"

"Yes, sir."

"I'm to the can and take a leak. By the time I reach my office, you will have hung up my coat, ordered my limo, and disappeared. I'll see you in two days.

"Enjoy your time off. Sorry, you can't spend it with your wife, Rick." Then he walked into the nearby restroom.

The senator rode down the winding road through the woods catching the first sight of his retreat through the surrounding trees. The large structure was more of a lodge than a fishing shack, and he loved the place. The faint light from the vertical windows of the fishing lodge gave it a homely appearance, especially in the dark like this.

He'd hardly ever gone fishing while there, although below the cliff face, over which the lodge jutted, a wonderfully secluded portion of the North Fork River was perfect for it.

He saw his orders before leaving to turn on a few lights had been carried out by the staff. His chauffeur let him out in front of the massive, weathered oak doorway, and he grabbed his overnight baggage. Slipping inside, he placed his bag on the floor. The red-oak walls and ceramic floor spread out before him, and he took a deep breath. The odor was always great here.

Simply smelling it put him at ease again. It had been a rough couple of days.

The news of Gillian's death had been a shock, but he'd carried on with business. Brushing up the speech and giving it had been exhilarating. Then there was the relaxing journey to his hideaway in West Virginia. He'd had a few glasses of single malt, sipping as they drove, eyeing the fall foliage that drifted past his window. He'd also mulled over the last night and day. Everyone searching, wondering about Gillian and why she died. It was a shame, but there was nothing to be done about it now in the middle of the night. At least there was the sympathy vote.

His ear picked up something and he stood still. The small noise came from the next room.

Now he wished he hadn't told his driver/guard to take the next two days off.

Another noise.

There was a .32 automatic inside the kitchen. If he made it in there ... Turning the first corner, he saw a shadow move.

Damn. They're in the kitchen.

He backed up and tried to think. He needed another weapon.

The bedroom.

He hot-footed across the great room to the bedroom as quietly as possible, where he ran to the end table and grabbed Gillian's .22, which she kept loaded.

Halfway back through the great room, he stopped. This is stupid. I need to leave.

He turned to the door and his ears picked up something else. A smile crept across his face, and he backtracked to the kitchen. Quietly he entered the room.

Naked except for the apron, her dark honey-colored skin contrasted nicely with the cream-colored apron. Engrossed in the little tune she hummed, she was unaware of his presence.

This close, he made sure not to make extra noise.

Slipping behind her, the humming was stronger, a popular tune from a few years ago.

He listened and watched the way her naked buttocks swayed with her humming. Then he stepped close and wrapped his hands around her under the apron top cupping her breasts and gently pinching her nipples. "Guess who?"

She stood stock-still. "Hmmm. Doctor … no, fingers don't feel right. Too warm. Not a doctor." She wiggled her rear and pressed her breasts further into his hands.

He leaned over and kissed her neck.

"Ummm. That's good," she purred, and her hands caressed his head, playing with his thinning white hair and then slithered down to fondle his package.

"I didn't think you would be back so soon," he said between nuzzles. "Figured you'd be here late tonight at the earliest."

"Made quick connections." She giggled a bit and turned to press herself into his hardness.

"We have plenty of time. Rick thinks I won't be back for another few days."

"I know."

"Oooh."

CHAPTER SEVENTEEN

Arousal charged the air. The aroma of hers added to mine, and together it helped us focus. I stroked her breast, nuzzled her nipple, the softness of her skin as exciting as anything imaginable. My God, she intoxicated me. My need for her increased with our rhythm.

Small tremors raced down her body, and the sound of her breathing grew louder in my ear. Her soft mewling— Gunshots outside.

I rolled away, grabbed my handgun and ran to the window. As I raised my head for a better view, the window shattered, shards flew everywhere, and I ducked.

A quick glance reassured me she hadn't been hit. She'd rolled off the other side.

More glass shattered above, showering me with shards, and I heard another bullet *thunk* deeply into the frame. My arm trembled with the effort to curb my urge to shoot at the bastards. I had no idea where they were, and my shots had to count, limited ammunition.

I took another chance and peered outside through the bottom corner of the window. As soon as I did, more shots followed. I still had trouble seeing from whence they came.

Behind me, I heard more shots. Several bodies pushed and shoved, all men. A hard shove and my mind cleared; reality coalesced around me.

The room faded to become the inside of a truck.

Wake up, p*encil neck!*

Always count on Hank to help.

Quit dreaming about her and get the fuck out the door, ya wanker.

The confusion around me was total.

Where the hell am I?

The back end of the truck was open. More than half the men in the back were already out.

They'd jumped out into the night, disappearing as they did. I heard more shots. Again, no direction.

I need a weapon.

No response from within. I inched down the trailer bed, trying to figure things out. Ahn's nose told me that the smell of gunfire came from the right and there wasn't any wind. I dropped to the ground and rolled to the left, my breath clouding in the cool air as I moved. I kept rolling until I was behind the rear tires.

From there, I saw three men firing AK47s into the air. Two other men stood nearby laughing, their weapons leveled at more men bailing out of the truck. They fired into the air again, the muzzle flash from each round lit the layers of cordite smoke filling the air.

I grabbed a handful of gravel and stood. Hank fell suspiciously quiet. I trotted toward the front of the eighteen-wheeler.

We need to be careful, mon ami.

Not now, Jacques. I'm busier than a cat covering shit.

Hugging the vehicle, I inched around enough to see.

The firing had stopped, and they all held their weapons at the hip, ready to execute everyone. The silence echoed in my ears. Indecision is a killer and mine was shivering its way through with the chilly air. I stood shaking with as much clue as a five-year-old kid asking a whore for the specialty of the day.

The driver's door opened and he stepped out, grabbing his AK by the top cover, nowhere near ready to fire.

"Hey," I said, barely loud enough for him to hear and turn. I tossed the gravel into his face and attacked. The gravel in my other hand beefed my fist solidly. I hit him under the nose with a phantom punch that would have made Mohamad Ali proud. I drove it upward, and he dropped straight down.

His rifle clattered on the road. I snatched it up before anyone noticed and carefully made my way back to the front of the truck. Hiding behind the front tire and fender, I aimed the weapon at the ground in front of the firing squad and squeezed the trigger. Most of the rounds burst where I wanted. I say most, because I did get one of the men in the foot, and when he dropped, the others stood immobilized.

Not bad, said Hank.

I heard him laughing.

Now you show up? Where the hell were you whe—

"Drop it, boy."

The pistol pressed against my temple stopped me scolding Hank.

I put over the AK down.

Hank's turn to scold me now. *It was a 1911, moron, and it was pressed against your head. The damn thing won't fire if the barrel is pressed against something. It's a safety.*

I let it go. I was busy. It wouldn't do any good to argue anyway. Besides, Hank was already dead. I was the only one who would've bit the dust. Added to which, the man's other hand functioned suspiciously like he wanted to try to re-break my nose.

You're an asshole, Hank.

Piss off, wanker.

The nudge between my shoulder blades suggested I saunter forward. As I did, Ahn commented on the air. From the smell, or maybe the quality of the air, he divined that we were in the mountains. Wyoming maybe? Ahn said it was very like Switzerland.

I had no idea how he might know what Switzerland would be like; we'd never been.

Would've said something to him but I had to keep my wits about me and didn't have time. Hell, I was actively ignoring all my inner horde.

We walked up to the other men. Their leader stood over the poor bastard I shot in the foot, while he rolled around like a scared armadillo. With a sigh, the leader took out his pistol and fired right next to the man's head. "I said shut up, ye doaty bampot. That's betta. Now let

Tommy have a look at yer foot."

Steam shot from his mouth as he spouted off. I thought I saw spittle too, but I tried not to think about it, as the trajectory landed on the toeless man on the ground.

The leader turned an eye to me as if taking my measure while the medic tended to the squalling, bleeding guy. "Ye're ain't very fearsome tae look at, is ye. Well, goes tae show." He grabbed my shoulder with his free hand and walked me off into the night.

Acute awareness of the semiautomatic he had in his other hand made me hope there was a warm fire in our future and not a place for him to fire at my head. After about fifteen paces, we stopped.

Shit. No campfire.

"We stopped like we always dae. Want ta know ef'n anyone had a bite in 'em instead of ainlie a bark. Already kened about the barks. Ah wanted tae find someone like ye – willin' tae act mair than a wee bit."

He turned more toward me, and the light of the gibbous moon lit his eyes enough that I was able to read them, or rather Hank was. "We didny want ye tae train in Wyonin'. Want ye tae take the Amsterdam Corridor."

"Why there?" That was Hank.

"'Cause at's whit we want."

"That's it then?"

Something flickered in the man's eyes, but Hank couldn't read it. I asked Sybil, but she gave no answer either. Maybe she was off somewhere shivering from fear, but I doubted it.

I had no idea where she'd run to, and without her, I didn't know what to do but take over myself. Then I remembered the TV screen and the heterochromatic girl. That aircraft had flown to Europe.

I shrugged. "Let's go."

CHAPTER EIGHTEEN

Dressed for the evening ahead, and befitting the neighborhood, no one gave her a second glance. The entire time the woman walked the street, she neither stared nor turned her head at anything the inner city had to offer – the man dealing drugs out of the car, the girl blowing the sailor barely inside the alley, not even the homeless woman squatting for a piss between the parked cars.

Without pause, the woman walked up the stairway and along the short hallway to the door, her stiletto heels clicking on the floor. She belonged here.

In front of the door, she glanced askance in both directions to ensure no one was about and knocked. Seconds later, the door opened. "You Johnson?" she asked as she paraded inside without invitation.

He licked her with his eyes as she walked by.

"Shut the damn door." She turned with a scowl, unbuttoned her blouse and dropped it to

the floor. The black bra concealed her small breasts rather than lifted them.

His mouth curled in approval, his eyes dancing over her body. "You'll do."

A mirror positioned near the doorway caught her eye and she gazed into it. The sternness around her blue eye was less dramatic than around the green. The disparity fed her impulse, and the harshness within her grew, explosively, like the flash of a spark when metal struck flint.

Her clothes matched her mood much better than when she'd worked undercover at the doctor's office. She didn't care for that little wimp, Lacy. In her heart, she was a dominatrix. Her eyes slid back to her evening's entertainment and cruelty snapped into place.

The slap on his face was equally as quick. "I said shut the door!"

The sting on her hand pushed that bourgeoning whim into full-blown self-indulgence and his shocked expression pushed it onward even more. She struck again. "Shut it!"

His anticipation evolved slowly as if his mind always had trouble on the uptake. Then she saw his rising pleasure bat surfacing like a fishing bobber.

He closed the door with a click. "Yeah. I think this will be fun."

The back of her hand struck again, stinging him even more fiercely. "Now shut your mouth." She stepped forward and dug her heel into the top of his foot. And again.

Seizing his hair, she yanked his face in close and shook it only inches away. "I see you ogling my breasts. You are not to peek there until I give you permission." She shook again. "Understand?"

"Yes."

The stiletto heel dug deeper. "Yes, what?"

"Yes, uh, Mistress?"

She dropped his head and walked away, fully aware that his eyes were devouring her ass. "This is an *I Tell You* night. Got it? You will do what *I tell you*, only what *I tell you*, until *I tell you* otherwise." She bent over, slipped on elbow-length gloves, then turned lazily around, putting her right foot up on the chair next to her, almost revealing her crotch to him.

"Get over here and kneel in front of me."

He scrambled to obey, his face on the same level as her upraised knee. His eyes tried to burrow up her skirt.

Another slap. "Did I tell you to gawk there?"

"No, Mistress."

A simple glance told her he was even more aroused. Easy to see with him. Damn, I like that.

"Lower your eyes to the floor. Now! Nobody told you to do anything but kneel."

Shuffling through her bag, she took what she wanted, bent over, and cinched the choke collar tight.

She struggled to remain aloof, especially when he started to breathe heavily. It excited her, almost as much as the burst of fear in his eyes when she'd slapped him. Snapping the leash, she reminded herself it was time to control herself, but the thought was for naught. His eyes bulged enough to tell her how tight the neck cinch was, and that was too much. She had to close her eyes.

After the tremor ran through her, she took a deep breath.

What the hell. Why not enjoy this?

Holding the leash higher, forcing his chin to lift, she slapped him again, much harder, strictly for her pleasure.

He worked a smile across his face and turned to her. "This might turn out goo—"

Another whack and his words morphed into moans. Experience told her the sound he made was a mixture of pain and pleasure, and his erection had grown, too, if that were possible.

Yes. I believe I'll enjoy this. With deft fingers, she fished around in her bag. She gave a good tug on the leash, pulled his face down, and forced him onto all fours. In a whirl of motion, she hiked her leg around, and over him; she straddled his neck, placing her spiked heels on his hands.

Now she let go of the leash and forced the ball-gag into his mouth and tightened the strap.

She patted the back of his head and cooed," Don't rub your head on my thighs. We'll get to that later." She slapped him again, stinging her hand. "I said don't! Now crawl."

The Mistress sighed in contentment and climbed free of the man. He was dead, eyes staring at the ceiling, arms still tied to the frame. She remembered the way his eyes bulged when she tightened the neck cinch; his frantic struggle to free himself from the bed frame had pushed her so close to another orgasm. With the final stab of her knife through his neck, up into the brain, he'd bucked so intensely that she'd remained on top. Death throes were so titillating during a cum.

She showered, dried with her own towel, and then cleaned the shower with it, and with the same precision, she gathered her clothing and dressed. Her normal care in wearing gloves while she worked always minimized the things she had to wipe down. A last kiss on his forehead, a quick check in the mirror, and out of the door she went.

On the street, she strolled through the night with an easy gait, carelessly clicking her heels on the concrete. No one was about. This early in the morning, even the night owls dozed.

The crisp air was perfect for late October. She'd always thought this the best time of the year.

The closer she came to Mu'izz's warehouse, the quicker her pace. It had been a long day, and she'd only had a short nap on the plane before she'd jumped. By the time the ship met her, and she received the message about this little job, she hadn't had time to rest. They'd picked her up in a helicopter, dropped her at the airport in Southern England, and she'd flown straight here. She slept a little on the flight, but she'd needed to do extra planning for the evening events.

The foul smells as she turned down the alleyway didn't register at all. Expectation of her destination drove her home; by then, exhaustion filled her so completely she could barely care about approval.

An exchange of nods while he had his cell pressed to his ear was all she had energy for.

Mu'izz pointed to his bedroom and waited for the other end to answer. After the emotionless greeting from the other end, he relayed the news of the aide's demise.

Mu'izz crossed to the door, told the guard not to disturb

them, and entered the bedroom. He stood by the door and gazed through the soft light at the slender frame of the Mistress as she lay on the bed. He crawled in, spooned up next to her, and grabbed her tiny breast. "Got another job for you."

"Later." She scooted her buttocks toward him, and he humped in closer yet. "What about your precious Allah?"

He snorted and pinched her nipple, "Don't give a damn about Allah. Do give a damn about the money."

They both chuckled as they drifted off to sleep.

CHAPTER NINETEEN

They had connections. I gotta give them that. After the stop where I shot that poor bastard in the foot, they put me in another vehicle. This new one an ordinary pickup, a little dilapidated, but my ass decreed that the engine was anything but stock.

Ahn had been right when he said it felt like Wyoming, and the farther we drove, the more the place had the appearance of winter. They'd had their first snowfall of the year when we were in a park near Medicine Bow while doing tryouts for the side trip to Amsterdam. There were huge boulders piled on top of each other in a semblance of gigantic piles of deer turds, and snow drifted near each pile. Currently, we were backtracking, heading toward Cheyenne, and the closer we came to that city, the more I saw drifting.

Neither the driver nor the ape-looking guy sitting on my right said a thing until we entered Cheyenne, and then it was the Neanderthal. He sat scratching his neck with a muscular index finger and said, "East. Base is east of here."

That was it, the extent of conversation while driving for a couple of hours. Talkative sonof-a-bitch.

The driver nodded and grunted. The exit for Warren AFB came into view and he slipped off the Interstate and drove right up to the gate.

Hank clued me in on how notorious air-base security was, so I waited patiently for us to be stopped, but it didn't happen. Well, we did stop, but only long enough for the driver to hand an ID card to the guard. The guard scrutinized it, saluted, and we were off again.

Both of them snickered for the next mile or so. Hank sat back and brooded. Jacques made me take another deep breath. He'd been doing that ever since we jumped out of the truck before I shot up ol' boy's foot with the AK47. Said he loved the pine and faint smell of sage in the air.

The problem was all I was able to smell was the Neanderthal and the driver; don't know how Jacques missed that stink.

I mentioned it to him and Jacques was disappointed, but Ahn said the two idiots had eaten mostly burgers and fries for the past couple of days.

These assholes are military, Hank observed, *but not the regular boys, an' not commandos. These guys don't belong, but they do.*

Consternation bubbled around inside me, leaking out of Hank, and now that the subject had come up, I saw his point.

The driver didn't slow at the airfield, as we bounced over a few packed snowdrifts. He did ease up a bit for curves but not enough. Ice covered the road and we slid around like drunken sailors. We also had to yield to other traffic, but that meant slowing not stopping, not even when we drove right up into the ass end of a huge aircraft.

Under its tail section, a cargo door lowered an oversized ramp that allowed my chauffeur to drive right up. Inside, a mean-spirited woman, a sergeant, used a variety of hand signals and some very explicit language to tell us where to go, both inside the aircraft and figuratively, too.

A rough bitch, I believe she could've quickly pinched ol' ape-man's scrotal sack off like a swollen tick and experienced undying pleasure as she did it.

Positioned, the driver crawled out. The ape opened his door with one hand, grabbed me by the scruff of the neck with the other, and high-stepped me out as if I were in a Nazi boot camp.

Hank kept telling me what to do to escape, or at least to stop the bullying. It was hard, but I kept him under control and endured. We didn't have far to go, about thirty or forty paces as we passed several shrink-wrapped piles of crap on pallets. Then they made me sit on a webbed seat that stretched along the inside of the fuselage. We fished around, grabbed some seatbelts, and clicked ourselves in securely.

It wasn't until they sat down that I saw the passengers on the other side. I knew one of them: Doc. Buckled up like me, she sat between two other people, a swarthy man and a fairskinned woman (couldn't see her face) both armed to the teeth with sidearms, knives, and rifles.

Hank agreed with my observations, except he drew my attention to the hand grenades hanging from their web belts.

Ahn was surprised. He hadn't had any indications. I guess the noise of the engines, along with the smell of the jet fuel and exhaust, masked his senses.

Loadmaster bitch presented herself up front. "All right! It's time you listened up. This is *my* C-17 Globemaster III. It is the best aircraft in the skies." She turned her attention to Doc and her guards. "You better pay attention and quit screwing around. I'm telling you."

I tuned her out. I had my hands full keeping Hank from escaping. He wanted to slap the shit out of Doc, and I needed Sybil to help reign him in, but she was nowhere around.

In the midst of all this, Doc turned her head toward me, and her eyes sucked me into them. It was like falling into a dream. No, more like remembering another life.

Shots peppered the air outside my hotel window, and I knelt near the sill trying to see without being shot, but early twilight and low clouds nixed that. Bullets zinging close to me always set my adrenaline pumping. The sound of them tied up the viscera, cut off messages from the gonads, and prevents clarity of mind, all in that nanosecond of the first sound. The net result was an acute sensitivity to all things dangerous such as the muzzle flash of a weapon.

More rounds boomed and whistled through the air, and I still couldn't see who fired. All I saw were the mountains surrounding the town, ghostly and magnificent with clouds partially obscuring them, stretching straight up like gargantuan ramparts on castle walls.

Sweat still ran down me from the bed exercises the attack interrupted. Deadly encounters tend to deflate the urge to make love rather quickly.

"How did they know?" The voice whispered from behind me in the shadows, but when I turned to answer, she'd moved to lie on the floor behind the bed. I heard her slipping into her pants. "I don't understand. Do they know about Sigma?" Her words made me dizzy, but I didn't have time to think about it. A hand grenade shattered the window next to me and dropped at my feet.

I bounced over the bed almost too late, catching some of the shockwaves from the explosion, numbing my left hand and arm. The fragmentation missed me, but I don't know how.

My hearing blanked out, blood dripped from my nose, and I was even dizzy. My eyes told me she was talking, but my ears were ringing. Billowing plaster dust made it hard to see, and the concussion from the grenade made my whole body hurt, especially my eyes and ears.

Nothing worked right. Hell, I couldn't even crawl. Kept falling over.

The next thing I knew, Sally had her hands on my back, shaking me hard, and yelling.

The ringing barely let the sound through. "Stan. Let's go." Seconds later, things came back into focus; the noise was unbelievable. More bullets *thunked* into the walls and ceiling. The dry fog created from flying plaster made it hard to breathe. Both Sally and I had a hell of a time catching our breath.

In a running stumble, we bent over through the doorway and into the hall.

The extra layers of walls gave us a little more protection, stopping most of the small arms fire, but a few rounds zinged through. We crouched, running with our heads down like wounded beasts. My heart thumped like a dog's leg scratching fleas. Although not calm, Sally carried herself as if she'd done this before. I mean, her eyes still bulged.

I debated whether to let my intuition work out how to pick a lock to get us into another room. Another explosion happened in the next room. I decided against the lock thing. "That way." We scooted down the hall and turned the corner instead. Lucky thing, too. There was an open door on the left. We scurried in like a couple of squirrels running from a hound.

I slammed the door. "Lock it!"

We sat with our backs against the wall, and I checked for brass in my 9mm. Saw the golden glint of it and nodded. "Don't worry. We'll be fine."

"How the hell?"

Another explosion nearby.

"How did they know where we were?"

Good question. I shrugged, too busy to take a poll of my intuition. She took it at face value, well, shoulder value. Either way, it was clear the enemy knew more than we wanted.

The small arms fire dwindled to sporadic, replaced by a room-to-room check. The sound of boots clumping down the hall sounded almost like mortar fire, and the heavy pounding of shoulders hitting walls smacked of muffled grenades. Above it all, I heard the short barking commands of soldiers coordinating.

The closer they came, the harder my pulse hammered. I wiped my hands on my pants.

My eyes shot to Sally, and she wasn't doing well. With wide eyes growing wider, she started to stand. I waved her down, my thoughts buzzing. Where was all of the chatter inside when I needed it? There was always odd shit flying through my head, and now …

Before me, through the window, loomed that majestic mountain unveiled by parting clouds. Thousands of people think the Matterhorn is only a ride in Disneyland. It's not. It's a real mountain, a huge mountain, and right now, it was framed by the window right across the room from me.

"Come on," I yelled.

I didn't wait. I ran straight to the window, opened it, and

leaned out. Only two stories.

Great! We were on the second story, maybe jump? Concrete lay below us but so did escape.

I stuffed my weapon between my back and belt, urged her to hurry, and I leaned further out.

"Stan!"

"It's okay, babe. It's not far to the ground. We'll hang and drop."

I turned toward her, there was a terrific crash, and darkness grabbed me.

Consciousness came back with garbled voices running through my head. I hurt – my head, face, and shoulders, all of me. Somebody had whipped my ass, and I lay crumpled on the floor.

It took slow seconds before sounds made sense.

"… doesn't matter." I didn't recognize the woman's voice. It was sharp, crisp.

Demanding. "The Berne Caucus wants him delivered. You've done that. Get gone."

"But—"

"Shut up."

I eased my eyes open a crack. Two of them argued – my woman Sally, and a flat-chested redhead who conducted herself with the demeanor of a rabid badger. There was also at least one man in the room. His smell tipped me off. I'd had a nudge from one of my intuitions, telling me to pay attention to the smells, and again they were right.

"Listen, you little bitch," the crisp words cut the air. "I don't give a damn about what kind of deal you had. Berne wants him gone."

"Not 'til I get my—"

The redhead backhanded Sally. I was ready to jump her, but the amount of determined reserve in my Sally's face stopped me, that and my hands were zip-tied. But there was something else from Sally, another focus. This one clearly in my direction –

hate.

My Sally's contralto filled the room, "I handed him to you because I needed to find out what he knew."

"What do you think they will do?" the redhead fired back. "Will Berne be—"

"Stan! For God's sake watch out!"

I'd rolled over, reaching with my zipped hands for my 9mm. If I could get off a shot ... Darkness thudded down on me.

I woke up tied to a chair. Somebody had rearranged the zip ties because I couldn't move at all. The redhead scowled and did her best to cut me in half with a laser-like stare. In her hands was a scary hypodermic with what resembled vulture puke in it.

"Well, Stan. Hello. You're getting ready to tell us everything. After that, I'll do what I do best." She sauntered forward, the dead glow of a badger's eyes controlling her face. Liquid dripped from the hypo.

Doc watched from behind her, a sly grin on her face, as the redhead pushed the needle into my arm.

The aircraft folded around me again, but my eyes focused on one thing. Sitting on the other side and still in handcuffs was Doc. Her eyes pleaded with me, I suppose for me to understand, but there was no way. All I wanted to do was unleash Hank. Staring at me was not only my doctor, but my past lover Sally as well.

That woman betrayed me.

The memory was clear, and it hurt. Like being eviscerated and watching rats eat your
entrails.

What a bitch.

CHAPTER TWENTY

Exactly as Carbonella commanded after the redheaded streetwalker hooker bushwhacked Tom, Alice produced a new task force HQ. The new place was an apartment in a brownstone in an anonymous neighborhood made up of similar buildings. Carbonella supposed it had been a safe house someone decided to turn over to them. If not, it was extremely fortuitous that they'd found it. The place was perfect. It was a corner flat, diagonally facing the precinct house Sigma had escaped from.

It was spacious too. The place had enough room for all to sleep if need be.

Carbonella sat at the kitchen table and stared at her laptop while the rest of the team scurried around and squared things away. After scouring the Task Force Command File, she had a much clearer idea of how things fitted together. They did have a name actually, but unfortunately, it was a simple string of alphanumerics that correlated with the black budget.

"That's why we've only used the name Task Force," she muttered.

They'd come into being because a year and a half ago, a man, code-named Sigma, walked into a top-level office at Homeland Security with a claim that an until-then-unknown organization, with ties to the American political system, was preparing to unleash terrorism on a global scale.

As outrageous as that sounded, the man produced proof. The file didn't elaborate on the proof. But clearly, it had been sufficient. Within a month, the Task Force was established, the money allocated, and Sigma himself in deep cover pursuing the would-be ISIS terrorists. His mission: to stop the group and produce a list of the influential people involved.

What puzzled Carbonella more than anything was Sigma himself. He was an enigma, his identity exceptionally classified.

His past shrouded, he'd simply appeared out of nowhere.

That's not to say he wasn't skilled. According to his Homeland dossier, his abilities were off the charts. Almost every time he needed a certain craftiness, he excelled at it, as if he had an artesian well of knowhow. Incredible. What made it even more so was that he appeared to be an idiot.

At any rate, Sigma had been incredibly useful, funneling information about the group known as the Berne Caucus. Involved in everything from prostitution and gunrunning, all the way to the original premise – inciting terrorism on a global scale. Exactly what Sigma warned of in the beginning.

The list of names involved should have been possessed by the task force months ago, and would have been, had it not been for his capture and subsequent disappearance. Details were sketchy. He went missing in Switzerland several months ago, but he'd resurfaced weeks later in New York City, Bellevue.

His shrink at Bellevue was Sally MacPherson, a doctor, who until about a year before her appearance in New York, had a practice in Israel. The town she'd lived in had been destroyed.

Her home and family gone; she moved to Switzerland, telling her few friends that she needed the neutrality.

That was about the time Sigma dove into his deep cover. There was no known connection to Sigma, but Sally moved to New York about the same time he disappeared.

The coincidence of her moving here and there at the same time bothered Carbonella.

Something wrong there. And then the good doctor picked up his case here pro bono, too.

Doesn't even have a practice and she's donating her time? There had to be a stack of money at her disposal. Then, after a couple of months of treatment, she discharged him, keeping him on the hook for weekly appointments. Awfully hinky.

Somehow Sigma was connected to the murder of Gillian Stonegate,

The wife of the prominent senator from Massachusetts, who

happened to chair the antiterrorism committee.

The whole situation made Carbonella scratch her head.

Behind Carbonella, Alice worked at setting up her desk computer, and while crawling around connecting what Carbonella estimated to be a thousand cables, she whispered, "'Bout time we had a woman in charge. Glad to see it." She burrowed back under the desk.

"What?"

Alice resurfaced, "Good girl."

Carbonella blinked a couple of times. "Hey, you guys, both of you. Come in here a second. I need to talk a bit."

Both Sam and John wandered that way. Sam came in first, then John after he stopped off to freshen his coffee. They always knew when she was pissed. That husky quality in her voice that made it scratchy became stronger, making it almost throaty.

Carbonella stood before the three of them. As much as she controlled herself, her face was flushed and her breathing hard. She stared at her subordinates. "Alice made a comment to me, and I think I need to tell everybody that it was not a smart thing to say."

"I meant—"

"I know what you meant. Another victory for womankind when they gave me command.

But it implies they gave it to me because I have a vagina, not because I earned it."

Her eyes moved back and forth over each of them as she talked. "To say that one or the other gender gets a job because of where their appendages hang and jiggle from is counter to everything we *say* we believe. We all have talents. Some are because of our genders. Some are not.

"Tom out-ran me on any given day. Males have a larger lung capacity. However, I can think two different thoughts simultaneously. Him? No. His muscles were stronger than mine. On average, all male primates are much stronger than females. Females can detect more odors than males. These things are gender-related. A kind of trade-off between sexes.

"It is what we do with our own skills and abilities that make the difference. Not genitalia." Her eyes made another track. "Are we clear?"

They all nodded, and no one said a thing, content not to have to gaze into her eyes again.

Sam shrugged, stood up, and sauntered off to the kitchen.

She watched him for a few steps. "There are indications at play that I have to be a bitch here, which I will do, but …"

She took a deep breath. "Sit down, Sam."

Once he had, she continued, "I once knew a Major in the Marines who, when he assumed command of any type – an office, a squad, even a task force – he religiously hunted around for the one senior son-of-a-bitch he would fire. Said it was the quickest way to snap some starch into everyone and cut the bullshit."

With another breath, Carbonella sat back in the chair and folded her arms over her breasts. "Right now, I'm in charge. Not Tom. He's in the hospital."

Her eyes raked her subordinates. "So which one will it be? Professional, or bitch."

"I like to do things professionally," ventured Alice. Both men agreed.

Carbonella glared at them for almost a full minute. "If I ever have to wait on any of you three again, someone will go. I know it's tough that our commander was shot, and I had to move up, but don't test me on this. I will not accept a lazy task force."

She leaned forward. "I thought this Sigma was important. Tom never told me how important, though."

"Guy's like a real squirrel." John tossed a small packet in front of his new commander.

"Don't know how he got all that info."

Carbonella thumbed through the papers. "He was about to give us a list of names." She flipped several pages. "It's not anywhere that I can see."

Alice jumped in, "He never passed it. Disappeared. There was a big firefight in Switzerland and he vanished. About a month later, he showed up in New York, acting like a homeless lunatic and somebody checked him into Bellevue."

Sam stood up and stopped. "I need some coffee. Okay, boss?"

She waved him on. "Bring several cups."

"Anyway," yelled Sam over his shoulder, "went to see him a few weeks ago to try to pump some more info and it was like talking to a roomful of straitjacket candidates at the same time." He walked back in with the coffee urn in his left hand and a stack of foam cups in his right.

"Fill 'em up, Sam." Carbonella held out hers for the first pour. "Nobody leaves until we've made some sense out of this shit."

CHAPTER TWENTY-ONE

Carbonella parked her vehicle and walked up the short sidewalk to the house. She loved the area.

It was the kind of neighborhood she'd always envisioned for herself when she retired – clean and well-kept.

Not only was the air filled with the chill of early autumn, but it also held the almost bitter smell of leaves before they turned. An underlying tinge of chlorophyll, layered over with an unmistakable nutty roughness. Infused among it were mouthwatering aromas from several suppers up and down the street, either in the process of cooking, or on the table for consumption. Someone had fried cabbage with onions and perhaps bacon; another family was enjoying pizza; there was a definite odor of Chinese, too.

The house needed a lick of paint, maybe some putty on the windows, but all in all, the upkeep had been done to a reasonable schedule. A few flakes of paint curled away, and a modicum of attention to the porch would improve the property in her eyes considerably. It had the earmarks of the owners intending to work on it in summer. Something must have changed their minds.

She rapped on the door then spotted the button for the doorbell and pushed it. The soft chiming drifted through the wall. A few subsonic thumps of someone's uneven gait to the door and it swung open. A man, maybe in his early forties, with prematurely graying short hair, stood before her. Dressed in a sloppy blue sweatshirt and jeans, he leaned to the right, supported by a metal cane.

"Detective George Nancy?" A gust of wind blew her hair, but she ignored the unkempt

feeling it produced.

His eyes narrowed. "And you are?"

Carbonella held up her ID, no sudden movements, and kept her hand clearly visible. The door had not opened fully, and she never saw the hand that operated it. That, together with the way his eyes studied her, told her to be wary.

He took his time worrying over the ID but at length nodded with a grimace. "I'm Nancy." He turned and walked back inside, "C'mon in. Shut the door, and have a seat. Don't see many of those IDs. Homeland Security's pretty vague. What the hell's that all about?" He turned around and dropped his service revolver on the table as he passed.

Mu'izz sat in his car and watched the agent walk from her vehicle. He'd had his driver, Jarib, pull over behind the van advertising a plumbing outfit. It was large enough to hide most of their vehicle and enable them to watch without being seen. A good spot, the two of them could stay here for a short time without raising suspicion, but they needed to stay alert.

He sipped his drink and leaned back into the seat.

The driver gazed at Mu'izz through the rearview mirror as he talked, "Berne say why we need to follow this bitch?"

Mu'izz shook his head and patted the air with his hand while he swallowed, telling his driver to keep it down. "All I know is we have to follow her and tell them where she went. I'd rather shoot her and go. In fact, you sit here and keep the motor running."

He stepped out and abruptly leaned back in, "Keep the radio on. I want to know when it happens. If I'm still out, you need to honk two short bursts as if you're waiting for someone." He slammed the door and strolled down the street, keeping his hand in the pocket of his windbreaker curled around the handgrip of his pistol. A few leaves chattered down the sidewalk in front of him, and the gentle breeze caught him in the back of the neck, giving him an exhilarating chill.

As he rambled by the house, he kept an eye on it, ready to

turn away should anyone exit, he paid particular attention to the nearby trees and bushes, checking for something close to the walkway.

The sun beamed down, and his shadow preceded him. After about twenty feet, he found the perfect solution. An overgrown cedar bush encroached halfway across the concrete path. He walked beyond a step or so, and knowing it would block him from the house, he ducked behind it.

His index finger traced the trigger guard on his handgun. A warm glow of confidence spread through him. This was what was needed doing, whether Berne agreed or not. He already had plans for Berne and would take care of them later.

Close to the house, he inched around the bush, without rustling the limbs, he brought out the pistol and craned his neck around to peep through the window.

He cocked the hammer and raised the weapon.

Carbonella followed Nancy into the living room, "I command an autonomous task force. Technically we belong to the Intelligence Committee, but the funding bypasses them and comes straight to us." She smiled more to herself than him while thinking about it.

The television babbled away in the background.

"Intelligence Committee, huh? Isn't that Stonegate's committee?"

"Technically, but I've not seen a slip of paper from that committee. I don't think Stonegate has a clue we exist." About to park herself in an armchair, a quick glance around told her to stop and move to the couch. Something was awry. The room had that aura of decoration by a woman – little doilies, knickknacks, and the plates hanging on the wall over the table were rose-colored. Add to that, he'd dropped into an identical chair, so she knew this one wasn't his.

She'd also caught the flicker in his eye when she'd prepared to sit.

The chair had been his wife's.

Equally plain, she wasn't around anymore. The house smelled of a man, no hint of perfume, not even a lingering scent of bodywash. She slipped onto the couch. "Well, to begin with, I understand you were shot less than a week ago."

"Yeah." He held up his cane and scowled at it. "In the leg. Said I lost too much blood and they made me take time off. Tomorrow's the first day they'll let me go back. Light duty." Another snarl.

"That's what I'd like to talk about. I want you to work with me for a while."

He scowled at her for a full three seconds. "Well, what does your little task force want me to do?"

A slow smile creased its way across her face. "Do you know a man called Wilburn

Stanton?"

Nancy humphed. "Stan? Yeah, I know the little bastard. I was trying to help him out when I got shot in the leg."

"We are delving into Mister Stanton."

Nancy snickered and then his glower returned. He stood up and headed toward his kitchen. "Ms. Commander—"

"Call me Carbonella, simply Carbonella."

He turned, contemplated for a second and then resumed his trek to the kitchen. "All right,

Carbonella. I'm not too thrilled about helping Stan or even your little task force, but I do crave a little company. So. You hungry? I was sitting down. Fancy a little New England dinner? Corned beef, cabbage, and carrots." He turned around again. "I cheated a little with the cabbage. Put a bit of bacon in it. The doctor would shit if I told him, but what the hell."

She stared. After a moment, while both of them tried to force the other to blink first, she said, "Sure. I'm kind of hungry. Sounds good."

"Get the plates over there. The silver is in that drawer." He waved her to the stove. "If you don't mind, we'll fill them up here. Can't haul all this to the table with a bum leg." They filled their plates and chatted.

"Stan's a weird guy. He's got this thing. He can't remember what he's supposed to and remembers what he's not."

"That makes no sense."

Nancy placed his plate on the table and rubbed his neck while he waited on his guest.

"Doesn't it, though? But he described it to me like that the other day."

Mu'izz watched as they came back into the dining room, both chatting away. After they sat down to eat, he considered the best angle of attack. They were both in a direct line with him.

No clear shot.

He tried the next window over, but it opened into another room. They weren't visible at all from there.

He tripped his way back to the first window.

A horn honked in the distance. By the time he peered in at his target, both people were gone. The horn blew another set of two blasts, and he turned his head toward the noise.

A smile stretched across his face. It had happened.

He refocused on the people inside; his finger traced the trigger on his handgun.

Still not at the table.

Mu'izz hopped over to the other window.

They stood in the middle of the room, glued to the television, clearly riveted to the news story there.

They must know.

Pride puffed him up, and he settled against the window frame to steady his hand. He let out his breath and took aim.

The sight picture was perfect. Her back was toward him.

Mid-back. Her spine.

Squeezing his finger, the memory of his instructor fluttered through his mind – the incessant heat of the desert, the constant berating of the man, but most of all, the unrelenting drive for perfection. He'd learned.

Supporting the weapon with both hands, his finger tightened more.

"Hey!" A jab to his shoulder came from the rear.

Bang!

The hit on his shoulder pushed him forward, the pistol broke the glass, and Mu'izz's grip foiled. A nanosecond later, the gun kicked up, uncontrolled. The pistol bounced out of his hands, the heavy metal wreaked havoc. Shards from the window sprayed back at him, lacerating his face and hands, some fragments cut into his eyelids and forced him to keep them closed.

Unable to see, hands from behind spun him about, seized his coat, and pulled.

Two gunshots sounded, and his ears reported wood splintering. He tried to open his eyes, but it was hopeless; even if he could, blood flooded into them and he couldn't see anyway. Lashing out to find his balance and protect himself, he flailed at the air, but the pulling on his jacket persevered. He dug his heels into the ground and connected with his captor.

"Abdul! Stop hitting."

The hands grabbed his head, and garlic-laden breath enveloped Mu'izz.

Jarib!

Now that Mu'izz recognized both the voice and breath, he didn't resist.

Without waiting for a reply, Jarib pulled, hurried Mu'izz along. "We must move, or they will catch us." They stumbled through the bushes and crashed out onto the sidewalk. Jarib hauled him back into the bush again.

Mu'izz wound up to slap the man, but Jarib whispered fiercely. "We must be quiet, Abdul. The woman you followed and the man I shot in the alley are hunting for us. Both are armed." Holding his hand on Mu'izz to calm him, he said, "She is close and heads this way."

His eyes followed her. "Looks like a pro. The man walks away from us …he is circling the house." Humor laced his voice, "He moves slowly, and hobbles like a cripple searching for a place to sit and beg."

Mu'izz heard the stumbling and silently joined in the mirth.

"Why were you about to shoot, Abdul? I thought we—"

"Why did you ruin the shot?" Again Mu'izz wiped his eyes. He saw light and dark, but no more. "You caused me to miss."

"It happened."

"What happened?"

"The thing you wanted me to listen for. The explosion. It came over the radio and I honked, like you said. But you didn't come back. Good thing I found you. They're hunting for you now."

Mu'izz smelled the cedar tree and knew they hid behind the one he'd seen before. He still couldn't see, but his nose indicated where Jarib was, and he felt for him. From Jarib's chest, Mu'izz slinked up until he touched his chauffeur's chin.

He slapped hard. "They wouldn't be searching if you hadn't hit me! Now give me something to wipe the blood from my eyes."

A cloth was pressed into his hands, Mu'izz dabbed his eyes, feeling the sharp cut of tiny glass fragments. He could see again, although it had a red haze.

Jarib is right. The woman still hunts for us and is well trained.

We are trapped here, and her direction of search is directly toward on us. She will be here in moments. We need to move.

She has a two-handed grip on her weapon. Pro. If we run, we are dead, especially at this range. To stay and fight is equally bad.

He took stock. They had only one weapon, and there were two enemies, both trained and well-armed.

Shit.

Jarib danced from foot to foot while peering through the bush. Abruptly he stopped, both hands stroking his beard. "Abdul. It is truly important that this woman die?"

Mu'izz dabbed at his eyes, watching the woman, and answered absently, "Of course,

Jarib."

"Then when I distract her, you shoot her."

Mu'izz's head snapped toward his driver. "When you what?"

But Jarib didn't answer. Instead, he stood, raised his hands, and screamed, "*Allahu*

Akbar." He charged straight for the woman, a knife clutched in the offensive.

Carbonella whirled at the sound. The man came from nowhere. The knife flashed, dazzling her. By reflex, she turned, aimed, and fired. Her movements were perfect, but his momentum was too much.

He only stumbled. Still yelling, he lurched again.

Another shot as his blade swung down. Pain lanced through her side. Now both rolled on the ground; she pulled the trigger again.

The man lay lifeless, draped across her.

"Carbonella!" Nancy's voice boomed through the air. She couldn't see him, but he wasn't far, perhaps rounding the front corner of his house. She heard the odd noise of someone hopping over the grassy ground with a cane. "Carbonella. Carbo ..."

He bent down to pull off the attacker. On his knees, he dropped the cane but still held his weapon at the ready; he retrieved his cell phone from his pocket and punched the speed dial for his precinct number. "Detective Nancy. I have shots fired at my home, an officer down.

Requesting ambulance and back up." Then he bent down and examined Carbonella's wound.

Mu'izz watched as his driver attacked and stabbed the woman. Jarib wanted him to kill her, but the chance of escaping presented itself while they fought, and he crawled away.

Hidden on the other side of the bush, he stood, pocketed the gun and walked calmly around the corner, pressing his handkerchief to his face. The action stung like a hundred bee stings, but sirens sounded everywhere, and it was imperative he cover himself. Doors opened as the neighborhood sprang to life from curiosity.

He thought about Jarib as he walked away from his car. He would miss him.

CHAPTER TWENTY-TWO

I studied Doc, my internal conflict excruciating, and I'm not talking about the mouthy busybodies inside. Don't get me wrong. They had plenty to say. I heard everything from sage advice to testosterone-fueled expletives, but I ignored them all. None of their advice helped, because I muttered the same crap myself.

Also, it was pretty similar to the way they have described me on occasion, so I gaffed them off like a gob of spit.

Lots of my questions were answered, but I sure didn't feel any better with all the fomenting memories that surfaced. Turns out that my name really isn't Wilburn B. Sanford. My brain simply remembered a detail from a significant conversation: "Will Berne be ... Stan! For

God's sake—" I can see now how I remembered the name that I did. It's not a long jump.

She keeps looking at me.

Damn! I hate looking into those eyes. They always melt me and stiffen me at the same time.

Somebody plunked a box meal in my lap. The bull of a woman sergeant didn't say a thing, merely pointed at it and then at me. She did the same for the Neanderthal and idiot driver. The two bobbed up and down like drooling dicks and dug into the boxes. She made her rounds, and then before the woman climbed the small ladder to the cockpit, she turned to face us all. "The C-17 Globemaster III is the safest aircraft you will ever fly in. Unclassified specs outline extremely slow stall speed when properly trimmed. It will even make an about-face ..."

She shook her head, snarled at us all, and turned to her ladder. As an afterthought, she turned back. "Don't get up during take-off and don't loosen your belt. You're part of the load now and I'm the loadmaster. We will maintain that safety record."

Her eyes hinted at giving each of us third-degree burns if any of us defied her. "You follow my directions, or you don't fly."

She stepped out of view.

I glanced over at Doc and her two guards, and the last memory surged again. I thought my stomach would yuck.

A hell of a deal. The whole thing pissed me off, and when that happened, the specter-like visions receded.

It struck me that now I don't even have that stupid name to lean on, and that damned woman doctor's the one who turned me in for whatever it was I did. She's key here somehow,

but damned if I know how. She screwed me several ways.

I told you that bitch would be the ruin of us. She turned you in!

Didn't need Hank needling me, but he is hard to ignore.

God, I hate your constant yelling about how it all makes sense. Shut up, Hank.

I know she's a bitch for what she's done, but the memories that swooped back included the feelings I had for her too, and those make the whole affair about as hard to believe as little old ladies only wear perfume to impress other little old ladies. It may be true, but I don't believe it. I mean, she did try to have me identified by running my fingerprints twice by the police.

Something is awry.

The whole issue makes no sense.

The lame-ass next to me crunched on his apple as Doc's eyes raked over me, her eyes pleading. Then the sound of the engines ramping up overpowered most everything. Ape-man punched me in the shoulder, pointed at my box lunch, and pantomimed putting in some earplugs. He even smiled like a chimpanzee. I gathered that he expected me to do what he would — ape see, ape do.

The aircraft rolled over the tarmac and before long we were airborne. The gentle rocking, the obnoxious rumble of the engines, and all things military had an unexpected effect on me, as though it was an everyday occurrence, which was strange. I had no memory of ever flying this way, or even being in any military before. Crazy.

Hank? You trying to take control?

No. Go to sleep.

"Atten-n-nshun." The sound of boots slapping together felt solid as I stood before my class, watching them snap to. The building behind the formation loomed over us in the midmorning air. The sound of an occasional vehicle driving nearby faded into the distance, taken over by the noise of troops marching to a cadence sung by a strong baritone sergeant.

I was comfortable. The inner turmoil I'd lived with all my life somehow was quieter now because I was in the Army. I was used to it. My dad was a colonel, and I'd been raised an armybrat. Well, in a way. Good old Mummy had seen to it that I'd been schooled in the best places and well-traveled. Her family money helped, especially after she'd inherited all of it.

But back to the army. Been up for hours. First, the callisthenic free-for-all while the TAC

Officers berated us, telling us not to get dirty because officers don't get dirty. We blew that off.

By now we were pretty much immune to their caterwauling. Besides, any minute now, another

TAC would yell for us jump into the mix, not worry about dirt. "Who in the hell told us never to get dirty, anyway?"

After that, we had our four-mile run, followed by a shower, shit, and shave. About three and a half minutes for that. Then double-time down to the dining facility for fingernail inspection. Officers don't have dirty fingernails.

Then breakfast.

Stand at attention while we filed past to receive our trays, marched to a table and eat (careful not to cast our eyes on anything except the tray and the bottom of the glass). Yelled at the whole time. "Hurry up! Use your spoon! We haven't got all

day! Put it in your mouth and swallow. Don't even chew." And on the other side of the room, another voice told us to eat like ladies and gentlemen. "Use your fork. Take small bites and sit up. Congress is ready to make
ladies and gentlemen of you."

A candidate caught with errant eyes looking somewhere other than the bottom of his tray or glass had to stand at attention and talk to Walter the Clock for five minutes. Have you ever tried to talk to a clock for five minutes?

Insane, huh.

Welcome to the Benning School for Boys. Specifically, Officers Candidate School, 51st
Company. The "for boys" part was erroneous, several females took the same verbal beating as the boys. The Army logic abounds, huh. Oh, and my name here is Candidate Swizzle Stick, a nickname given me by my TAC officer. On formal occasions, they do use my last name but usually, it's Swizzle Stick.

"Candidate!" barked the officer in the doorway behind me, forbidden for candidates to use, only true officers were allowed through there. I intuited that she stood At Ease while scorching everyone with her gaze. "Make them march, Candidate." Her voice was deep but not sultry, and she filled out her uniform nicely on top but a little too much in the hips. It might be in my mind, but I was sure not going to say it.

I ignored her.

"Riiiight face!"

With the sound of a hundred feet thumping the parade ground, the formation changed to a column that now faced to my left.

"Forrrward march! First Sergeant."

The scrawny female candidate ran up and with a shrill voice called cadence for the company, and all of them in the column sang it back. Regardless of how scrawny she was, the candidate was good. Her eagle eye was sharp, and a motion of her head told any slackers to get in line. But there weren't many. We were graduating in a couple of days and all of the chaff had been left behind weeks ago, blown away by all the TAC officers' bawling.

"Not you, Candidate Swizzle. Stop where you are." My TAC officer as he exited through the 'Officers Only' door. He was a cocky little bastard, but I'd learned to be oblivious to the smartass part of him and listen to his commands and wishes.

I snapped-to and waited. The TAC officer swaggered up to me. Still amazed me how he dragged the knuckles of one hand while he walked and dug in his ear with the other hand.

"Captain James needs you. Go report." Then uncharacteristically, his voice changed, "Go ahead and use the officers' door this once. He needs you now." The compassion in his voice unnerved the shit out of me. He even patted me on the shoulder.

Oh, shit.

He acted as though I was about to be recycled back to a junior class or relieved and kicked out of the school.

Except, I reasoned. He wouldn't be concerned about either of those. The little prick. "Yes, sir."

Itchy between the shoulder blades, I pulled open the door and strode inside as if I owned the place and for the first time in fourteen weeks, walked down the hall not caring in the least that my boots might scuff the floor.

I turned into the real First Sergeant's office (not the candidate's). "Hey, Top, uh First

Sergeant, I was told to report."

The NCO's head snapped in my direction, and he held up his hand. "That's all right, go ahead, Candidate."

I knocked on the door, in the ritual of reporting and forced myself not to make eye contact with anyone, only the wall ahead of me.

"Enter. Come on in."

I opened the door, took two steps in, and stopped at attention. I hadn't gotten my right hand even halfway up when he told me to stop.

"No need to report this time, Candidate. At Ease." Then he stood up and walked around his desk. "In fact, go ahead and have a seat."

I turned to the couch, where I saw General Mackinsey. He had been a friend of the family for longer than I'd been alive. Normally we joked and kidded to the point that Mummy always had to frown at Dad, and then Dad would be forced to say something to us. Hell, I've called him

Mac my whole life. Now it's General Mac.

Mac wore a stern expression on his face, with that thousand-yard stare in his eyes. They drifted to me. Then, inexplicably he used them to order me to sit right next to him.

As I did, his tension contaminated me.

He took a breath. "Son, I'm here in an official capacity today."

"Yes, sir."

His eyes caught me straight on. "It is my duty to inform you that your parents are dead."

The bad news hit me full in the face, and the next second, whooshed through me as if it had been a foul wind. I heard what he said, understood it even, but there was no residual pain, like a through-and-through gunshot wound. Just the impact, and the initial wound it caused, but there wasn't any nasty old bullet lodged anywhere, nothing to dig out, nothing to fester.

He continued. "They were ambushed in their vehicle on their way to a dinner party on the

Northern coast of Israel." He paused to let me absorb everything.

The captain chimed in, "I can offer you compassionate leave so you can take care of everything. Or you can wait for graduation and take your normal leave after you're commissioned."

"Normally, I don't interfere with anyone's command, but Captain, that's bullshit." The general stood and faced my commander, "Is he on course to graduate?"

"Yes, sir."

"What does he have yet to finish?" The captain simply shrugged.

"My point." Then the general turned to me and recited the pledge, swearing me in as an officer of the U.S. Army. It was all done in a matter of moments. Afterward, he turned back to my CO and told him he would take care of the paperwork, but as far as he was concerned, I was a 2nd lieutenant and fully commissioned. "Do you have bars in your room, Lieutenant?"

I gazed ahead, thinking about the bastards who had killed my parents. My father didn't bother me much. He was a soldier. Mum was different. She never said, or did, anything to threaten anyone.

"Lieutenant?"

I pulled my eyes back up to the general.

"That's good, son. Keep the fire, both in your eyes and your heart. Now, do you have bars?"

I shook my head, "No, sir. The colonel was bringing his."

The general stood silently for a few seconds and then nodded, "Thought so." Quietly, he reached into his pocket and handed me a set. "My own butter bars. They aren't your dad's, but

I'd be honored …"

"Thank you, sir." I palmed them for when I changed into my Class A uniform. "Sir?" He answered with his eyes.

"Who were the motherfuckers?"

"We'll find out, Lieutenant. I know you wanted Infantry, but I made a few calls and had your branch changed. You're Intelligence, now."

"Sir, I need to let someone in my chain of command know I will be OCONUS for a

while. I have to go pick up my parents."

"You just have, and now you have permission to leave the States. I can have the paperwork ready for transport before you leave."

I met the general's eyes, "Thank you, sir, but I will fly them back in the Baker family

Gulfstream. I need the flight hours to maintain my license."

He nodded. "How long do you need?"

"Don't know, sir. Can I start with the thirty days I have right now and ask for more if I need it?"

"Sure, son. Sure." He leaned his chin toward his shoulder and barked, "I want his leave paperwork completed by the time he has his bag packed, Captain. My aide will pick up the rest of his gear. You can have an NCO turn in his TA50 field gear."

He pushed me toward the doorway, "Go, Lieutenant. Do we need to run by transportation?"

We marched down the hallway and out of the building. "No, sir. I'll square up when I land. I'll use my Trust Funds. I have plenty there."

He nodded. The vehicle sat directly before the two of us. I stopped to climb in, he patted me a couple of times on the back and stood there like a statue in mourning.

Something was different about me now. From somewhere down deep inside, I felt, or heard maybe, something unrecognized. Voices? Although I couldn't distinguish between them, a sensation of great fullness, and all of whatever they were, boiled inside me, fighting to be heard.

It puzzled the crap out of me.

I shrugged and climbed into the general's vehicle.

I woke up burning with that same desire to kill the bastards responsible, and the first thing I saw was Doc. Damn her.

I continued staring. She leaned back in a doze and had that expression that told me she was dreaming. I don't know why, but I thought she was pretty sitting there like that. I still wanted to slit her throat, though. Her dream smile made my little dream that much more vivid, and thinking about it raised some questions. The most obvious being, why did I still remember it? Usually, my dreams fade quickly. This behaved like a memory.

A memory?

Was that your memory, Hank?

No.

Then why did I remember it?

Why do you ever remember things?

Shit.

The NCO poked her head down from the upper level where the cockpit was and yelled for our attention, "Threat level has gone up. Some asshole bombed a mall in Pennsylvania, killed dozens, including the vice president. There will be more security than expected."

CHAPTER TWENTY-THREE

"Goddamn it!" shouted Captain Beaufort throwing an ash-tray across his office. "I want to know where the hell he is." The detectives in there ducked and generally moved out of his way.

Experience advocated that the best way to handle one of the captain's tantrums was to keep their heads down while he vented.

His fierce glower leveled at his underlings quieted them even more. Reaching for his coffee, he took his chair, leaned back and turned so his eyes could drift through his window at the brownstone across the street. "I want an update every hour, and I want to know how in hell this son-of-a-bitch can vanish with not one single trace. He killed a senator's wife for Chrissake.

Now it appears he set off a bomb in Pennsylvania."

Beaufort swiveled his chair to face his detectives. "How in the hell did he escape from us to begin with?" He placed his cup on his desk, picked up some paperwork, and held it in front of himself. "I want answers. Now get the hell out of here."

They shuffled through the door, mumbling, and before the last two exited, Nancy entered, his cane making odd thumps against the floor. He nodded. "Cap'n."

"What do you need, Nancy?"

"Information." He yanked a chair over to center it about-face in front of the desk, straddled it, and sat, easing his gammy leg out in front of him. "Now that I'm on the Fed's Task

Force, I'd like to talk about Stanton."

The captain had no expression. "What in a donkey's dingleberry are you talking about?"

Nancy rubbed his thigh absently. "Homeland's requested to transfer me."

Beaufort shook his head, "Why'd the Feds want you for an investigator anyway? A puddle of piss would be better." He grabbed another stack of paper and pointedly ignored the detective in front of him.

"You know, Captain, you never have liked ol' Stan very much, have you?" Beaufort gave no indication of hearing Nancy at all.

"It makes me wonder what your interest in him is." He leaned back in the chair and picked up his cane to fiddle with.

"Listen, Detective," the captain rapped his desk with his pencil a couple of times, and then he too leaned back. "Both you and that ugly little prick have been a carbuncle on my nut sack for quite a while."

He lay down his pencil. "But to answer your question ... my interest in Stanton? I want him to pay for killing the senator's wife, or at least off the street so he can no longer plant bombs in malls. Now get out of my office!" His eyes bulged and skin tone darkened several shades, his fist balled. "I said get out!"

Nancy took out an ID from his pocket and tossed it onto the captain's desk.

Beaufort's face pinched together, "That piece of plastic is only a temporary card sayin—"

"It says, dear Captain, that I belong to Homeland Security now. The Task Force

Commander came to the house." He snickered. "Had me attached to her before she even asked

me. Said they bypassed you altogether. Talked to the chief instead."

Nancy planted his cane on the floor and stood. "The point here, is that I am not the only person who suspects you have your own motives concerning Stan." He limped to the door. At the doorway, the detective turned.

"Get Out!" Beaufort jumped up and took off toward the door, but Nancy had already hobbled out. The detective turned around and stood slightly on the other side of the threshold.

The door clunked, and Nancy's teeth blazed an obnoxious white through the window. He mouthed the words bye-bye.

Then with a wave, he limped away.

Beaufort swore under his breath the short walk back to his desk, retrieved his chair from where it rolled, and sat. He put his hands on his desk for a couple of seconds, tapped the top of it lightly with his pencil, picked up his phone, and punched in a few numbers. "Yeah, it's Beaufort.

What can you tell me about Nancy? First name George ... detective. When? Who did it? Okay, Thanks."

He hung up with his finger and rapped the desk a couple of times with the receiver, took a sip of coffee, oblivious of how cold it was, and then unlocked a drawer in his desk. Reaching to the rear of the drawer, he pulled out a cell phone and punched in a preset code.

Seconds later, a gruff voice answered. Beaufort wasted no time, "They took Nancy from me."

"He wasn't helping you that much, anyway, so I made a call and suggested they take him."

"He was the best connection to Stanton we had."

"Let it go, Captain. Send your people out to find him."

The captain paused for a beat; the man on the other end jumped in first, "It's federal, Beaufort, not local. Now let them tackle it."

"But—"

"Goddamn it, Captain. Go find him!"

"We're searching now. If he's here—"

"He's not."

"What?"

"He's not in the city."

Beaufort paused to process.

"Damn it, Beaufort. Do as you're told." Beeping signal ended the call.

The captain exhaled slowly. He leaned back in his chair, crossed his legs, and interlaced his fingers on his chest. He tapped his index finger on the knuckle of the other hand while he thought.

CHAPTER TWENTY-FOUR

The senator lounged on the bed as he lay the cell phone down. He returned to tickling her bare buttocks. "Was the captain. They're still searching for Stanton in New York. Told him to keep at it."

Amy chuckled and wiggled her rear. "Stop."

His fingers kept moving. "Did you hear me?"

After several heartbeats, she swatted at his hand. "I heard you. Why did you tell him that? Stanton wasn't there. That was stupid."

He popped her on her honey-colored butt cheek.

"Ow!" She whirled around, rolling over to face her lover. "That hurt. Keep it up and I'll call the Mistress! What was that all 'bout anyway?"

"I don't like anyone telling me what to do." He sounded stern.

"What I was trying to say—"

"I know what you were trying to say. You let me worry about strategy. You ride the wave."

He crawled across the bed and rested on his elbow to gaze down at her. "My God, but you are pretty."

He diddled lightly with her left nipple. Shaking his head, he moved some of her hair from her face. "Speaking of the Mistress, though, what's the deal with her eyes? You know I have only met one other person in my entire life who had two different eye colors, and she was a—"

"A what?"

"Not important."

Amy scrunched her face at him, and he shrugged, indifferent. "She was a whore, a whore with two eyes of different colors. Strangest thing I'd ever seen."

"*Heterochromia iridum.*"

"What?"

"*Heterochromia iridum*. It means two different eye colors in the same person."

Her breasts enthralled him again; they captivated his attention as he kneaded one – their perfect shape, flawless color, their dark nipples.

She slapped his hand. "Stop."

"What the hell is the matter with you?" He moved his hand away and stared at her face.

"You always like it when I play with your tits."

She rolled away, flipping off the sheet as she did, and snatched some clean undies on the way to the bathroom. "Well, I don't like it today." The bath door slammed shut as the sounds of running water filtered through the door.

The senator followed the trail of his clothes from the night before, kicked them into a pile, and sauntered into his closet to dress.

Seconds later, her voice filtered to him. "So what have you done about the other thing?" Her tone was sharp.

"It's on track." He walked out of the closet tucking his overly starched shirt into his suit pants, and zipped up. Facing the tie rack on the back of the French door to the closet, he fingered through them to pick the right color. Pulling out two, he walked to the mirror, flipping them onto opposite shoulders.

He spoke while watching her bathroom door in his mirror. "I sent condolences to Dumb

Ass Jack's family. Never really thought he ever had a clue. He was always too busy getting strangled by his sphincter. That is the reason he was VP and not the big guy." He nodded to himself and flipped one of the ties away, and pulled the other around his neck. "Also, I've fielded several queries about my availability for the VP position." He twisted the neck cinch into a knot.

The bathroom door opened. Amy walked out briskly, clad only in bra and panties, to her clothes. Pushing up the thin plastic cover, she worked her blouse free from the hanger, put it on, and then fished out her slacks. With a last check in the mirror to ensure coordination, she stepped into them.

Stonegate sauntered up behind her and peeked over her shoulder. "Why'd you dress so formally? Bra and Panties? You know I like to ogle." She glared at him over her shoulder.

He shrugged. "Okay. The plan is fine." He turned away, "Tell Mu'izz his people did a good job." He slipped into his shoes and turned to see if she'd acknowledged him. "Why're you so pissy today?"

She turned, tucking in her blouse. "But I'm not." Her smile was disarming.

"Okay. I thought maybe you were in mourning for Rick. I mean, his death was pretty sudden. I had to spin the shit out of the circumstances to keep from getting mud slung at me."

"No, honey." she hugged up against him. "I'm more than willing to trade up to the future.

Rick was becoming tiresome. He lost his magic almost to the day he started working for you." She skewered him brazenly with her eyes and then gave him another hug, this one with a sexy wiggle.

He reached down for a squeeze of her buttock. She purred quietly, "Think of me as your brown sugar."

"But I'm diabetic."

"Oh. That's too bad."

CHAPTER TWENTY-FIVE

The dream came again. The vision rolled through the night until it unfolded for her, and she lived it again.

The night air was crisp and dry, and the gibbous moon shone brightly. Its light beamed down, revealing many things to a casual observer. To those who had already learned stealth and night movement, the pale light was more than adequate for killing.

She stood motionless, dispatching her target in her mind.

It had taken a long time, but an understanding had come. This was the way to go.

Violence was exactly what she needed. She remembered the instructor as he stood before her. Arms akimbo, the man fixed his student with a withering glare. He quietly explained what most people didn't understand the goal of violence.

His voice was crisp and he pronounced his words in a clipped fashion, like his English teacher who had indeed been English, or British. "Overwhelming violence brings paralyzing terror. That terror can be generated in many ways. All anybody needs is a sudden burst of energy. Any kind of energy. The more violent the energy, the better the result. The other extreme can be as petrifying – killing up close. Case in point. Decapitating an infidel with a sword and letting his head roll in the sand terrifies our enemies."

She let the memory go. Instead, she used the instructor as a model. She practiced using her peripheral vision to track her target. A practiced stab through the ribs, between the third and fourth rib, was usually best, although different places had been taught to her.

There was also slicing with the blade.

In truth, the practical aspect of trying the different techniques of the weapon captivated her. She found she liked getting in close to kill, and she'd decided to kill her target using a Kabar knife. She wanted to delve into his eyes while gouging or slicing him to death, whichever mood took her in the moment.

Her smile vanished thinking about her enemy. She quit woolgathering, sat up straighter. She absorbed the philosophy of terrorism: it thrived in her guts and filled her with the urge to kill.

The few lights inside the aircraft, dim blue, cast barely enough illumination to see the other people sleeping in their web seats.

I tried to sleep, but between the memory of Sally's betrayal and Ahn's nagging, I knew some shit was about to happen. Sitting up, I eyeballed everything around me, but no matter what I did, my ire would not go away.

We are not headed where you think.

Shut up Ahn. I need to sleep.

The Neanderthal and the other guy dozed like bookends on either side of me. Rough snoring came from across the fuselage where Doc and her guards slumped together, and now that my mind had cleared a little, I discerned two people snorted away over there, a kind of duet. One of them was Doc.

Bet she's drooling too.

A mean little grin teased across my face thinking about it. I remembered how upset she always was when that happened.

The grin hadn't gotten past my nose before my anger killed it. Unbidden memories flashed through my head, the kind of thing I didn't need – lovemaking, swearing undying love, betrayal.

That reminded me of Hank. I didn't need him bitching about Doc. I knew she had trashed me, but I'd squashed the recollections before Hank woke up. It was bad enough that Ahn wouldn't leave me alone about whatever it was he wanted to tell me. I needed inner silence to figure out what the hell to do.

I had all of New York turning over trying to find me. I was on an aircraft headed toward Europe, preparing to dig myself into an ISIS organization. And my past personalities, the things I most trusted to help me, were disappearing. I hadn't noticed the gradual absence of petulance. Nothing loud or boisterous, more like a toothache fading away. It took a while for the absence to become noticeable.

We aren't where you—

Shut up, Ahn.

A loud snort came from across the way.

Damn it! Here I am, flying across the world to find out what I'm supposed to do, and I have no flipping clue.

What I did know, however, was my inner selves have spent months trying unmercifully to force me into doing whatever they want, and now that I genuinely need some help, they've gone away. Conversely, I'm ball deep in a conspiracy I apparently knew everything about before I lost my memory.

My eyes shot to Doc with her mouth open and drooling.

Why the hell?

I stood up, not caring one diarrhetic shit if the Neanderthal and his underling bookend cracked heads. I don't even know how I walked, because the aircraft was flying through turbulence. What I do know is I found myself standing above Doc, feeling the rumble of the aircraft through my feet, staring down at her. It was hard for me to breathe.

Lying there with her mouth open and leaking was the woman who had the answers to so many questions.

"… hell, did you have to give me more questions?" I spoke to myself and the inner horde, but the words popped out.

Her eyes fluttered open, half glazed, her kisser still open. Her tongue ran around the inside of her maw. I thought it strange that her tongue appeared to drag over the top lip. The irony of how sexy it was made me chuckle, which in turn warred with how pissed I was about her.

Maybe I should wake Hank to help me stay pissed.

We aren't goin—
Shut up, Ahn.
Doc's eyes focused, and she sat up. "What are they saying, Stan?"
"Who?"
She shrugged and sat up straighter. "Don't know. That's why I'm asking you. One of your past lives is talking to you." Mild disgust scrunched her face into a scowl. "I simply wanted to know what they were talking about."
"Ahn. He's telling me that we aren't flying to Europe."
"Of course we aren't."
That made me chuckle. "Of course we are. Amsterdam."
No Stan. We made a huge circle for several hours. Now we're heading in the direction of where the sun leans in winter. Amsterdam is toward the rising sun.
Ahn. Sometimes he captivated me. You can't even see outside this plane. And where did
you learn geography?
Hank. And I don't need to see. I feel direction inside.
That was true. I trusted his feelings as much as he did. "Damn it!"
Doc had a sick expression on her face that I didn't understand until her female guard turned to gaze at me. It was the redheaded bitch from Switzerland, the one who put me on the floor, the one Doc betrayed me to.
What the hell is Doc so piqued about?
The barrel end of a handgun poked in my face. Hank was busy telling me that it was a little popgun, a .22 semiautomatic, and that she'd have to hit me directly in the head or the heart to stop us cold.
Regardless of what he touted, emotionless eyes drilled into me, and the whole mess made my ass suck up so far inside of me that it felt like my rectum was squeezing my heart.
Can that little pop gun bullet stop a heart if it's encased in a rectum?

De eyes. Holy shit, De eyes; Fox Boy screamed. *De danged Mistress!*

I did a double-take. The two-colored eyes stared right back at me. "Lacy."

"Shut the fuck up, dick weed." The pop gun came in close to my eye, so close I smelled the gun oil.

"What the fuck is happening in my aircraft!" The loadmaster's voice, shrill with anger, filled the air.

Lacy, the Mistress, whatever her name was – the redhead's eyes never wavered. Nothing in her face did.

"Goddamn it!" continued the loadmaster. "Put that little piece of shit away before you blow a hole in my aircraft."

Redheaded bitch rotated her weapon just enough to fire, and then quickly re-centered her aim on my nose. While I suffered ear pain from the concussion, the wispy smoke drifted from the barrel, fascinated Ahn, and Hank babbled on about the way the redhead bitch had stopped her talking meant the kill shot probably hit the loadmaster in the face. He sounded as if he was proud of her.

Everyone was awake now. My bladder was ready for action just from the unexpected sound and violence. The redhead eased to her feet, keeping me covered. She did it perfectly: too far away to jump her, yet close enough that even a blind man would be able to kill me by squeezing the trigger. Pop gun or no, an eyeball shot would certainly end me.

Even Hank was stymied and growled in admiration.

The man guarding Doc stood.

My eyes were a magnet to Doc's. Her's were wary, busy taking in everything.

"Well," said the redhead, "So glad both of you are here." She shuffled around me, keeping her feet in contact with the floor. Once around, she backed up to the loadmaster's station. Still keeping her aim, she half squatted and pulled out a package from behind a bulkhead. Then, with well-practiced moves, she unfolded a few straps, stepped into them and pulled others over her shoulders. All the while, I had an excellent view down the barrel of her handgun.

A click, a shrug, a couple of snaps, and she had the parachute donned. A couple of pulls and another set of shrugs – adjusted. Her face morphed from grimace to snarl as she fished through a cargo pocket on her thigh. Then she pulled out a small device. "The only reason we needed her," she nodded curtly at Doc and motioned with the .22 for her to stand, "was to pinpoint you. The Amsterdam Corridor was out there, but we weren't sure you would take the bait." Her face brightened. "Now, I'm sure." She turned her attention to the Neanderthal and his buddy and fired, dropping the smaller one. Head shot, neat and clean.

Before he hit the deck, Doc kicked the man next to her in the knee, bending it sideways and put an elbow into his neck. He was gone.

Holy shit, did you see that?

I felt Hank nod, albeit silently.

The bitch whirled back to Doc. With deadly aim, she took the time to shake her head. "No more, or I'll shoot you right there where you are." She chuckled, nodded sideways, and turned to the Neanderthal. "You were next. Reprieved." She used her head to indicate the cockpit. He disappeared up the ladder, a sick little grin plastered on his face.

The redhead's expression directed at Doc was almost admiration, "Learned a little something along the way, hey, honey?" She still held her weapon trained on us, but perhaps more on her than me. He dug in her pocket and pulled out a little device. A small movement with her hand and muffled explosions rocked the aircraft, and the regular vibrations became distorted – rougher, a loss of speed.

"Exploding bolts exchanged for engine mount bolts at Wagner." A tough-shit expression played across her face, and then it changed to quizzical. She shook her device, "Feels like at least one set didn't work."

With a shrug, she dropped the small case onto the floor,

strolled to the bulkhead, and slapped the large button next to her. The back hatch began to lower, and wind-whipped everywhere. I stood amidst the deafening roar and watched.

Two more muffled pops in the cacophony and I turned my attention back to the woman who held us captive. Her new partner, the Neanderthal, stepped down out of the cockpit stairway, "Let's go."

A crisp nod signaled her understanding and she edged toward the tail. Yelling over the thunderous air blasting through, "Alas, both the pilot and copilot are dead, and there is one engine still attached, wobbly though, maybe one or two bolts still intact. Only had three to begin with."

Ol' Ape-Man threw the remaining parachutes out of the tail and tightened his own, nodding for her to jump. She shuffled the last few steps to the open hatch, her pistol still tracking dead on my third eye. She stepped in front of Sergeant Ape, then turned and her Ka-bar sliced his throat. Quick jerks on their rip chords, their chutes opened and out they both flew, his blood misting in the wind.

"Well, shit."

I was unable to tell exactly who said that. Actually, and more correctly, it was beyond me to figure out who had not said that – Doc, me, my inner horde. Everyone said the same thing at the same time. Then there was a deathly hush. That is, assuming you can have that kind of quietude in the middle of ear-splitting wind clatter.

The extraordinary thing about the voices was they all had different aspects to them – curiosity, anger, puzzlement, the whole gamut. The most bizarre thing, though, was the silent voice, kind of an extreme whisper, almost visceral, like muscle memory, and too insistent for me to ignore.

The cockpit. Go to the cockpit.

I wanted to move, but my legs stayed put. The whisper had something in it that fascinated me. I stood there feeling the timbre of it. The familiarity of it.

Doc latched onto my arm, and at her touch, I was aware of everything around me again.

Doc's focus clutched me with more force than her hand on my arm. Even her hair, dancing like

Medusa's wild-assed coif didn't distract me from her eyes.

Cockpit!

The non-sound sliced through me. I tore myself away from her eyes and ran.

Surprisingly, her grasp turned out to be the death-grip kind, and she attached herself to me like a shadow.

The bumps, the sudden rising and falling of the deck, made it almost impossible to run. I tripped once, and Doc stumbled a couple of times. We only made it by being together. It was dicey getting up the stairway, ladder, whatever the hell it's called, but we made it.

As I kicked the door open, the view from the windscreen stopped me.

"Ah, shit."

That was definitely Doc this time, and she delivered the right sentiment. The ground was close and zoomed along. A quick glance to the right, and the one engine was hanging from a bolt about as thin as half a thread in a spider's web. Well, maybe two threads.

The left was even more frightening. Seeing the wings all naked, made every muscle I had clench tighter than a whale's ass at the bottom of the ocean. I wanted to piss, felt like I had, too, but there was no way to squeeze out any juice through that hole.

Lowdy. Lowdy. Lowdy!

I had to ignore Fox Boy. He just kept yelling.

I pulled the pilot free from his seat and bailed into it.

Lowdy.

"What the hell are you doing?" Doc's voice filled my ears.

I didn't even look at her. The roar wasn't so bad inside the cockpit, and even the internal cacophony had quieted to an explosive roar. I did my best, nimble fingers and all. My hand busily trimmed the flaps and equalized the whatevers. I'd had a dream about flying a Gulfstream, but I hadn't a clue what I was doing. Somehow the silent voice inside directed my movements, and it worked. The plane flew, well okay, coasted, glided.

Damn! Was that dream mine?

It wasn't falling, and it had some semblance of purpose. Instead of plummeting, it moved more or less forward with several of those quick drops and sudden rises I mentioned before.

At least there is still one engine.

That damned non-voice again — but what it said was comforting, and I muttered it to myself.

Stan, you stupid wanker. We gotta find a way to survive. Just believe you've been a pilot before, old boy. Follow your instincts and bob's your uncle.

Shut up, Hank.

Jacques drooled over the view, Ahn grunted agreement to Jacques, and Fox boy continued with his mantra, *Lowdy!*

The sight of the ground approaching made me want to puke, and I didn't have a clue what the hell to do. Doc's expression made my bowel want to void, not because I saw hatefulness there, but because she smiled. Smiled!

One engine or not, my sphincter cramped up so hard to keep everything inside, it was probably bulletproof. I guess that would solve the problem, huh?

Doc reached over to rub my shoulders.

What the hell?

Anyway, her contact worked. My hands moved on their own, flipping this switch then that one. I watched in horror. I obviously didn't have anything better to do but knob-dick around.

Doc leaned back and took a deep breath. "What are you doing, Stan?"

The wind flap and the inner arguments and expletives made

it hard to hear, but I did. We sat in a plane, falling out of the sky, and she casually asks me what I'm doing.

Hank's voice zeroed in on me, *Shoot her and let's get ready to ditch this fucking plane.*

I thought it was well said, although I still had no idea of how to survive the crash.

Besides, I didn't have a pistol.

"Stan!"

My head snapped back to her.

"What the hell are you doing?"

I gawked and blinked rapidly. After what seemed to be couple of minutes of eye flutter, but was probably only a nanosecond, the non-voice inside whispered to me and I repeated it,

"Dropping airspeed to lose altitude enough to jump."

WHAT! You fucking moron.

Hank had a way with words.

"How do you know what to do?"

"A voice." *What voice?*

Shut up, Hank.

"Whose voice, Stan?"

My hands worked on their own again, extremely confident in what they did. The aircraft change, minutiae, a subtle pitch change, a settling of vibrations.

My eyes flicked to the windscreen. Blinding sunlight lit the view. Below, the mountains slid to my side, their sandy brown shades boring in the blinding sunlight. Ahead, near the horizon, a brilliant reflection stabbed me in the eye.

"Stan. Whose voice?" She had the same tone of voice she used in my clinic sessions.

I didn't make eye contact with her, kept my hands free to do their thing. "I don't know who it belongs to. I can't even tell whether it's male or female. I keep thinking something with the first initial of B. B … be … ba …" I nodded. "Ba something."

She leaned back into the copilot's chair. "Okay." A smug

expression ran across her face. After a blank visage for a second and another semi-smile, she lifted her eyes to gaze out of the windscreen. "What's the plan?" She eyeballed the rest of the cockpit, amazingly immune to all carnage around us. Then she centered on me again. "Think there's anything Irish out there?"

"How the hell should I know? I'm in a plane with no pilot. It's crashing. And you are fucking looking for Ireland?" I checked the progress of our doom, and then stared at my hands that gave every indication that they were on their own. To me, they had the same thoughts as I did: Holy shit! What do we do?

"Well, okay." She leaned back, more intent on watching me.

My hands started in again, flipping some things, adjusting other controls. Hopefully, I appeared to know what the hell I was doing, but I doubted it.

"I love you, Stan."

"What!"

She's stacked well, but she's full of shit, yelled Hank. *That bitch turned you in. Kill her and let's go.*"

I know.

I stopped long enough to flick my eyes over to her, full, I'm sure, of the anger I felt. Hank was right, but there was something else. I went back to work. The engine dropped pitch, the fuselage shook harder, and we slowed considerably, pulling me forward in my seat. Thank God for that remaining engine.

"I said, I love you."

I punched the instrument panel, "Damn it, Doc—"

A very loud thump interrupted me, and the plane fell deathly quiet, like a fucking graveyard. That is to say, I still heard the muffled sound of the hurricane taking place behind us in the cargo area ... but no engine sound.

"Holy Fuck." I muttered to myself, a new mantra. "Holy—" My head swiveled like an owl's as I checked the wing, but it was hard to see with my eyes so engorged. Besides, I knew what had happened before my eyes confirmed it.

The remaining engine was gone, broken loose, dropped

away. "Now we're really in trouble."

My eyes searched the terrain below.

Goddamn it!

Only mountains, and we were falling like a burro's turd bouncing down the Grand Canyon.

Wait … something flashed up ahead.

Water!

A lake nestled in those mountains, long and skinny, but maybe ... I banked the craft toward it as gently as possible while lowering the flaps. At least, I did something, and the flaps extended. Pushed the tail down, elevating the nose.

The plane dropped so fast that my body contracted even more than when I flopped to the sidewalk to hide from the Shannie-a-like. Doc still smiled, but it was strained, her jaw muscles popping. Her boobs bounced up and down with every turbulent swing, and her eyes remained locked on mine.

I nodded curtly. I don't know why. I was still pissed, but half of me felt something else.

More turbulence rocked us and I turned around.

Pay attention, Pencil Neck.

I ignored Hank. We were almost at the lake before I saw it – Hoover Dam. At least I knew where we were crashing. Lake Mead.

The plane dropped, leaving me in the air above the seat for almost a full second and I almost ate my own butt. Then I plopped down hard and my balls screamed in pain. "Doc, listen to me. Doc!"

"What, Stan?" The tension in her voice screamed louder than my heartbeats.

"When I tell you, get up, run to the back and jump out that back end. Don't look back."

What? Are you crazy? She—

Shut up, Hank.

"Sta—."

"Don't 'Stan' me now. Did you hear me?" My hands did

something and the aircraft dropped again. It sounded as if it was slowing, but honestly, without an engine, there was no way in hell to really tell. We were traveling a hell of a lot faster than I wanted. "Doc!"

"I heard you. I jus—"

"Goddamn it. Do it!" More adjustments. We were coming in low, and I banked enough for us to fly down the long axis of the water. "Get up. Ready? Run like hell!"

My hand hit a switch and I clambered free of the seat, slipping on the pilot's blood. I had to scoot.

Running down the fuselage, the air was damp. We were so low that the ramp kept slapping the water, and heavy mist filled the air.

Standing at the top of the ramp, I grabbed her shoulder. I yelled loudly, hoping she heard.

"Get as close to the edge as you can. Then jump out, cross your legs, wrap your arms around your chest, and grab! Hold on and jump in feet first. If you're still alive after you go in, swim hard in the direction bubbles float."

She nodded.

I nodded back and moved to the edge.

I hesitated for what might have been a year, and then I squeezed her hand, wishing like hell that she hadn't betrayed me because I still loved her. With a huge leap, I tied myself up tight and hoped I would survive.

Oh, crap. Holy Shit. Mercy fu—

I'd rolled down Mount Everest with a family of Yeti kicking turds out of me every time I bounced, and man, did I bounce, coughed and gagged, well-nigh dead. This was way more than getting my ass whipped, more like getting kicked, whipped, eaten, and digested. The gorillas finally got me.

Black smoke covered the sky. About a kilometer away the plane stood nose down into the lake. Flames boiled up its side to the tail, consuming it and dotting several areas of the water with all kinds of shit. Smoky as hell.

My entire body screamed as I trod water, and my nose felt as big as my fist. I made myself search the area. Doc was nowhere.

I should have told her how I felt.

You're better off without her.

Eat shit, Hank.

He was probably right. She did betray me.

I rolled onto my back to rest before I shinnied off my pants. I needed something that floated. It was possible to tie the legs and blow air into them, but God, I was tired.

CHAPTER TWENTY-SIX

The Mistress floated down from the doomed aircraft, the sun white-hot above her in the sky. She didn't care. With her downward view, she knew luck favored her; she would land in the high pastureland of Southwest Colorado.

She buried her chute and walked through a vast open field filled with large boulders toward the only road she'd spotted from the air. The sweet aspect about her landing in the boonies was nobody would have seen her land. The sour factor was nobody would drive by, and she needed a little traffic because finding a vehicle was high on her list.

That next half-hour presented plenty of time for her to grumble and gripe at her failure to plan for something like this.

Maybe she needed to reevaluate the luck thing. Something wasn't right. Still hyped from the adrenaline high from the bloodbath and the jump, fatigue betrayed her body, plus the sweat dripping into her eyes irritated the shit out of her. She cursed to herself while she walked, sometimes mumbling, sometimes much louder, and waved her arms around constantly. A passerby might have thought she was a tad deranged.

They would've been correct.

The car zoomed up and over the hill, practically airborne at the crest. The screech of the tires as the vehicle crunched down fully was the first thing she'd heard. She ran to the roadside and it's fishtailing almost took her out. Her lightning reaction saved her.

The screeching stopped several yards beyond her; acrid smoke and the stink of melting rubber burned her nose. The young driver, maybe nineteen, shook his blond mane of a Mohawk from his eyes and crawled out of the Mustang, leaving the engine running. A sly smirk spread across his face as he sauntered over.

"You an air jockey or something?" he pointed at her flight suit.

She smiled back, "You always drive like that? Almost hit me."

He grunted out a couple of chuckles, rubbed the back of his neck, and widened his last two struts, placing him next to her. "Never anyone walking way out here."

"You gonna give me a ride?"

The guy eyeballed her up and down. His smirk widened to a grin, revealing a deep dimple on his left side and a calculating eye that continued to measure her. "You gonna give me something?" His eyes lingered on her crotch, then up to her face.

She stared for a full minute, her hand behind her back resting on her handgun. *Do I screw him, or shoot him?*

Fatigue crept through her and made up her mind. "I'm a bit tired. Been walking you know. How 'bout you drive me to where I can get a flight while I sleep, and we'll see what happens when I'm more rested. How far is the nearest airport?"

"Crop-duster, or commercial?" His eyes hardened, yet they still licked her with pleasure.

She chuckled silently to herself and took her hand away from the weapon. He'll do.

"Depends. Need to get back to the East coast. Crop-duster take me there?"

He grasped her arm and led her to the car. "Nope. But maybe get you to a bigger airport."

"How far?"

Draping his arm over her shoulders, he reached down and gave her breast a rough squeeze. "If I drive about two hours. Or I can take you to my buddy, John, twenty minutes to him and about half an hour after that by air."

She patted his hand on her breast and then sat on the passenger side of the Mustang, her fatigue almost overpowering her. "Listen, John."

"Mike. The name is Mike." He walked around to his side and

eased into the seat.

"Whatever. I need sleep." She leaned back into the seat and closed her eyes. "Drive me to a decent airport an' I'll give you a little action."

His hand fondled her breast again, and she let him have a good feel. She nodded, eyes closed, "A promise. Things to come. Now let's drive."

I heard something and pulled my head out of the water.

"... an! Over here, Stan."

Turning toward the sound, my eyes caught the most beautiful sight. Doc, about fifty meters away, and she was in a life raft. A life raft?

"Lie there and float, Stan. I'm coming." She leaned over and paddled with her hands.

I don't know how long it took her to reach me, because I gained consciousness in the little raft, puking water and blood. I felt like hammered dog shit. Apparently, I sank, she dove in, grabbed me, and hauled me back to her little raft before I drowned. Said she reset my nose too.

Couldn't tell, coughing up all that water.

"You okay?"

I lay there like a sick dog. For once, the inner horde was quiet, and I had to fight to stay alert. "How? A flippin' boat?"

"After you jumped, I turned around to take one last deep breath before committing. Immolation had to be easier than what I'd just seen you do. I took a deep breath and was about to jump when I saw the emergency equipment locker, half-open, I guess from the tail banging around. Anyway, I grabbed a life vest, but it was really a raft and when I tugged, it inflated.

Acted like a sail and we went out together." She grimaced at me, "It hurt, but not like the beating you had. My bottom and back felt like I took a hard spanking."

Mu'izz studied his reflection in the mirror, fingering the little scabs around his face and eyes. It had taken that whole evening to pull the glass shards out and apply steri-strips. Most of the cuts would heal, but there were a couple on the right side of his face that would definitely grow scar tissue.

Facial scars. Even during my first attack while training with Hezbollah, I never got a scar.

I was terrified, but that's when I learned how to be cruel. Still, no marks.

He turned around.

They'll give me cruel look. He snorted. Can't hurt.

His eye checked his beard for a neat trim and nodded.

Unfolding a crisp white shirt, he put it on, careful not to bend the fabric and cause an unsightly crease. He liked things tidy, his person, apartment. He preferred everything orderly, strange for a man who directed mayhem and terror.

He glanced at his cell phone, resisting the urge to pick it up and call the Mistress. She should have called by now, but the last thing he wanted was to appear anxious.

He buttoned his cuffs, straightened his sleeves, and checked his reflection. Satisfied, he headed out, snatching his cell phone on the way.

It had taken Bobo half the night to retrieve his car. Said the cops were climbing around the neighborhood like ants on a melted candy bar.

Mu'izz chuckled. The man was a reasonably good shot and would step into a fight with a smile, but he wasn't near as smart as he thought he was. Mu'izz had found him in the ghetto, and the struggle to train him in the ways of jihad had been huge.

"Let's go, Bobo. To the precinct house. You're my driver now."

After slight confusion, Bobo opened the door to the street and headed to the car.

Mu'izz ignored him and climbed into the back as always;

Bobo needed to figure things out alone. Mu'izz had to spend time reviewing his position in the meeting to come. It would be like priming a pump. The more he thought about what he wanted, the more his mental juices flowed. The drive didn't even register. By the time they pulled up outside the precinct house, Bobo had to yell to get his attention. "Mu'izz!"

Mu'izz's eyes snapped.

Bobo's head dropped as his voice trailed. "Sorry. Didn't think you heard me." Mu'izz glared for about fifteen seconds, and then moved his eyes toward his door.

Bobo took the hint, jumped out, and opened the door.

Mu'izz walked past, ignoring him.

Without stopping, he strode past the desk sergeant and through the bullpen. One of the detectives tried to stop him as he entered the captain's office, but he closed the office door quickly, and they didn't follow.

"Hello, Beaufort."

The captain said nothing for long seconds.

Mu'izz thought the man's face reddened by at least three shades. "You know, Captain, I will not be ordered around."

Leaping to his feet, the captain exploded, "You'll do what—"

"We're in this together. Or did you forget that all of us were in the room when we captured Sigma in Zermatt?"

That stopped Beaufort. Mu'izz watched the man labor to keep his breathing even.

"Yep, Mu'izz. I was there when the Caucus decided what direction to take. All of us, including you, agreed on the hierarchy and you ain't doing what you're required to do."

Mu'izz snorted. "First of all, the real test of rank is, do you need me more than I need you?" His eyes leveled on Beaufort. "Well, do you think Berne wants the money I bring in, or the thin veil of protection that is your responsibility?"

The captain sat back in his chair and ran the back of his hand over his chin. His eyes never lost focus on Mu'izz. "You shot at two federal agents."

Mu'izz chuckled, "If my money dries up, what will you do? If you dry up, we'll simply buy more." He stood, walked to the window and gazed out of the new pane, and studied the fresh paint while tapping absently on the glass. "Go ahead. Make that call you're thinking about. Have your people run up here and lock me up."

"Berne will—"

"Fuck Berne." He spun around to glare at the captain again. "We all agreed. The Caucus puts Stonegate in the White House. After that, we receive appropriate compensation."

"Lower your voice."

Mu'izz strolled back to his chair and sat. "I'm thinking I might use my little organization for bigger things." His neat fingernails tapped lightly on the chair arm. "If you ever order me around again, I will gut you on the spot."

"Don't play shit with me, Abdul." Beaufort jabbed his finger straight at Mu'izz's face.

"You screw with me—"

The *thunk* of Mu'izz's knife as it stabbed into the table stopped him, but he grabbed his revolver from his holster, cocked it, and pointed. "What the hell do you think you're doing? This is my office. Nobody can come in here and do that."

"It's a gift."

Beaufort stared. "What the fuck are you talking about?"

Mu'izz glanced at the knife jutting up from the table. The point of it pierced an envelope with Beaufort's name scrawled across. Saying nothing, Mu'izz lifted his eyebrows, reclaimed his knife, and walked calmly out of the office.

The captain scowled, lay his weapon on the desk, snatched up the envelope while chewing his inside cheek, and sat in his chair. Almost absently, he opened it and pulled out the missive. The damned thing was a record, a list of dates, deals, and people he'd somehow influenced.

"Shit."

He threw it onto the desk and grabbed his phone. As soon as he heard the voice on the other end, he wasted no time. "We got trouble." Silence greeted him; he wiped the sweat from his upper lip and scanned the list again. "Hey! You hear me?"

"I'm waiting for you to explain."

The maddeningly calm voice made Beaufort rub his chin with the back of his hand.

Bastard. "That prick gave me a list all the things I've done for the Caucus."

"He's keeping track?"

The calculation he detected in the senator's voice helped Beaufort breathe easier. His eyes ran down the list before him, and he pursed his lips. "Bastard's jotted down all our names. I see a few things you did down here." He tossed the paper onto his desk. "And I think I know why too. The son-of-a-bitch told me he was leaving the Caucus. Going into business for himself."

The senator snorted.

CHAPTER TWENTY-SEVEN

Nancy squirmed in the car. He tried not to, but he found it impossible to get comfortable. His wound hurt, screamed no matter the position he found. Not like hers. She only needed a few stitches, and it didn't even slow her down. Carbonella drove like a cheetah chasing a scared bunny.

The SUV lurched, airborne, after a small rise in the road, and jiggled hard when they landed. He grabbed the handle above the door to settle himself and gritted his teeth to contain his groan.

"Sorry." Carbonella kept her eyes on the road. At first, Nancy thought she had extraordinary patience, and maybe that was true as long as the investigation made progress. Times like now, on the road, drove her daft. Luckily, the roads had scant traffic because of the hour, and most of the occasional drivers around shopped the whores strutting back and forth.

He glanced Carbonella's way with a nod, trying to hide the grimace. "S'okay. A little twinge."

A throaty chuckle rolled from her. "Twinge my ass. I've been keeping an eye on you.

You do try hard to keep it to yourself. But I can tell."

A smaller bump, not quite so enervating, and he didn't have to grab the handhold.

"Like that." Another chortle. "It's okay, Nancy. I get it." She drove in silence for a second or two, and then, "Never been shot, but I've heard it hurts like a bitch." Now it was his turn to laugh.

"I know. The bitch herself saying it must hurt like a bitch." Both her hands lifted off the wheel for a quick shrug.

"Why call yourself that?"

"It's my nickname with the team." Her husky voice rolled through the car. "But speaking of a bitch, that Mistress bitch seems to be floating everywhere. Did you see the report identifying her as the terrorist who blew up the plane? The crazy eyes were the giveaway."

He nodded with a grunt and adjusted his leg to no avail. "She gets around."

Carbonella nodded. "Quantico doesn't even know who she is. Now Mu'izz is different. We do have a file on that little shit. Have you had a chance to check his file?" She slowed down, made a turn.

His attention drifted from her to the growing population of hookers.

"Hey, you listening?" Her voice became throatier. "Focus on Mu'izz. This guy was a small-time moron, doing little hustles up until about five years ago when he made his way over to the Middle East. A few months later, he stopped off in Europe on the way back from whatever training camp he'd been in. After a couple of months of intense training there, he's a new man.

No more small-time thug."

Nancy pointed to a spot not far away, "Pull over up there."

She swerved to the curb and parked, amazing Nancy that the whole thing happened so smoothly. He didn't even have to grab the handle, and his leg throbbed only a little.

She scooted around in her seat, turning a knee toward him, her face stern. Nancy's eye caught sight of her breast jiggling as her arm plopped around the seat back, and he forced himself to stare directly at her face. The time since he'd been with Vivian weighed him down, and he was acutely aware that his supervisor was a woman. Definitely female.

Damn biology.

"Listen." She shook her head. "Mu'izz is a badass, the mystery redhead too, but there's a bunch more at work here." A quick wince and she held her side, and then sat back breathing deeply. "I shouldn't have to explain this. Maybe I made a mistake putting you on my team."

"Maybe so. I thought I was here to lend my knowledge of Stan."

"You are. But the task force's primary functio—"

"Wait." He held up his hands in surrender. "Yes, ma'am."

Her face didn't lighten up, but her silence let him think he might try something else. "I'm sorry. Can we start again?"

She nodded sideways.

"How 'bout you tell me what you want me to do, what my function is, and start from there. Tell you what. I've got an idea. Drive. I'll direct you. It's not far."

He squirmed under her leveled gaze. She chewed the inside of her cheek, pursed her lips, and gave him a slow bob of her head, she grabbed the wheel and drove off. "You're here to help with Stan, but I need you to be on the team, not as a consultant. Savvy? Tomorrow I want you in early to catch up as best you can."

"Sure. Turn right up here. Then take the third left." She nodded.

The streetlights threw shadows through the car. Nancy watched Carbonella's hair illuminate with each passing light.

Damn biology.

"You know," Carbonella talked as she drove, "Tom, the last commander, and I were really close. We shared each new revelation as it appeared. It's different without him and I need you to catch up as soon as possible, not to replace what I had with him so much, but I function best when my partner is up to speed. I don't need you to know everything I do, but you have to have your feet solidly on the ground."

"I got ya. Pull over up here."

"Here?"

"Pull over."

As soon as the vehicle stopped, he sat back against the seat and pointed to the working girls primping next to the buildings. A couple of the streetwalkers strutted toward the car.

"You wanted to show me hookers?"

He waved her closer still but continued to look the other way. "Something you need to understand about Stan," he said without turning toward her. "He's a little pissant prick. One minute you think he cares about you and the next, he cuts your throat and leaves you for the wolves."

A car dove by slowly, and the street girls were back to business, bending forward, backward, spreading their knees, one adjusting her breasts, another rubbing her crotch, all heckling the driver.

"You talking about the way he made you feel like an ass about your wife and the lesbian thing?"

He glared askance at her. "You know about that? Figures." He gazed back into the night.

"Nothing like that. I'm sorry about her, by the way."

Nancy chewed his cheek for a few seconds and then grunted.

"Sure. But back to that other thing, I meant that I read the file."

He turned half toward her, "It's not in the file."

"I read the case file." She rushed on, "And before you say it wasn't in there, you're right.

I talked to your captain. He filled me in."

He shrugged. "Sounds about right. He don't like me much. Thought the lesbian thing in particular was a real chuckle. But that's what I'm talking about. Stan was real sorry about that part, but he still laid the bomb out there anyway. He didn't bother to tell me about it the entire way back to the precinct. Then when we got there, he flapped his mouth to everyone in the bullpen." He shook his head to clear it. "In the hallway, he claimed he didn't know either. Has some kind of split personality. He's got a shrink, real good looking, and − hey."

Movement down the street caught his eye and attention.

"Anyway, this is where he sniffed it all out, right down this street, whores and all." He mumbled to himself, "The cases are connected."

"Meaning?"

Nancy turned back to her, his face almost grotesque in the street shadows. He pointed to a bunch of streetwalkers "That case and this one, they're connected. Stan told me that when the senator's wife got shot."

His eyes glowed and he found it hard to sit still, "There was a redheaded bimbo who had a thing for Vivian."

Staring out of the window, he became more intense, "She's over there, leaning against that building. No one around her."

Carbonella leaned over to have a better view, and she patted his arm. "She liked the lesbian thing, huh?" He nodded.

She unbuttoned a couple of buttons on her shirt and tucked the collar underneath the rest of the shirt to reveal some cleavage. "Hand me those shoes in the back behind you. Wait here." While he fished around for them, she reached under her coat and pulled off her pants, exposing her legs. A sly smile roamed over her face as she reached into her glove box, retrieved her leg holster, and cinched it around her thigh. She slipped her weapon into it, and then slipped the shoes onto her feet.

"Wait here and I'll get her." She opened the door and stepped out onto the street, like a sexy woman out for a stroll.

"What the hell, Carbonella? A man with a cripple leg out—"

She shook her head and he shut up.

He waited for her to reach the first working girl, climbed out, and limped after her, his cane keeping him about twenty feet behind her. He kept as far into the shadows as possible.

The redheaded Mistress leaned next to the building. It had been years since she'd worked the street, although she technically wasn't working. Mu'izz had asked her to watch the stable of girls while his face healed. What a prima donna.

She didn't care, though. The trade was a family one. Her mother had traded sex for them to survive, and family had always been extremely important to the redhead. She had started on her back, spreading her legs, but her personality and sense of adventure drove her to widen her options. She liked variety.

As a few of her customers became violent, she discovered

new talents. Mu'izz showed up, and when he did, he helped her talents expand even more, sending her to training camps and exercises to refine her skills.

A disturbance down the street piqued her curiosity. She quit leaning on the brick wall and walked over to the girls. Several of them hassled a couple. The guy had a cane and hung back, letting the woman take the lead. It was the usual kind of thing.

Several catcalls and whistles added to the confusion, and then Sweetie's voice sailed through the air, "Hey, Lorraine! Got a lezzie for ya."

She smiled and leaned back against the wall. She was content to let the girls do their hustling. She preferred to reminisce about her latest kill.

The boy had driven her but before driving into the town, his anticipation had gotten to be too much. He turned down a dirt road, wearing an evil little smile, parked, and dragged her to a nearby grassy area. There, he pulled her flight suit open and worked it down past her hips.

She didn't make a fuss. And when he started slapping and yanking her around, she let him. She actually enjoyed that part; the pain aroused her and kept her interest. The best part though, was her climax. It came at the perfect point. Plunging into her, she imagined he thought of himself quite a cocksman, impaling her with his magnificent tool. He never saw her fish the Ka-bar from her boot.

She timed it between his thrusts and stabbed upwards from his throat to his brain. His sudden jerk helped her peak, and letting him flop onto his back pushed his almost average penis into her further. She watched his horror gurgle away and rode him 'til he gave the slack-jawed stare.

A great orgasm.

She left the body, slipped into the creek to wash up, and drove to the airport.

"Hey!" one of her girls yelled. "That your man, honey?"

She focused back on the street, turning in the direction of the yell, then the man.

Stepping close to the building and away from the brightness of the streetlight, the Mistress stared. Too far to make out his features, but she recognized the shoulders. He stayed so close to the shadow, and his gait with the cane wasn't the same, but she knew him.

A quick flick of her eyes back to the lezzie-john and it made sense. The man was a cop working the investigation of the senator's wife, and now that she was closer, it was plain that the lesbo bitch was working with him.

"Shit," she mumbled and, grabbed the little .32 pistol hidden under her coat in the front of her pants. She inched away and peeled around the corner of her building.

"Hey! Stop! Police!" The shout sailed up the street.

Doubling back, she peeked around the brick wall. The woman ran, he hobbled.

Mu'izz's girls scattered.

The Mistress fired blindly, then sprinted away. No time. Have to go.

"Stop!" The man's voice echoed off the buildings. Shots returned. Chips of brick flew, stinging her head. A glance back said the woman had fired, and the man was not far behind her.

She turned another corner, ducked behind a dumpster and froze, straining to control her huffing. She waited.

Maybe the rank smell will help them move on.

The woman ran past but stopped about twenty feet away, clearly studying the alley.

The urge to run coursed through her but the Mistress resisted, forced herself to stay still, fingering the pistol in her hand.

"You lose her, Carbonella?" The man's voice filled the alley.

There was no answer, and she saw the hand signal telling him to shut up. Another pointed to the opposite side of the alley.

His legs and cane hobbled through her line of sight, his cane clicking each time it touched the ground. She watched him move through the shadows from the streetlight. He took an overwatch position behind a brick corner to cover her as she searched.

The Mistress's heart thumped in her ears. She visualized the woman's progress by careful listening. Once, a noise down the alley tricked her, probably a rat scavenging. Then the sound of a scrape much closer. Her pistol hand was slippery, but the thrill of it all surpassed everything.

She saw his pistol move, pointing toward her. She needed to focus better but it took effort, and awareness of that disgusted her.

This is bullshit.

Myriad scenes flashed through her mind, all from her memories of being denigrated, beaten down, and beaten up. Her hand closed tightly around the pistol grip, and the feel of it brought her back to herself.

Bullshit.

Slowly she switched weapons. It would feel so much better to do this with the Ka-bar.

The deranged screaming spooked Carbonella enough to spoil her aim, and her shot ricocheted away. The redhead leaped from the shadows, behind the dumpster. The knife in the woman's hand flashed briefly and then disappeared. It stabbed upward, and Carbonella lost her balance.

Then she was on the ground, her leg screaming. Two shots fired from a long distance.

CHAPTER TWENTY-EIGHT

The blackness of sleep was omnipresent, not only an absence of color and light, but sound too. It had more to do with texture and quality than anything else. Velvety black was the norm, fuzzy and blurry, but warm and comfortable.

Occasionally a disturbance raced around the periphery, and when it did, stark colors and pain crossed through.

That damn near killed us, mon ami. Jacques appeared, almost ghostlike, a middle-aged Frenchman. A disheveled appearance differed from his usual, tasteful likeness.

Piss off, Jacques. Irritation edged the English voice.

An image of Hank appeared. He busied himself by inspecting an arsenal of weapons that surrounded him. He picked up a 1911 .45 to clean and sat at a table. *"As a commando, I received wounds several times. Mind you, they all hurt more than that landing. I'm glad he's been listening to me about getting in shape."*

You may've been a soldier, mon capitaine, *and while he is in better shape, it might've been better if you'd helped him in some other fashion.*

Hank talked as he broke the weapon down, pulling out the assembly stop, and removing the slide group and barrel. *It matters not what I've taught him, Jacques.* He picked up his gun oil.

Fact is, he's quite coming along. So, why don't you go stick your nose up some bloke's perfumed arse?

Oh, shut up!

Just because you have no idea what he should have done.

Jacques ran toward Hank, out of his area and into the velvety blackness, *You're—*

The *thunk* of two bodies colliding resonated in the

velvetiness and the fuzzy image of Jacques bounced down onto a floor that winked into existence in time to catch him. Above him flickered Fox Boy. *Ahm sorry, Mistah Jacques. But—*

But what? Mon Dieu! What was that? Sneaking out of the dark.

That's what he does, Jacques." The crisp voice floated through. *He has always been sneaky. It is his nature, why his name is Fox Boy.*

Sybil? asked Hank. W*here in the seven hells of Beelzebub have you been?*

Dante had nine levels, Hank.

Shut up, Jacques. He ran the slide back onto the receiver and turned toward Sybil's voice.

Finally back with us, are we? Ol' Stan's been worried about you.

Sybil's image sat cross-legged in a hut. Blue smoke floated through the air in thick lines, drifting around her. She sat as if she were a mountain and smoky clouds floated around her. She gazed placidly at the others. *As a novice, I spent hours listening to my Adept explain how the world around us worked. Said I had to understand it before learning, the mysteries would come.*

A grunt sounded from Ahn, squatting on his haunches in a glade surrounded by saplings.

A gentle breeze ruffled the leaves behind him.

Thank you, Ahn. Sybil turned back to the others. *At my initiation, I learned about next lives and how that happened, about the way time doesn't move at all. How it's all an illusion – everything happens in the same instant.*

"*Sybil,* mon petit, *what are you talking about?*"

She beamed a gracious smile toward Jacques. "*We are all parts of the same whole. Stan's Doc MacPherson, his Sally, is convinced that we are the same person too, except not individual personalities and parts of the same spirit. To her, we are simply fragments of Stan's mind and memory. She thinks that Hank here is that portion of Stan's mind that went through combat training.*"

Hank let the slide slap forward, a signal that he'd finished with the weapon.

And Jacques, you are the product of his quality upbringing. Ahn is his primitive self, and

Fox Boy is ... his secretive life in intelligence.

Velvety quiet covered them again as they all wavered and quivered.

If I may, Sybil, the voice of Brother Mick, the monk, broke the silence. *By that reasoning,*

I would be his early training at church. But you? Where do you fit in? His latent homosexuality?

Bullshit! Exploded Hank. *None of us is queer!*

It doesn't matter whether I was, none of that matters. I simply am the part of us that relaxes with the rest of us. Sybil raised her hand for quiet, but it did no good. They leaped at each other, and the ruckus exploded into true cacophony. It was almost comical the way they abused each other, like brothers fighting over the last piece of fried chicken.

"*Stop!*" The voice held sufficient command that they all stopped; but there was something else too. It wasn't volume, which was minimal; instead it was how unfamiliar the sound was to everyone.

Who the hell is that? barked Hank.

No answer. Not even a glimmer ruffled the luscious blackness, but elements stirred and solidified. They all became crisper in their images.

Hank picked up his .45, eyed the rest of the personalities, and finally settled on Sybil.

Who was that?

The only answer she gave was a deadpan face.

God, I wish ... The voice again.

Sybil cocked her head slightly to the side. *What do you wish? I wish I had a drink.*

What kin'a drink? asked Fox Boy. *Watah?*

The sound of lips smacking, *Naw. Maybe a shot of Irish whiskey.*

Sybil's eyes crinkled as a hint of a grin pushed the corners of her mouth upwards.

I woke to something poking me in the ass cheek, and it irritated the fuck out of me. No matter how I moved, the jabbing continued. I swatted at it. Missed, swiping benignly at nothing.

Laughter bubbled around me, a woman's giggle.

The smell of grass from the sprigs stuck up my nose combined with a whiff of lake water. Something else wafted through the air too, but I was still disoriented from my recent beating in the water. Opening an angry eye, I took stock. Woods, ground cover of moss, twigs, and rocks near the lake, and a determined prodding behind me. Then I saw Doc. My heart flip-flopped with instant pleasure, but before a second flip, it flopped flatly remembering her betrayal – perfectly waylaid following a glorious set-up of actually getting laid.

Bitch, growled Hank.

I let his remark go.

She had a goofy-assed grin plastered on her face and a stick in her hand that had clearly poked my butt cheek. My inner group shuffled around, releasing the memory of the Traitor bitch in splendid Technicolor, which pulled my focus back to the dream I'd experienced.

"You awake yet?"

The contralto voice sent a quiver through me.

I stared pointedly at the stick in her hand, sorely tempted to ask her to turn over and let me poke her in the ass, but I thought she might construe the comment as a sexual advance and clamped my mouth. I grumbled under my breath and sat up. "What the hell was that?"

She openly laughed. "A wake-up call." Hank made me snort.

"Tell Hank to stuff the snorts," commented Doc.

I opened my mouth to answer her but trying to control Hank kept my mind occupied. She continued without pause. "We've got to move. Sooner or later, some idiot will come investigating the little landing out there. Can you move yet?"

I tried but ended up moving about as fast as the bowels of an eighty-year-old sloth. I didn't see it, but I knew that stupid grin was sliding further across her face. "Guess not."

"I feel like a dung beetle's pet that got hit by a twenty-pound sledgehammer."

"You ought to. Care to guess how many times you bounced across that water?"

"No. But my mind is trying to use calculus."

"It was Hank again, wasn't it?"

"What?"

"The one who gave you that stupid idea." My shoulders shrugged all on their own.

"You know he's a great visceral reactor, he's saved your life so many times, but he's also shoved your fingers in so many fans that I can't count them, either." The rustle of her clothing brushing against a nearby bush indicated she'd walked away. I lay there stewing, about what she'd said. Also, I imagined her clothing brushing against her bush. By God, that was sexy.

Maddening.

At first, there was no inner-horde noise, and that unnerved me even more, but it didn't last long. Before I took in a nervous breath, Hank, Fox Boy, and several others barked about the betrayal while Jacques and Ahn worried more about our dream. My mind still lived in confusion, and it was impossible to shut anyone up long enough for me to think.

I rolled onto my side to find a little inner tranquility, and instead, I found myself feasting my eyes right on her. The lake odor was strong, darkness had stared to conquer the sky; the beginnings of what promised to be a spectacular show of colors, with the black smoke underlying the natural hues of all the other pollution that displayed so vibrantly in the normal course of events. At least I knew which direction was west.

Part of me enjoyed the shape of her hips as she walked, but it was short-lived. The view was identical to my memory of the day she betrayed me – the same sway of her hips. I heard Hank chatting away. My pleasure deflated flaccidly.

Doc tended a small campfire, and Ahn observed that she'd have built it better by digging down a bit and building a rocky wall to the side as a reflector. It would give off more heat and simultaneously shield the light from illuminating the night.

"Tell me, Doc. What the hell are you doing?"

She ignored me while stirring the base of the fire, releasing sparks and the smell of iron into the air.

"I don't understand you, Doc. You turned me in to the police. By the way, Hank is furious with you."

"But you're not?"

"What? Oh, well, I'm miffed. What really pisses me off is knowing that you turned me in to the Caucus in Zermatt."

"You remember that?" Her head had snapped up and she focused hard on me.

I was unable to tell if she was about to laugh or what. Her eyes sparkled with pleasure.

Goddamned eyes.

Hank tightened my fist around a rock to hurl at her, but I wrestled control from him and put it down.

"What else do you remember, Stan?"

John, the band director, pointed out that the soothing quality of her voice had an undertone of excitement. Ahn agreed because her eyes did the same thing. Hank told both of them to screw off.

"Why, Doc?"

"What else, Stan?"

"Listen, Doc. Do you know how to defend yourself?" I didn't trust Hank, and it was really hard to keep the prick in line. Asshole was using everything he knew to force me to hurt her.

"Sure. Didn't you see me take care of that guard on the

plane?" Her face took on a darker quality. "I paid a guy thousands of dollars to teach me. Not martial arts, though. This guy said to forget defense. Attack. The defense comes on its own when the enemy has to defend. Best defense is unyielding offense."

Her expression was vulnerable yet predatory.

Sexy as hell.

"Now, forget combat. What else do you remember?"

"I don't know." The memory of us entwined swooped through my mind. "Making love.

We were making love when it happened."

I sat up and scooted closer to the fire, not for the warmth but for the light. By now, the sky was as black as the inside of an elephant's ass. The orange flames mesmerized me. "Who the hell are you, Doc? I thought you were my shrink. Now I remember you from before. And it's not a pleasant memory."

Her eyes painted me with sorrow, pleading, and hopefulness all at the same time. "The sex wasn't pleasant?"

That took me aback. Of course — was. The wispy memory aroused me right this moment.

Hmm, cooed Jacques. Even Hank quit being an ass and reveled in the feeling of all the blood rushing down there.

"No. It was good. But you still haven't answered me. Who the hell are you? Hell, I'm having dreams about you, and not your betrayal."

"So?" She leaned over and propped herself on an elbow. "Like what?"

I tried my damnedest to keep my eyes on hers and not her breasts. "The inner horde. Last night."

"I was in that?"

"No," I shook my head and then drew on the ground with a nearby stick. "Not in it. Mentioned."

She snorted with a chuckle. "These days, it's normal for Hank to deride me. How many times does he need to call me names before it's a part of the verbal wallpaper?"

I erased my ground etching with my hand and took stock of her sitting across the campfire from me. "We knew each other before." It was a statement I knew to be true. "But you made it seem as if we met for the first time during my session with you."

She didn't even blink.

I continued, "Now I seem to remember us being more than acquaintances, too. That wasn't the first time we shared a bed."

Still no blinks, but her gaze softened.

C'mon, mate, slap her hard enough to move her nose to the middle of her cheek.

Shut up, Hank.

Ignore me all you want, lad, but she needs—

Shut! Up!

I stared at her, concentrating with the single-mindedness of a baby screaming for a bottle, and at the same time, battled to drown out the inner gang.

Where the hell is Sybil?

Every voice inside me screamed that one question – except Sybil's.

"Are you Sybil?"

Her expression never changed, but she did sigh, a small one, and if I weren't so enamored with her breasts, I would never have detected it. I tried not to lust after them, but my steely little eyes reacted as if those things were magnets.

"Why would you ask that?" The fire murmured, and a plume of sparks erupted into the night, the increased orange light made her face shine and eyes glow. They pierced me deeply, searching.

I forced my eyes from hers and told myself not to glance at her boobs. Alas, taking that away gave them no place to gaze. They circled around and came straight back to return her stare.

"Why, Stan?"

"The Inner Tormentors."

"They think I'm Sybil?"

I shook my head. "Couple of them do. Others think

167

differently. She hasn't been around for a while, like you." I picked up Hank's rock and tossed it into the fire sending more sparks floating.

"Is she back now?" No.

That dawning insight gave me pause, and I relaxed more. Shrugging, I shook my head in answer. "I could go for a finger or two of Irish right now."

"What?" Her timbre made my eyes pivot to her. She studied me like a hungry prospector eyeing a nugget of gold.

"Wouldn't a shot of Irish whiskey taste good right now?"

Doc smiled and leaned back, "Yes, it would." An expression of relief covered her like a sexy blanket. "Welcome back, Stan. Welcome back."

CHAPTER TWENTY-NINE

The senator popped his desk with an open palm and pushed himself back into his chair so hard it almost tipped over. With his jacket off, shirt sleeves rolled to the elbow, and tie still in place, he appeared professionally busy, yet extremely tired. The bags under his eyes would never fly in a television interview. His deep, almost melodious voice, however, would. "If that is that Mistress bitch, tell her that she needs to stop screwing around and take care of Mu'izz. I haven't got time for his bullshit!"

Dressed in a tasteful form-fitting white dress with a brown scarf and belt that complemented her honey-colored skin, Amy held her hand over the speaker on the phone. Her mime through the doorway urged him to lower his voice.

Amy appeared as fresh as if it were early in the day for her, although it definitely wasn't.

None of the other staff remained in the office, but she felt he needed to display caution.

He waved the air to dismiss her. "Don't care." He had a trace of a pout in the two words.

All that did was produce an icy glare from her. She turned her back to him.

"Tell that little whore to get on with it." He slapped his desk again, and several papers took flight. "And remind her that Berne is really in charge. Not her, or that little pissant, Mu'izz. I don't care if he's connected to ISIS or not."

Amy's eyes flashed.

He snorted. Let her be upset. The plan was working, so he didn't care. He let her talk quietly into the phone for a second; his view distracted him. Great ass.

She started as soon as she hung up. "You know," she turned and walked purposefully into his office, "you are an ass."

169

A dirty little smile crossed his face, "As it happens, I was admiring your—"

"I know what you were doing," Her eyes held no expression at all as she parked her hip on his desk corner. "Which makes you even more of an ass. This isn't about the two of us. The Mistress has been unavailable. Had to leave a message. She's to return my call." A chuckle escaped from him, but her expression choked it off.

"The whole idea of the Caucus had nothing to do with us playing daddy loves mommy. If you remember, the goal was to—"

"Politics." His head bobbed quickly. "To grab power." He rubbed his face with both hands and exhaled deeply.

She dropped into the other chair in his office and crossed one leg over the other at the knee. "That power has nothing to do with getting even with Mu'izz."

"It has everything to do with getting even. Why do you think power is so desirable? Simply to say we have it?" He glared at her as he stormed around the desk for another cup of coffee. He knew she wouldn't get it for him. Besides, it was late and he needed to stay energetic.

Am I too old for this shit? He pushed the errant thought away. "We take power so we can do what we want, so we never have to listen to fools dictate to us. Why do you think that blithering idiot in the White House right now wanted to be president? How about any of them who lived there?"

He held an empty cup out to her. She shook her head.

"We certainly don't need some punk terrorist and a killer whore to—"

"She is an enforcer, which we need. And he is the means by which you gain money and fame. We need them both!"

Noise in the outer office filtered into the room. The cleaning crew had arrived, and the senator closed the door to keep things private.

At first glance through the window behind his desk, the

lights of the Capitol Building shone tranquilly. The longer he stared, the more tarnish he saw — the dirty gray clouds, the flashing emergency lights of first responders heading to some tragedy. He talked, mostly to himself. "We need them to a point."

He turned his face to her and growled, "I'm tired of lip. I still want him dead. No one threatens blackmail like that. Not to us. Not to me!"

Amy chewed her cheek for a second. "There wasn't any backtalk. The Mistress damn near got caught last night, had to shoot it out with the Feds. She's been shot and needs to hole up.

Said she would take care of Mu'izz in a day or so, but she has to heal some first."

He sat in his chair and took a sip of coffee, wishing it was Scotch. "Where'd she get shot?"

"In the love handle. Nothing serious, but had to be stitched."

"She kill anyone?"

"The Feds?" She shook her head. "Doesn't know. Bullets filled the air and she tried to stab one of them, but she didn't hang around."

"Shit."

It had been a quick trip to the nearest drinking hole. Doc hurried me the entire way. It was as if she wanted to set a new land-speed record. Once on a road, she flagged down the first car to drive-by waving a wad of cash so the driver could see it. They screeched to a stop; Doc talked to them about three seconds; in we climbed. She held my hand tight when we jumped free of the car.

Then, I sat in the bar, staring at the stars through the window while Doc sat across the table.

Hank wanted me to take her out back and snuff her, a quick dispatch and gone. I'd already told him to cram it I was going to get a drink before anything else. I figured he would understand that, and I was right. It did calm him down, which was fine. There was still something I needed to know.

In my hand, I held a double shot of Irish whiskey. I smiled to myself remembering that satisfied smirk Doc had worn as she handed me the glass. It didn't add up. That smug grin was the spark that set Hank off again – thus a renewed push to snuff and go.

You should snuggle with her, mon ami. The smell of her neck will help.

At least Jacques tried to help.

Ahn agreed too, but when I pointed to their example, thinking I might find agreement among the rest of the inner pricks, Hank interrupted. *I think you should forget the shot, snuggle with her, snap her neck, and then drink.*

Damn it, Hank. Let it go for a few minutes, will you?

He finally buttoned up. For once, I was able to think without interruption, and I studied the stars trying to figure things. But there was a big "but." Not like the song, this "but" was idiom, like however, although, on the other hand, never-the-less. But, the problem was the silence of the horde. It unnerved me. Never in my memory was there a silence so … inaudible. I felt naked.

In the midst of the quiet came a little voice, Sybil's. *It's time to open doors, Stan.*

Where have you been, Sybil?

Guarding doors.

Why did Sybil always make sense even when she didn't?

Stan, do I need to take you back to my beginning as a weird woman?

I experienced an old feeling, creepy, yet familiar. Tenuous. I had no idea what she was talking about, but an ominous inkling danced the Stanky Leg up and down my spine.

No, Sybil. I don't need to remember that right now. What I need is to … open doors.

Give me the key.

She snorted. *You have to be ready, and you are. Drink your drink, Stan. And relax.*

I tossed the whiskey back, and as it burned my throat, I sat back and relaxed. God, the stars were beautiful. They swirled around exactly like Van Gogh's *Starry Night*, only right then, they actually moved.

CHAPTER THIRTY

I shivered in the night. The air was crisp, but that wasn't why I shivered. Adrenaline made me tremble. The last few weeks, I'd lived on it. Of all of the skills I had, the one I least liked was burglary. Crouching on a balcony with a clear moon beaming down, trying to open this door was wearing me thin.

At least Sally kept watch for me down on the street. The last thing I needed was one of Berne's police force curious about me. We agreed beforehand that should anything happen, and we were separated, we would meet at the hotel room I rented in Zermatt, a town at the base of the Matterhorn. I'd booked it under another name, and it was our rally point.

The door clicked open, a rush of warmer air blew out at me, and I quickly entered, shutting the door behind me.

I crouched into a shadow to my left. A quiet feeling warned me to stay immobile and canvass the room with my peripheral vision. Nothing moved. Someone snicked away with a good snore in the other room, probably the senator, and I stood for a visual recon of the room.

The place was a mess, like revelers had pushed a pause button during a Bacchanalian celebration. A couple of champagne bottles lay on the floor, fruit baskets littered the room, and various items of clothing lay draped, dropped, and wadded all over.

My guess? Someone had been playing, "If you can catch me, you can hump me!" games. Certainly, the room had heard a lot of giggling and heavy breathing, not to mention a little spanking and tickling. I shrugged.

Another rogue feeling inside drew my attention to all the smells in the room, booze, perfume, and sex, as I eased to the closet near the door of the suite. Most hotels hid their room safes near there. Made no sense to me. Why always put what you want to protect in the same place, and near the entry point at that? Someone like me would always know where to go.

The snoring stopped.

My damned heart felt as if someone was strangling it, but after a vicious snort, another round of snoring, the heart killer let go.

I hate this kind of shit. That's what I'm here for, though.

I searched for the safe.

Moving so slowly it took a while, I finally reached the closet. And I was right.

The safe sat about knee-high and halfway hidden in a cubby. I leaned down to get a closer look-see, a devilish smile lighting my face.

The snoring sounds were regular and robust. Too bad senator, I chuckled to myself.

You're about to be screwed harder than you were in this room an hour ago.

I clenched everything I had, except the hairs on my arms. One of my hunches turned into a voice, telling me it heard something. I listened intently, between the sounds of the senator's saw blades.

Nothing out of the ordinary.

I sifted the night sounds for a moment more, and then bent to my task. The safe changed combinations with every use, the kind where the user supplies a four-digit code. Most people use their birthday or anniversary, and I remembered them all from his dossier. Unfortunately, this guy didn't use any of them.

I worked my brain as if auditioning for Einstein's understudy, but none of my ideas worked.

Damn! Why didn't I pay more attention when they explained this!

The temperature seemed to increase with every second, and I had to wipe my brow a couple of times. Between the snoring, the combination, and listening, I was about as jumpy as a mongoose watching an angry cobra.

Another voice in my head whispered to me, and I relaxed. It was so simple. I reached out and pushed zero, zero, two, five. The little lights popped, there were clicks, and the door popped open.

My cocky grin was back.

All I had to do was remember what happened in the little meeting, the one where they ended up calling the Berne Caucus, and I knew. The whole point of the Caucus was to raise money by way of hookers, drugs, and terrorism and use that money to jockey the senator into a position to use the Twenty-Fifth Amendment – like Gerald Ford. He used the twenty-fifth, not the hookers, drugs, and terrorism.

Among other things, the twenty-fifth outlines what happens if the vice president dies or leaves office. The president can nominate his own vice president and Congress votes on the selection to ratify. Tailor-made for the Caucus.

Then it is a matter of the president dying and *voilà*!

I opened the safe. The only thing in there was a thumb drive with what I assumed was a video recording of the meeting. I grabbed it and stuffed it into my pocket.

Why does anyone record shit like that?

Laughter from the hallway filtered into the suite and it unnerved me.

Time to go.

Click. The door swung open and light from the hallway outlined me full in the face.

The silhouettes of two women faced me. The one closest, a redhead, drew a sidearm incredibly fast, aimed at my center mass.

"What the hell are you doing here?" It was the senator's secretary's voice. She stood behind the redhead in the hallway, and I had barely enough light to make her out. My mind zipped along just below the speed of light in response to my adrenal glands doing aerobics.

I jumped to the side. The deafening boom from the shot

made unbelievable pain shoot between my ears. Dizzy, I rushed the woman closest to me and with a tremendous punch, knocked her on her ass.

She growled and stood right back up, blocking the door.

Crap, she's tough.

Behind me, I heard the senator yelling incoherently. I turned to protect myself from that direction and saw a sick sight – the senator, naked, waving his arms. Made my eyes want to puke.

The redhead tackled me. Her knee targeted my crotch, but I twisted and the impact caught me in the thigh. It hurt like hell, but I didn't turn blue. I punched her in the chest. She rolled with the impact.

The senator jumped into the mêlée, scaring the shit out of me. I didn't want any of his old wrinkly body touching me. And how the hell did that tiny penis do anyone any good anyway?

Horrible sight.

I fisted, kicked, and gouged, doing great damage to anything I came in contact with. I had a remarkable inner sense directing my pummeling.

Two more shots reverberated through the room, and everything stopped. My eyes flipped to the open door where my Sally stood, backlit by the hallway. The pistol in her hands smoked, she aimed it at the senator's tiny pecker.

The two women let me go and I bounced up like a kangaroo. Then without a glance behind me, I jogged the short distance to Sally, who motioned me into the hall. As I passed, she told me to meet her at our rally point.

I left her there to clean up.

The weather was crisp and clear at the rally point, and we cuddled like the lovers we were. Her soft smell invited me closer as much as her skin did, and I dozed, my head tucked comfortably on her back. I hadn't planned the lover part, but the stress levels while in deep cover … I needed an outlet, and I'd found a, uh, partner. It happened.

They tell you in all the training that sex should be used as a tool, that you can never lower your guard when you use it, because it can be a trap too.

I'd come to Switzerland hunting an arm of ISIS. My intel said this group might have had something to do with my parents' death. Furthermore, I discovered the group needed someone like me, well, my Sigma cover – rich and dissatisfied. It had worked too. They'd accepted me.

That is to say, the bankroll I represented was a desired commodity.

Like most good lies, part of mine was true. I had a personal fortune, inherited when my parents died, and I knew how to behave like a privileged brat. I was not dissatisfied with life, though. The truth was – I wanted these pieces of shit. If they weren't the people who had killed my parents, they were a lot like the pricks who did.

I still wasn't in the inner circle, but every day I found out more about my colleagues.

They were assholes, killers, and terrorists. They spent their time hurting people, not friendly at all.

Sally, on the other hand, was amiable, and right now, I was happy to be chummy.

Like me, her parents had been killed by ISIS. She was a hunter too, came on her own to hunt specific terrorists. I still didn't know the details but didn't need them. The word incredible described her. Saving me at the Berne hotel had been spectacular.

Not only did she have nerves of steel, shoot with precision, make love like a hussy, but she was a doctor. Not only an M.D. either, a psychiatrist to boot.

She rustled around, tucked her chin back over her shoulder, and opened lazy eyes. "What are you doing?"

"Smiling and dozing. Thinking about fondling again."

Her hand rubbed my head in an open-handed noogie, and

then she dropped her head back down onto her pillow. "To do that correctly, you need to roll me over and start lightly down there."

Instead, I dozed. It turned out that I didn't want fondling that urgently.

She woke me by talking. "What happens if they catch you?"

I nuzzled into her but didn't answer.

After a few minutes, she asked again, forcing me to answer her.

"It won't be as pretty as you." I batted my eyelids and put on a huge smile.

"Very funny."

I shrugged. "I'll have to make sure they don't catch me. They will probably shoot me up with drugs and I'll blabber everything they want to know. That's why we need that thumb drive you helped me steal. Thank you so much."

"Uh huh. Well, If I hadn't been there, they would've caught you peeking into their safe a couple of days ago."

My eyes slid askance toward her, "By the way, what did you do to them after I left?"

"Convinced them to leave you alone for a while."

That told me nothing. "My intuition tells me you prolonged things. They probably followed you here. Now quickly, what did you do?"

She stared. I speculated her brain worked like a Trojan. Her teeth chewed the inside of her cheek. It was a great opportunity to don my boxers, visit the restroom, and let her sit in her cannibal's pot and stew.

She sat with her back to the headboard when I came back, the sheet tucked tastefully around her under her armpits. Her hands pinned the sheet to the mattress.

I took all this in as I sat on the bed. "Okay. You are pissed, but I need to know. You aren't a pro. You are a very talented person who wants to help." I leaned over and tried to touch her leg.

She moved it.

"Damn it, Sally. These people are dangerous."

"They may be the people who killed my parents!"

"True. All the more reason to quit screwing around and tell me what I need to know."

She chewed her cheek again, and I got up to fix a drink. I swished my glass of Irish around and asked, "Would a drink help?"

A lightning bolt flashed from her eyes. A small voice inside whispered for me to pour a shot of vodka. She didn't like my Irish. I mixed a vodka tonic and placed it on her nightstand, then walked around to the other side and sat.

"I asked them if they were responsible for the attack that killed my family." She sipped and swallowed. Her expression softened and she wasn't throwing lightning bolts at me anymore.

I looked at the ceiling and sighed. "Of course, they told you no. You think they would ever tell you yes? You had a gun on them."

"I knew what they would say. I'm a shrink. I know what to listen for, and what I heard was, the really mean woman, knew something but wouldn't tell. So …"

"So what?"

"I'm watching her."

The way she said that unsettled me, but I clamped my lips.

Her face softened even more, and her eyes embraced me. "Stan?"

"Huh?"

"Why don't we get married?"

Now I'd already thought about that, but right then life was dangerous, and I was about to say that when she dropped the sheet exposing a wonderful sight. My eyes locked on the view and my automatic nervous system kicked into gear. I had to control myself.

My insides, really conflicted, thought it a good idea to think things through, but …

I ignored them as I jumped onto the bed. It took me a couple of seconds to shed the boxers, but I did beat the world record.

Afterward, we lay together and she asked me to watch her necklace. She twirled it artfully in her hands, talked to me soothingly for a few minutes, and told me to close my eyes.

I did. Unable to help myself.

"Do you have anything to hide from me?"

I smiled, still with my eyes closed. "Sometimes I need to hide how much I care for you."

"And that is?"

"I love you."

"Okay. Just checking."

It sounded as if she was laughing to herself as she continued in her soft voice. "Stan, I am giving you some suggestions. Upon specific signals, you will be compelled to do certain things.

Do you understand?"

I nodded. This was strange. It was like watching a stage show with me in it.

"Stan, your first signal is when someone gives you an injection. After you feel the needle pierce your skin, several things will happen. Your memories of this entire lifetime will be hidden away, locked tight, and you will be unable to retrieve them no matter what. This will continue until you ask me for a drink of Irish whiskey, and you actually drink it. Is that clear? And Stan, the instant your memories lock, your mind will relax, and … you will be open completely to your inner voices, as deep as they go. They will keep you safe.

"Lastly, you will retain all of your skills." Again, I nodded.

"One more thing, Stan, you will never actually ask for that drink unless your subconscious tells you that you are safe."

"Safe."

"Yes, Stan, you have to feel safe, deep down."

She paused, ruminating, I guess. It didn't last long, maybe

thirty seconds or so, and then she said, "When all those things happen, your memory will come back in total." I heard her licking her lips. "So, you understand all of this?" Another nod.

We went through the whole thing three times.

"The last thing is this, Stan. When I wake you in a moment, you will remember nothing of this conversation until your memories are restored. Then, you will remember everything. Now

I'm going to kiss you. As our lips touch, you will wake up as if you'd dozed off."

I felt Sally's lips pressed against mine and my eyes opened.

"I love you, Stan."

"Me, too." Then I had a great idea. "What the hell. They warned us all against this in training, but they aren't here. C'mon." I threw the sheet back. "Let's go. I know I'm not supposed to, but if you think you can live with me, even though you don't know everything about me—"

"I will find out."

God, I loved this woman.

I had an obnoxious voice inside tell me to hurry because he wanted to take her to bed again, another one told him to hush up. I had to laugh.

"What?" Her eyes dripped with caring.

"Never mind. Inner turmoil."

"About us?"

"Never. Impossible to do anything to stop me from loving you." I grabbed my jacket,

"Let's go find someone to marry us. When this is over, I want to come home to you."

I watched her get dressed and didn't give a diddly-squat that women tend to take a long time to get gussied up. I blithely draped my jacket back over the chair and enjoyed the sights.

Half an hour later, we walked through the doorway together,

into the bright sunlight.

Well I'll be a buggered son-of-a-bitch.
Damn it, Hank, shut up and let me think.
Still doesn't change the way she smiled when we were captured.
I know, Hank. Don't forget she's the one who opened your door. Quit screwing with me.
I stared at the stars above, trying to digest my epiphany. Sally's face eclipsed my view.
Understand now, Stan? It was Sybil.
It certainly makes sense. I mean, at least now I know what in the hell happened.
"Stan?" Sally's voice interrupted me. "You mad, honey?"
Damn! Dat girl really know how ta tie it all up.
Not now, Fox Boy.
I felt her hand take mine, but she stopped in half squeeze. "Stan?"
I sighed. "It's okay, Sally. I know you did it to help me, and you didn't know they were coming."
She drew her hand back. "No." The way she said it chilled me. "No, Stan. I did know."
My eyes rolled to hers. Hank started to mouth off, but I stopped him before he twisted the knife more.
"How?" My edge was back. Hadn't even known I'd had one to begin with, but I had one now. I knew how to use it too.
"How?" I said it without emotion. My eyes matched the sound.
"I had to know, Stan. I had to know if they were the ones who killed my family."
"So, you served your own husband up to answer a question?" The quiet intensity of my voice was deadly. "Or, did that not matter?"
"Of course it mattered." Her eyes and face contradicted each

other. Her eyes pleaded; her face expressionless. "But it was the only way to find out."

"Bullshit! You gave them the drive, too."

"Oh, no. No, no, no, no. I have the drive. Have it hidden. I wanted to know about my family."

"Did you get an answer to your question?" I puffed myself up like a striking cobra.

"Yes! Well, halfway."

"What do you mean, half?"

"Listen." Her voice was venomous. "They said they knew who, but wouldn't tell without the drive, and that wasn't happening. So all they told me was the brutality of this terror raid impressed the Islamic State quite a bit."

Even Hank drew quietly sullen.

She thought for a second and then added, "I think it was that redheaded bitch."

I crossed to the bar, poured a double shot of Irish and tossed it back, never once glancing in her direction.

Her perfume is wonderful, Stan. Your favorite.

I didn't answer Jacques, but he was right. It took strenuous concentration to ignore the aroma. She was my love and having all the fences removed made things complicated.

"Stan, eyes on me." I turned.

Ahn took over both my eyes and nose, and my heart rate increased like any other predator's.

Cut it out. Ahn.

Yeah, chimed in Hank. *Let me lo— and dream. Hell, I'll remember.* He caused a couple of X-rated memories to flash through.

Butt out, Hank. In fact, all of you put a bung in your mouths. I need some quiet. Now leave me alone.

I poured another shot and sipped it as I turned toward Sally. "Okay. You did it to find what you needed, and you prevented them from finding out about me. Did you also know you unleashed all these lives in here?" I pointed at my head.

Concern covered her face. "Are they still there? I thought they would flounder and fade away once your memory returned."

"Well, they haven't. It's like having an asylum full of freaks having a continual argument in my—"

Asylum? Jacques's voice sounded as if he'd stepped into a disgusting water closet on a hot day.

Freaks! screamed Hank.

The timbre of Hank's voice ignited an explosion, a brouhaha so large, it gave me a colossal case of vertigo. The room circled and heaved constantly, and I thought I would throw up. I was barely able to stand up straight with all the fracas.

"Shut up!"

I'd had enough. My bellow filled our collective consciousness and the mêlée slowly fizzled. I'm not living through this kind of shit again. Now sew your lips shut for a second or two, so I can figure something.

I turned an impassive face toward Sally, "I can live with the others blabbering away—"

Blabbering, mate?

I'm serious, Hank. Keep it quiet.

Her eyes betrayed she was struggling to stifle a guffaw and my mouth slid sideways in a grudging snort. I nodded to her. "It's a pain in the ass, but I can control my past-life heathens."

Brother Mick objected to the use of heathens, but I appeased him by asking for, and receiving, a quick prayer.

"Sally, I need you to be very straight with me now."

She nodded, and those eyes of hers made me all squishy. Well, not all, as in everywhere; one place was anything but soft and tender. But her seriousness was not in question at all.

I toughened myself inside. "Did you marry me becau—"

"I married you because I wanted to, I needed to, because I loved you then, and I love you now. I don't know how to say—"

I grabbed her, kissed her, ignoring the crowd inside, and I

kissed her well. It was wonderful. If it hadn't been for the electric passion, our lips would've been exhausted. As it was, we settled into a warm embrace.

"C'mon," I whispered." Let's go home."

Happiness lit her face as she nodded. We left, but only after we made love most tender.

CHAPTER THIRTY-ONE

Nancy sat beside the bed, his arms propping up his head and eyes closed, coming to terms with his new boss lying in the ER. She, too, rested with eyes closed, and judging by the paleness of her face, Nancy supposed she felt like shit. The gown half-covered her, one leg sticking out like a member of the Rockettes doing their chorus line thing, except for the red line of her wound winding up the limb. The stitches looked mean, and no doubt she would be hobbling as badly as him for a while.

Tubes ran into her, one IV, another blood.

He chuckled to himself thinking about how comical they would appear, both walking with canes and limping in sync. It felt good to busy his mind on something other than Vivian.

That was hard to do, too.

The entire room reminded him of his wife. Even the smell of blood with the underlying antiseptic odors matched exactly the night he … That he discovered he'd married a bisexual.

That night, had completely gone from his mind.

All he thought about now was the way she'd been stabbed. Following her, actually causing what happened, everything sharpened his guilt so much he felt eviscerated by it.

His eyes wandered aimlessly around the room. The pain her death caused still throbbed in him. He'd tried to shove it all from his thoughts, tried never to think about it, much less converse on the subject, but now he was unable to block it anymore.

His eyes followed Carbonella's bare leg up to the suture line, then over her gown to her face. Her eyes fluttered open and then took in the whole room. He had no idea what to say. Deep inside, the fear of death still distressed him, not his own but that of those around him.

"Good thing I had my thigh holster on, huh?"

The mumbled observation was so wispy that he barely heard

it. The words took time to burrow down deep enough for him to feel their tickle. A couple more seconds drifted by before he recognized she had spoken and then the tickle had become razors cutting.

A weary smile forced its way across his face; he rubbed his eyes a couple of times and then dropped his arms onto the bed. He nodded. "If it hadn't had been there, her knife would've clipped the femoral artery, like—"

"Your wife."

He turned his eyes to her in answer. Innately he knew they didn't explain a thing. They were too hollow. He'd spent months seeing them this way in his own mirrors. "How did you know?"

She was exhausted and in pain but still managed to give him the "you're an idiot" eyeball thing. "Remember your damn file?"

He nodded, but kept his face down, hiding the clench of his jaw. Remembering the sight of the redheaded bitch standing there while he tried to stop Vivian's bleeding.

He rubbed his face to get the sound of the ambulance out of his head. Using his cane, he limped to the other side of the bed and tenderly held her hand. "Listen, Carbonella. This is my fault. If I hadn't shot my mouth off about that damn bitch who knifed you, you wouldn't have been hurt."

Carbonella tugged his hand and her mouth moved, but Nancy's ears were unable to hear,

"What?"

She tugged again.

He leaned down.

"Shut the fuck up." The words were soft but throaty, and when his eyes flicked to hers, he knew the boss still lived. Even so, or maybe because she lived, he moved toward the door.

"Nancy."

It was no louder than the background beep of the heart monitor, but to Nancy it exploded through the room. He stopped for a second, but the room closed in again with the memory of Vivian and he left.

It was time to find the Mistress. To do that, he needed Stan. Where the hell are you, Buttwipe?

Inspiration came before he walked halfway down the hall.

The Mistress clicked off her phone and maneuvered her way through the dark warehouse.

Mu'izz, you goddamn fool!

Barely enough light filtered through the windows from the streetlight to navigate, and her side hurt, really badly.

None of the damage had actually harmed Mu'izz's eyes. His face had cuts and slices galore, and it obviously pissed him off to have his face damaged, but there had never really been a challenge with his wounds.

With hers, she bled so much she couldn't stem it. Her blood, mixed with her victim's made her steps slippery, and she trailed the sanguineous fluid with each step.

She had to be a gruesome sight, but the men who guarded Mu'izz watched blankly as she moved. None of them moved to help.

Assholes.

Breathing in ragged gasps, she fumbled at the door, her unsteadiness apparent to any observer. If it hadn't been for the stickiness of the red fluid covering her hand, she would never have opened it.

She worked it ajar, and a sliver of light cut the darkness from the other side. Pushing it open, she almost fell through the door and rolled around the edge of the frame. She flipped the cell phone to Mu'izz who caught it, put down the bottle of water he'd been sipping, and scowled at her.

"Stop! Don't bleed on anything." The last thing he wanted was a mess everywhere.

Her eyes manifested her loathing. "Eat shit." She stumbled to the couch and plopped down, staring directly at him, she wiped her hands and arms over the fabric, staining it deeply. "I need help." She leaned back, her stomach pulsing blood.

The sight of Mu'izz stroking his beard with the back of his hand irritated the shit out of her, and she rubbed the fabric again while stuffing her pistol between the cushions.

He continued brushing his beard but drew his finger across his mustache. With a deep breath, he traipsed to a cabinet, opened it, and rummaged around for some med supplies. Picking and choosing what he needed, he dumped the stuff on the couch next to her.

Flipping the packages around, he searched for what he wanted, and then sat back. With a squint and an absent rip of the wrapping, he opened a gauze sponge and poked it hard into her gut. "Lie back." Next, he ripped her shirt for better access and picked up a syringe. Turning her torso for better light and more scrutiny, he gave a slight nod.

She sighed, leaned her head back, and closed her eyes. The injection and burn of the local painkiller meant nothing to her.

"When did you plan on telling me?" He tossed the spent hypo into the trash.

"What the hell are you talking about?"

"Berne's order."

Dull numbness spread through her abdomen, replacing the surface ache of the wound. He started poking around for the bullet and her eyes fluttered open. "What order?"

She winced as the forceps in his hand probed deeply, searching. "The order Berne called you about. The one ordering you to execute." He glanced at her face and then back to his work.

"Put both of your hands on your chest and lie there. Do not move." Her eyes flashed as she obeyed.

"Are you telling me about it, or am I about to forget to fix you up here?"

The room was silent for long seconds, and then she took a deep breath and let it out slowly. "I don't know how you knew about that."

"It doesn't take much to figure it out. I told the captain I quit. What do you think that triggered?" He pulled out the bullet, and cleaned her, preparing to close the wound. Snatching another sterile package, he pulled out the suture kit. With measured progress, he sewed her skin together.

She watched his eyes, ensuring they didn't move from his needlecraft and inched her hand off her chest and down her side toward her knife. It wasn't ideal but it was possible. Would do it if …

"You need to stop moving that arm." She dropped her gaze to the scalpel in his hand.

"You think I don't know what you're doing?"

Forcing a smile, she said, "I did get a call, but I needed to talk to you first. Then I was shot."

He lunged to her head, grabbed her hair, and placed the scalpel against her neck, the edge slicing her skin. Both her hands dropped to her sides.

The warmth of her blood dripping preceded the irritation of the slice, and her mind calculated furiously. This wasn't the way she wanted it, but it would do. Staring into his eyes, a grimace crossed her face. She bared her teeth for a second. "Berne called, wanting you to die, but I have a better plan."

Mu'izz said nothing. His only movement was his finger tapping lightly on the scalpel.

She moved her arm slowly behind her, toward her pistol.

"A plan?"

Her fingertips teased the handgrip, moving the weapon enough for another finger to brush it. "Take your knife away and let me explain." A shake of his head.

The pistol moved again.

They locked eyes. His grip tightened. Her hand almost had the gun. "Damn it. Put it down!" She winced for show and pushed her hand down, grabbed the grip, and pulled it half out.

The movement caused the knife to dig in and more blood flowed.

"Okay." Mu'izz pulled the knife away from her neck and rested his hand on her upper sternum. "Okay. I'm listening."

Her finger found the trigger.

At a knock on the door, automatically his eyes flicked there and back. "Yeah." The door opened a crack and Bobo leaned in, "You need me to drive you anywhere soo— Oh, I'll come back."

"Get rid of him," whispered the Mistress.

Mu'izz chuckled and pushed the blade back into her neck.

"Stop with the blade and look at my hip. While you were distracted, I pulled my weapon."

He snorted, "It's aimed at your hip you stupid bitch."

"And Bobo can't see it." Her eyes blazed. "True, if I pull the trigger, I'll shoot my hip, but follow the bullet. It'll take out that cock of yours that you're so proud of, probably your balls too. My hip muscle will be mangled but it will heal. I'll walk again, maybe with a limp, but you won't be able to …"

She chuckled. "We'll both live, but one of us will lose a hell of a lot more than the other.

Now, *stupid*, get rid of him."

Mu'izz motioned with his head and Bobo left.

"Get off me."

Mu'izz sat back, taking the blade away from her neck and stood. She followed him with her pistol, keeping it aimed at his genitalia. Motioning with a wave of her hand for him to back up, she inched further back along the couch. "Stupid." She glowered, and a smile appeared like a feral dog's warning to stand back. "I'm not killing you." He stared.

"I told you I have a better plan."

He raised an eyebrow but said nothing.

She took Mu'izz's bottle of water and sipped. The wetness of it tasted like swallowing a piece of heaven. Her face softened, and she nodded. "Berne wasn't happy with your pronouncement about quitting. The phone call was very specific." She lowered her weapon, wincing as she did. "Where is the stuff you threatened the captain with?"

"So you can collect it all before killing me? Screw you."

She raised the pistol again. "Listen, stupid. You give that stuff to me, I set it up so it's like you're dead, and everybody wins. Berne gets the stuff you have on the Caucus, and you get away – taking half your money as you go."

His mouth opened to object but she went on quickly, "They have to think it's still there.

Otherwise, they won't believe you're dead. Once you're gone, you can either hide somewhere remote and pleasant or go back into business again in a place where no one knows you."

Mu'izz quietly stroked his beard, and then he glanced around his comfortable warehouse.

His eyes finally stopped, focusing on the door. "How do I die?"

She exhaled, sat back, and closed her eyes. "Don't know yet, but it would be best to blow up or something … so they can't find your body. I'll work it out." She sipped some more.

"Where's the stuff?"

An evil grin spread across his face. He crossed to the cabinet he'd lately gotten the medical supplies from and pulled it away from the wall. It was heavy enough that Mu'izz had to put some muscle into it, but the cabinet rolled quietly, and as it did, it revealed a hole in the warehouse wall with another cabinet inside. This one held a safe. His fingers danced over the keypad and the door clicked.

She worked her way up and stood behind him as he started to reach in. "Stop." The Mistress tapped his head with her pistol. "Move back. Any traps?"

He stood back and folded his arms across his chest. "Not on the outside."

The door swung open. Inside were a large folder and a couple of handguns, a Glock 21, and Sig 1911. Both .45 caliber. There were also two doorbell-like buttons. Both had wires through the back.

"Don't touch those."

She turned back. "What the hell are they? They're like—"

"Suicide switches." He turned with a wide grin. "Yeah. The whole place is packed with C-4, all connected with detcord and will go up with a huge bang. ISIS wanted one. But I modified the whole thing. Here we have two." He pointed to the one on the left side, the slightly smaller box. "This switch will give you fifteen minutes to un-ass the building after you press it."

Now it was her turn to grin. She nodded. "Let's get Bobo and go." Careful not to touch the switches she grabbed the Glock and tossed it to him. After she picked up the Sig and tucked it away, she snatched the folder and they both left.

CHAPTER THIRTY-TWO

Nancy stood in the dark on the porch. He'd never really broken into anything before, never had to. He'd either knocked and showed his badge or had a search warrant. Regardless, it had always been legal.

Tonight, was different, and he was determined. It didn't matter to him in the least whether he was legal or not. Whatever he had to do to find the Mistress, was what he would do.

Besides, this was his second illegal entry tonight. He'd made the first about half an hour ago at Doc's office and he'd actually broken the window to climb in there. This time he used the spare keys he'd found in her desk at the office.

This is stupid. I'm a cop.

The key opened the lock. He hobbled in and stopped, standing alone in the dark.

How does she manage to make the place smell so good?

Even Vivian had never been able to do that. It wasn't only here, either. Her office smelled as good – crisp and clean. Could it be Doc was the only one living here? Vivian had always complained about the smells he made.

He nosed around without turning on the lights. The ambient light was enough to keep from tripping or falling, and his cane moved easily. No surprises.

The smell matches the digs too. Neat as a pin.

The living room had everything in place. Even the wet bar had the aura of a display, although it had clearly been used, judging by booze levels. Well-stocked, too. There was that Irish whiskey she'd ordered at the bar. He picked it up.

Humph. Still full.

He wasn't surprised.

She sure made a face when it touched her mouth at the bar. In this bar, more vodka had been used.

He remembered why he was here and moved around the room. The memory of Vivian dying flooded his head while he walked and renewed his determination to find the redhead.

That bitch.

He would find her somehow.

If it hadn't been for her, Vivian would still be alive.

His jaw floated back and forth under his tongue as his eyes searched the room. Nothing stood out.

He kept moving and walked slowly into the bedroom. It was darker, and he was careful not to hit the cane on anything while opening drawers and searching under clothes. A picture caught his eye. Displayed prominently in the corner of the mirror on top of the dresser, the photo was an eight-by-ten.

Why a photo like that?

He picked it up, and when he did, it revealed another photograph underneath. It had been purposely stuck behind the one he had in his hand.

Son-of-a-bitch!

The second one was the same size and had a simple image on it, two people standing side by side in front of the Matterhorn, arms entwined, heads together. Along the edge were two words, Our Day, with hearts drawn around the words. The kicker was in the corner of the actual picture; in a neat script scrawled in pencil, it had the word *Married*, dated July 10, two years ago.

On the back was neatly written, Mr. And Mrs. Baker.

Baker? That your name, Doc? Thought it was McPherson.

Nancy flipped the picture around, fanning the air with it.

The first picture was a dummy, a random picture, only meant to hide this one. Why?

Nancy chewed the inside of his cheek as he thought it over. Then it clicked. It was in Switzerland; the Matterhorn was behind them; the woman was indeed the doctor. It had been a few years and the couple was younger, but that was the doctor. The other person had lips too big, eyes too small, and Nancy wanted to kick the shit out of the guy. In that instant, he knew exactly who it was. He had longer hair, but it was the same guy.

Stanton! What The Fuck Are You Doing?

It took all his willpower to keep from ripping the picture to shreds.

This changed a lot, and he had to calm down to figure it all out.

He dropped the picture back onto the shelf, limped to the bed, sat, and rubbed his face.

What to do?

A deep breath helped him settle, but he sensed something wasn't quite right.

This is crazy. What is all this? And where the hell are you, Stan?

His eyes focused intently as he turned his head slowly, taking a fresh glance at everything, controlling his breathing.

Something clicked in the back of his head. He had an idea, and when it consolidated, his anger ebbed.

Ol' Buttwipe can't remember, but Doc can.

If the picture was true, then she'd known him a long time. He scratched his jaw with the back of his fingers.

That's why she'd kept such close tabs on him. It made sense, to a point.

He needed to find the Mistress, and for that Stan was still his best shot. He did want to help with the investigation, but before he could focus on that, the Mistress thing had to be resolved – one way or the other.

All this other mess is crap. I need Stan.

The corner of his eye caught the bedside table. Vivian always kept shit in hers.

He wallowed in the pain of Vivian for few minutes. Then he inhaled, shrugged, rolled across the bed, and opened the top drawer.

A sliver of streetlight sliced through the edges of the drawn shades, giving him just enough light to see – a book about some medical thing, a box of tissues, a small bullet-shaped vibrator (he chuckled to himself over that), and a pink notepad in the semblance of a skirt with a few pencils.

Pulling open the drawer below revealed a lot of panties and bras, all stacked neatly. He pushed them around feeling like a pervert, and finding nothing of consequence, he started to shut it, stopped for a second, and then finished closing it.

His head moved back in thought as he eyeballed the front of the nightstand, rubbing the side of his face with his fingertips. Both drawers were the same size on the outside. But when he opened the top again, it wasn't near as deep.

False bottom?

He tapped the velvety-covered bottom and nodded. Hollow.

He searched for a latch or tab, or lever. It took a while, but he found two straight pins jammed into the side walls, tucked next to the crack between the bottom of the drawer and the front facing. After about ten minutes of teasing at them, they sprang away, and the false bottom lifted right up.

Underneath were two things: a flash drive and a half-inch-thick folder with neat script across the front – Berne Caucus.

He picked it up and sat down. Thumbing through the folder, he nodded to himself. This is what I want.

He ran across several eight-by-ten photos, two of which made him pause. The first was Stan. It was years old, and he had some kind of uniform on, maybe army.

The other made his eyes bulge and his jaw clench. It was the bitch, the goddamn Mistress. She was part of the whole thing.

Pocketing the flash drive, he stood, tucked the folder under his arm and walked out of the bedroom.

After I find the Mistress, I'll get the drive back to Carbonella. The team will probably be able to open it.

Before he made it to the living room, he heard someone at the entrance door. He ducked into the kitchen, behind the bar that separated the two rooms.

The door opened and the light from the streetlamp flooded the air and two long shadows flattened across the floor and up the refrigerator. The shadows stayed for only a few seconds, the light in the living room came to life, and then died. The door shut.

He peeked around the kitchen bar, saw Stan had come in, and ducked back.

Well, shit. He's right there, and I need to talk to him, but I broke into this place.

"What the hell are you doing, Nancy?" Stan stood with a .38 pointed directly at him, and his face told Nancy it wasn't time to spout wisecracks.

Leaving the file on the floor, Nancy raised his hands and stood.

"What are you doing in Sally's house?" His dead tone matched his expression. Nancy definitely understood the implied meaning and he picked up the folder; then he followed the lead of Stan's nod toward the living room.

Stan sat next to Doc, so Nancy eased to the only other chair in the room and, keeping his eyes on Stan's pistol, asked if Stan would let him sit. A smile teased the corner of Nancy's mouth, Stan's face looked as though he'd barely survived a couple of rounds with Ronda Rousey. "Holy crap, Stan. You look like someone handed you your ass and then beat you up with it."

"Yeah, yeah," Stan nodded matter-of-factly. "The plane kicked my ass. I'm sure you would've enjoyed watching." He waved for Nancy to sit down.

"Sorry. You, uh, with Doc?"

Doc's face darkened, "You're in my house. I didn't invite you in. Stan, shoot."

Stan shook his head slowly, stood, and re-aimed at Nancy's crotch.

She shrugged and gave a small nod, "Now again." She stared. "What are you doing in my house?"

Nancy's eyes didn't know whether to plead, cry, or be pissed. "I'm trying to find that damned redheaded bitch and St—"

199

"You come to my house searching for Stan?"

"What?" Nancy leaned forward, forgetting what the gun drew a bead on. "After what I found in here?"

Stan dropped aim about two inches, and fired.

Nancy's eyes all but popped out of his head, his color deepened at least four shades instantaneously, and he talked quickly, "Don't get carried away!" He patted the air in front of him. "Stan, you've known about that damn redhead for a long time, and I knew the doctor here had more information about you than the rest of us. I didn't know how much."

She stared, not uttering a word, and Stan walked toward Nancy, still aiming at him. "Yeah, I know about the Mistress, Nancy. But right now, Sally and I are working through a few things and I don't have time."

"Stan, please. She was there when Vivian died."

The barrel of Stan's weapon pressed into his head.

Nancy looked straight forward. "Shit, Stan. What the hell happened to you? I'm a federal officer now."

Stan's face set like stone. "As it happens, I'm one too."

CHAPTER THIRTY-THREE

The Mistress stepped out onto the fire escape. The rain didn't bother her; it was more of a drizzly mist and actually refreshed her. The brownstone where she lived was quiet, as was the neighborhood up and down the street. Mu'izz slept in the guest room. Her place was nice but much too small to have this conversation with him in it, asleep or not.

She had to get Mu'izz's folder to Berne. It was flaming hot, and she didn't need it around here.

The wound pained her tremendously. She needed all of her faculties; otherwise, she would have drugged herself and slept, but right now that wasn't an option. Not with everything that had happened. She stood under the upstairs ironworks landing and backed against the brick wall.

Studying the fire escape both above and below to make sure she was alone; she pushed the button on her cell that connected her to Berne.

The voice came on the line after the second ring, "Do you have the information?"

"Yes, of course. You know I always do what's needed."

"Yes. Always."

The Mistress relaxed as she leaned even more against the wall. She hadn't realized how tense she was. She bent her knee to place her foot on the brick and the pain in her side eased.

"Where did you kill Mu'izz? His body must not incrimina—"

"I didn't kill him."

The silence on the other end roused a cluster of alarms to wail in the Mistress's head. The longer the deadly hush lasted, the greater her distress.

"What?"

The peach-orange light of dawn intensified by the second. "I had a better idea." There was more detail of the buildings around her than only moments before was in shadow, and it made the Mistress feel so vulnerable. Even the rough feel of the brick scratching her back increased her wariness.

She rubbed her forehead.

"Did you not understand the order?"

The redhead wasn't used to feeling this way, not since she'd been a child. "Yes. The order was clear."

"Do you know what you have caused?" Now it was her turn to clam up.

"Tess?" The voice came through the phone, "Tess, answer me."

The Mistress breathed in deeply and exhaled. "I'm here, Amy."

"Why didn't you kill him, Tess?"

"Amy, I know you've been in charge since Mama died, but this time I really do have a good idea."

"Then why didn't you tell me about it before you committed? Where is he?"

The Mistress stood and paced the landing in the drizzle. The light had increased enough that she was able to see the clouds off to the west instead of darkness, and they looked mean. They were only minutes away, and then she would be soaked, but the air now smelled fresh, especially for the city. A glance at her window. "He's with me."

"Which is where?"

"My apartment."

"Well, keep him there. Tie him up or something. You're nearest to I80, right?"

"Hmm … I think."

"Okay. I'll meet you about one o'clock. We need to hash this out. You do still have the stuff Mu'izz was using to blackmail the Caucus, right?"

"Yeah, I got it all. It's in my room." Her heart skipped. "Shit." She scrambled through the window. Inside, she found that both Mui'zz and the folder were gone, the Glock, too. She still had the keys to his car, though.

"Amy, I need to call you back." She hung up, stuffed the phone into the back pocket of her jeans, and grabbed her 9mm from the small of her back. She had no illusions about Mu'izz.

He was deadly. Even though he only posed as a terrorist, ISIS had trained them both and the violence he was capable of was real. She had to find him, convince him to go with her plan, or kill him.

After double-checking her apartment, she entered the hallway. A brisk walk to the stairs and a quick glance down them told her nothing.

Can't have gone far. The elevator didn't ring.

A quick search of the vending alcove produced nothing.

Damn it.

Blood tinged her shirt; the more she walked, the more it bled, and it throbbed. She tried to ignore it, but in the end, she had to grit her teeth and go. She turned back to her apartment. Halfway down the hall, she caught a fleeting shadow from the corner of her eye. It faded into a room ahead.

She slowed. Inching along the wall, her weapon was a part of her. At the door, she waited against the wall, ears focused intently.

"I'm here, bitch." Exhaustion colored his obnoxious voice so much it surprised her.

She twisted around the doorframe, weapon before her, and stared down the barrel of his pistol.

"Put it down." Total focus etched his face. "I have nothing to lose." Repugnance morphed his face, "If I don't stop you now, you will kill me. Do you think I'm an imbecile?"

"No. But you're not thinking through what I told you." He cocked his head and raised his eyebrows.

A small sigh escaped her, almost a snort. "I'll explain one more time. We can twist things around, but only if you come with me. If you don't come, I can, and will, follow through on the kill Berne ordered. I'm not playing here." Slowly and deliberately, she aimed her weapon at his head.

"It's your turn. Decide … now." Her voice acquired more edge. "I haven't got the patience to play with this, so, in about thirty seconds, I will decide for you."

She stood up slowly, keeping her pistol dead center on the bridge of his nose. "Berne already wants me dead for not doing what they ordered, so it's a wash. Like you, pointing that thing at me means nothing. Either way, I take my chances. My last word … you stand there, you'll die. Even if you shoot me, you will die."

He stared for a couple of seconds, and then he put his Glock on the floor.

With a curt nod, she motioned him past her and scooped up the Glock as she followed.

Keeping careful aim, she marched him back through her apartment. "Relax."

In the bedroom, he plopped down in the overstuffed chair near the doorway.

"No. Over there. The bed." She motioned him on with her pistol. There, she kept him clearly visible while inspecting herself in the mirror with a couple of quick glances.

Resting her handgun on an end table close to her, she drew up her shirt until she saw the wound clearly. The bleeding wasn't too bad. It seeped a little and was sore as hell. She poked at it here and there.

No sign of infection.

She nodded to herself and pulled her shirt back down.

"I want the folder, Abdul." She waited only long enough to tuck her shirt back into her pants. Then her eyes flashed, and an expression of malign boredom replaced it. She picked up her handgun, made sure the safety was off, and raised it.

"In a plastic bag, in the bottom of the ice machine in the vending alcove."

She nodded professionally at him as she passed by. "Sit right there, and don't fucking move." She disappeared out of the door. Seconds later, she returned with the folder in her hand and sat in a chair. A quick flick through it told her she had what she needed, and a smile of relief spread across her face.

"Okay. Now we wait until Berne gets here, then we hash it out." Her eyes flipped up to him. "Let me say it one last time. Screw with me, run away, do anything without checking with me and I will hunt you down and feed chunks of your body to rats up and down the quays. We may have been trained at the same camp, but let me remind you, I was better than you and since then I've refined my skills. I constantly work in the shadows, and in case you didn't realize it ...

I'm extraordinary at the job. You walked in a different direction."

CHAPTER THIRTY-FOUR

Nancy wore his confused expression, and I would have laughed had it not been for the tohubohu inside my head. The crowd inside all caterwauled simultaneously and had since I woke up with Sally. Right now, peace of mind was not anywhere in my universe.

Not now, John. Stop the humming, and for God's sake, quit tapping my foot!

No peace at all.

From what I remember after my awakening, these voices that vied for my attention were the same things that gave me my intuition before, only now they had obnoxious voices.

Damn it, Hank, leave me alone.

These voices have personalities, and they all think they are me.

Quit, Ahn! Both you and Jacques stop singling out Sally's aroma. I have enough trouble without you two being obsessed with her smell.

I remember talking to them, carrying on conversations when I was under the hypnotic suggestion, but I'm not now.

I need peace.

Shut up, all of you!

Well, hell. That worked.

Keep it buttoned.

"You all right, Stan?" Nancy's face appeared as if he'd seen Casper the Ghost. He didn't know whether to run or laugh.

My eyes sought out Sally.

"Stan's been having a bit of trouble concentrating." She sat down and patted the seat to her right as a hint for me. Nancy understood the hint better than I and sat on the easy chair near the doorway. My butt eased onto the cushion next to her.

"I'm fine, Detective. What are you doing here, by the way?"

I placed the .45 next to my right leg and kept hold of it. He's a pretty good guy, but lately I can't count on anything.

Thank God you realize that.

Shut up, Hank.

"Searching for you, Stan."

It was quiet in my head, but I still had no idea why he would be sniffing around for me here. "Why?"

"I need to find that redhe—"

"No. Why look here?" I turned to Sally. "You tell him something that you didn't tell me?"

She shook her head and I was sure her noggin worked overtime to make sense of it, too.

I was complete again, but I also had my fragmented pieces to deal with. What a dichotomy, but at least I'm not crazy. Along with all that, I had a realization about what needed to be done.

Of course, you aren't crazy, Stan. Never have been.

That was Sybil and it didn't help, either. I didn't know if she believed what she'd said, or had a case of Socratic irony. Why would anyone think a man with myriad voices in his head was crazy?

I know. Beats the bear shit out of me, too.

"I'm gonna let that go, Nancy. What do you need me for?"

"I told you. I need to find that redheaded whore from the last case."

"You mean the one you caught enjoying your wife's … uh …"

"Yeah, Stan. Let it go." Nancy's face was brutally cold. The only sign of life was the slight flush to his cheeks. The rest of it resembled baked granite.

He's in a mood.

Will you gag your trap? Not now.

"Sure thing, Nancy."

"Where?"

I tightened my grip on the .45. The inner squabbling started to stoke up again, but this time I ignored them by force of will.

"She lives in that brownstone we staked out."

Nancy burst out of the door and was almost in his car when a connection came. "Nancy, wait! Is that the same redhead we've been tracking?"

He was gone. All the loud noise in my head prevented me from thinking.

Shut the fuck up!

I grabbed my head and held it for almost a minute.

I felt like the town simpleton. Of course, the redheads were the same.

This shit in my head has got to go.

Stan?

The voice was soft, but direct. I took a deep breath.

Yes, Sybil.

Can you remember the first time you and I talked?

No. Why?

You will.

CHAPTER THIRTY-FIVE

I walked forward. Every few heartbeats, the wind transformed the clouds above to images of water in a boiling cauldron. The smell of rain floated in the air and mixed with the aroma of the incense escaping the shelter before me. Of the two sent, the natural one infused the air, but the odor of the smoky perfume amplified with each of my steps.

Sundown happened before I left the village and now the light had faded so quickly, it was hard to see to walk. In moments there would be nothing but black and a few flickering fires.

My feet bare, I had to ignore the grass between my toes that normally delighted me.

It was not the time for that, I reminded myself.

A gust whipped my hair into my face, and I had to stop myself from pushing it behind my ear. Let it fly, ignore the sting of it. I clutched the wolf skin that covered my nakedness.

On the hillcrest, the elders lined the way to the hut. Robed and hooded, they resembled statues carved from thousand-year-old oaks in the flickering light from the fire. Their only movement occasional wisps of hair tossed in the wind.

I stepped close to the fire as the flames danced and popped wildly in the darkness. The glow lit the elders' eyes, transforming them into red spots floating in the dark.

An ancient woman stepped into the light from a deep shadow and barred my way. "Who are you that comes to this place?" Her eyes glistened with curiosity and purpose and her voice creaked like dried-out oak limbs rubbing together in the wind before a storm.

It had taken me days to travel from my village. I had spent the time concentrating on my inner self, and this was the moment for which I prepared.

I am ready.

I knew the truth of it as deeply as I could delve within myself. I pulled in a breath for strength and dove into her eyes, fathomless, "I am a Mother of the Highest Level, and I seek entrance." I had said the words simply as befitted one who seeks wisdom.

"You lie." Her vehemence was enough to make my soul bleed.

Two younger elders dropped their cloaks and stepped forward naked, brandishing war axes as if to strike. A corner of my wolf skin slipped from my hand, but I snatched it back quickly.

"You are not of the Highest Level," the old woman screeched.

"I am."

Thunder rolled over us, deep and powerful. I felt it shake my heart.

The Ancient One tossed her head like an angry horse and waved me away. "Be gone," she spat and disappeared into the hut.

I stood my ground but did not dare to speak. Blue lightning flashed across the sky. The sharp tang stung my nose; in the same instant, thunder cracked hard, shaking the ground. I hunched over.

"Did you not hear me?" the shrill voice pierced the skin of the hut, like the point of a newly chipped flint knife. A heartbeat later, she burst through the flap, pointing her finger at me.

"Take her measure," her eyes ablaze like the fire. "After this night, she will be changed. This woman will either be so much more … or become like smoke in the night."

Can the whispers be true? It is said some Mothers fail, but do they never return from the Great Mother test? I fidgeted.

As soon as I realized it, I forced myself to stand still, but it taxed my will.

The two men threw their battle-axes to the ground and grabbed my arms. I jerked at their touch and when I did, I dropped my wolf skin. A cold gust made my nipples crinkle, and the immediate chill bit through my skin. Then the wind died as the remaining elders surrounded me.

An old man approached and stabbed my leg with a bone needle and then smeared the blood from it on a piece of leather. Another elder cut a length of hair with her flint knife, and yet another person took a strip of hide, draped it from my top knot to the ground and cut the length.

My measure taken.

One, so old and fat there was no way to tell which sex, even naked, leaned toward me. The fat gave breasts, although misshapen, and the stomach hung low, covering the sex organ.

"Who sent you?" The voice was soft and husky, not deep, and not melodious.

"The Gods."

"Approach and say your name."

I walked toward the hut and the old one ducked inside. I followed.

The temperature grew comfortable and I relaxed, free from the wind. A cloud from smoldering cedar and mistletoe hung in the air, and my eyes burned, dripping with tears, as they adjusted to the darkness. Tapers burned in the cardinal points and the worship circle had been cast.

The Ancient stood as naked as I. Her robe lay bunched by the entrance. She met me with an open arm hug. Her ear close to my mouth, and I whispered the names of the god and goddess, the ones who had sent me to this place.

This close, I saw broken teeth through her smile. Her age displayed itself with facial wrinkles so deep they were almost fissures. Brittle hair hung like straw to her breasts, which had long since held milk. They hung now like flatbread, drooped nipples pointing straight toward the ground.

She bade me sit and yet remained standing herself. "No, you are not." She sang and sang as she talked. "You are not yet of the Highest Level," she croaked.

A quick turn and her back faced me. She greeted the Great Couple – The Mother of Life, and The Giver of Peace. She walked the circle and talked to the cardinal points, always moving deasil, to the right, in the direction of the sun's apparent course, auspicious for the gods and casting circles.

The circle completed, and back at the beginning, she turned to me and spoke to the air above my head. "The initiate is an infant who crawls."

I envisioned myself the way I was when I began my learning. The crone continued, "The first level was the beginnings of being wise." I saw myself at the age when I first bled like a woman. It was then I stepped for the first time into the Circle.

"Second level, you tell us you're ready and we raise you." My pride at telling them that I knew the first big secret almost overwhelmed me.

The old woman grew somber. "Third level happens when you alone understand what you need to know. Others of that level can tell, but it is you who must raise yourself. That level is thought of as the highest, and only those who attain it can be a High Priestess or High Priest."

She stood above me now. "It is time for you to learn, and you will know the truth. Only those seekers who survive even suspect it, and if you live, you can never even hint at it. You can only talk to yourself about it and only when alone. Do not forget your measure has been taken."

Taking hold of a bowl-shaped stoup, she held it to my lips and poured much more than a mouthful of bitter wine into me. Standing ready and watching me, she cackled again. Then she pinched a sprig of dried mistletoe and casually tossed it onto the small fire. Blue smoke billowed.

She leaned into my face. The sting in my eyes returned, and the smell of moldy wood filled the air, making my nose itch. "Breathe deeply, Little Mother," she cackled. "Breathe deeply."

I did as she bade, and with the smoky air came a numbness of my mind and body. I felt similar to drinking too much mead without the rich, bloated feeling. I floated.

With fingers on my forehead, she pushed me back until I rested on the Blessed Earth. A smoke trail swirled above, turning gracefully, stretching lazily in the air. Two tendrils bent exquisitely around and pushed elegantly down and under me. After the smoke curled around and cradled me, the tendrils stopped for a several heartbeats as if thinking. Then they stabbed into my eyes.

"Mmmm," the moan escaped me. The smoke seared me deeply, and I felt myself lift, up into the rolling smoke cloud above, yet I still felt the ground below.

My mind turned to the impossible task of understanding how that happened, and even though I had my eyes tightly shut, my vision cleared. As I floated, I saw beyond, farther than the smoke, above the hut, and beyond the clouds. I had no boundaries.

My teachings before this test said life came from the Mother, full of vigor, and death was simply a transformation from one life to yet another life, one more chance to pass through the Mother's Great Cauldron of Life and be born again.

What I saw now exceeded all of that.

Life is limitless. The thought grew like a giant tree, stretching far into the distance.

Up close, I saw the way of my lives as they flowed one after another. After each death came a rebirth. One after another, I died and changed. One after another, I watched my inner self grow, until I arrived at a place where I saw the end, and vibrations of the truth filled my spirit.

I rolled through the air, riding the smoke, watching my colorful lives, each contrasting the others – until I came to a man with small eyes and large lips staring back at me. The others had never known of me. This person joined with me.

I experienced our sameness, and somehow, I knew:

Each spirit vibrates a certain way and produces a tone, like a string for a musician. Although the string never changes, the vibrations can; when portions of the string vibrate differently, the tone changes.

Each life has distinct personalities, always different from the others as are the tones, but the spirit is the string. It always remains the same.

I floated in my cocoon of smoke, and my new knowledge intertwined down to my deepest core. I rode the universe with the entirety of it. The heat of it in the center of my being, flamed intensely. I lived the rest, learning the truth of life, but as I absorbed that truth, there came a strong call to return home. It tugged, and I ignored it. Several times I turned my attention to something else, and several times, the tug came again, stronger.

Then I remembered the crone.

I'd forgotten her until now, and in the instant her memory blustered through me, my tone that is my spirit tensed − I understood why some never survive. They simply did not want to leave the outpouring of life. The filling gratification and the temptation and longing to stay was …

The old woman jabbed me again, and her craggy voice stabbed my ears. The sound rocked me. My grip on where I was faltered, but before I was sucked away, I reached for it again.

Another jab. And again. Each time my grip strengthened.

That was when I heard the voice cry, "Help." It was the one with the small eyes and big lips.

I turned inward.

"I need you. Please come."

I focused my attention on him, and as I did, my hold on the secrets vanished. The hut materialized around me again. My eyes fluttered open. Above me stood the Ancient One, smiling, her rotted teeth exposed.

"Welcome back, Great Mother," she cackled. Exhaustion played across her face, centuries of life rested on her shoulders, beating her down. "I am so glad you returned, for you are now the Sibyl and I am tired. It is time …" The Old One's smile dropped, and she crumpled into a heap next to the fire.

I nodded to myself and closed her eyes. I understood – she craved to go back.

Exiting the hut, the guards stood where they had lately been resting. The yellow light of dawn fanned across the sky, and the clouds were gone. Through the crisp air, I smelled the embers of the fire that had burned through my ordeal.

I bent to retrieve my robe of skin and wrapped it close.

All of them waited for the crone, and when she did not appear, they turned to me.

I shook my head, and they understood.

"What does the Sibyl wish?"

"Prepare the old Sibyl." Then as an afterthought, "Where is my hut? I want my clothes."

Stan?

Yes, Sybil?

Do you understand yet? All of us are the same. There is no need to fight within yourself.

I thought that through, and the clarity of it almost hurt. She was right, of course. I had to use it.

Sybil?

Yes, Stan.

It's a title isn't it, not a name?

Yes.

What do I call you?

I have no name. Sybil will do.

CHAPTER THIRTY-SIX

The quiet rapping at the door alerted them both. The Mistress stood by the door, pistol in hand, and peered through the viewer into the hallway. It framed Amy in her form-fitting white dress.

The Mistress's mouth teased a grin while she stuffed the weapon into the back of her pants, unlocked the door, and pulled it open. "Come on in, Amy."

They hugged briefly and the Mistress re-locked the door.

Mu'izz fidgeted uneasily in the overstuffed chair, his hands and feet zip-tied. Focused intently on the two women as they moved into the room, his jaw muscles popped.

Outside, the overcast sky shed a gray tint across everything. The rain had stopped several hours ago, but the sidewalks, grass, and trees still had that damp, permanently wet feel to them.

"Okay," Amy waded in before the Mistress had a chance to take a seat. "What the hell is this plan you have that you disregarded your orders?" Her eyes flashed at the Mistress. The redhead sat on a chair, and Amy sat on the couch, crossing legs elegantly at the knee, pulling them back at an angle, demurely correcting her hemline.

"Easy, Amy. First of all, Abdul knows we are sisters."

"What! We agreed—"

"I know what we agreed. But it doesn't matter."

"Bullshit it doesn't matter!"

"If you will let me, I'll explain." Tess stared at her sister. After a few seconds of Amy's measured glance back and forth from her to Mu'izz, Tess sighed and sat back in her chair.

Nancy quietly worked at opening the window from the fire escape, but his hands shook, as did his butt cheeks from squatting. It had taken too long to climb the fire escape. He'd had to do it one step at a time, because he'd left his cane in the car.

Don't blow it, Nancy. You're this close to that bitch but trip up now and it still might go wrong.

He'd seen a bunch of police down on the ground preparing, and God alone knew the plans they had. By the size of the crowd, he would have only a little time, certainly not enough to screw around.

Hell of a cat burglar, you crazy old gimp. The window squeaked and his heart thumped so hard that the hair on his arm moved like a wave clear up to his chest. His anxiety was acute, chest tight, hard to breathe.

He eased the window more slowly and his arms trembled.

Almost there. Another inch or two. There.

He sat back and tried to control himself, wiped a big dollop of sweat trailing down his face with his finger, and took a deep breath.

Tess waited for her sister. Amy waved with impatience, and Tess began. "It doesn't matter because he will either be with us, or I will kill him on the spot." She stared at Amy in defiance.

"There is a possible escape."

"Not from me." The redhead grabbed her pistol and pointed it at Mu'izz's head.

That gave Amy a little pause. The corners of her mouth tilted upward, and she gave a shrug and a nod. "That would do. Okay, we'll table that for now. What about the file?"

Nancy wasn't certain if he was pissed or scared, but whatever it was, it felt crappy. Gritting his teeth, he bent forward and eased himself through the window; as he did, he debated about shutting the thing or letting it go. He left it alone.

Open is good, might need to escape.

His ears picked up a voice.

She's here. But others are too, damn it. Should've waited until she was alone.

A vision of Vivian dying flashed through his mind, and his jaw muscle popped. It had taken too long to find the redhead. At first, he didn't admit to himself that he needed to find her.

Then the lieutenant died, and he thought, "What the hell. Doesn't matter now." Now though, with all the bullshit happening, he knew what he had to do.

And Stan. Stan has been a blithering idiot.

He limped toward the other room and peered through the crack between the door and the wall. Three people. Didn't know who the knockout in white was. He'd seen the guy around.

Why the hell is he tied up?

The redhead faced the other way, but while he'd been woolgathering, she jumped up and turned in his direction.

Oh, shit!

He hopped behind the door.

Captain Beaufort stared hard at the corner window three floors up.

That redheaded cunt lives in that kind of luxury. And I'm a captain and get to live where I do? Ain't right. He shook his head in disgust.

His men worked diligently setting up defensive positions as quietly and unobtrusively as possible. They were almost there. Ten minutes at the most.

He shook his mind free of pissy thoughts and returned to the Berne orders. The design of this exercise was a fancy way to kill that little bastard Mu'izz and that's what he intended to do.

He snarled to himself.

His eyes drew his head to face the window above. As soon as ol' secretary stands in the window. He nodded. She does that and we'll have the folder. Then we go in. Straightforward.

He grunted. All because I got a phone tip that the local head of ISIS would be there. He gave a low chuckle, at his idea. Important enough that I personally go in.

There you go you, damned little shit. Go ahead, threaten me, prick. Threatened me!

Beaufort eyed the window again.

"Captain," barked the radio on his hip.

He picked it up and spoke, "Captain. Go ahead."

"Sir, this is Team Two Spotter."

"Go ahead."

"I have someone who crawled into the apartment through the fire escape window."

"Can you ID them?"

"Negative."

"Okay. Keep watch. Stand ready everyone. Wait for my go."

Tess pushed the door open and strode into the bedroom. She snatched some papers on the bed, turned around, and exited the room. "Here, hon. This is everything. I tried to sanitize it a bit, bu—"

"Never mind that." Amy grabbed the papers and let them fall into her lap, shuffling them together, picking and choosing some of them to stack singly. "I'll do all that later. The senator has a lot of canvassing to do to put him in line for the selection, so I'll have time."

She bent back to making things neat again and became so single-minded in her work, she might have forgotten the other two people in the room. After muddling along for a couple of minutes, the stack was fairly neat, and she put it next to her on the couch. She smoothed her hair back into place.

"Now, back to Mu'izz and what we're about to do with him." A brief sneer at him and she turned her attention back to her sister.

Tess grinned like a kid wanting to keep the new puppy.

"Okay, Sis. He fits in without much trouble. Fact is, I think it's better." She gave him a sly smile.

"Hold up, Tess. Keep your legs closed for few minutes. You have to sell me on this."

"All right. But I'll have to explain the whole thing in front of him." She waited for the okay.

Amy went for the kill, "He's in or dead, right?"

Tess shrugged.

"I'm in," Mu'izz confirmed.

Amy's expression told him he was snake feces. "I was pretty sure you'd make that assertion, given the circumstances. Go ahead, Tess."

"Well, if we take the original plan and tweak it ..."

Nancy pulled his weapon free and edged nearer, but when he caught the conversation, he stopped. Something about the senator and a caucus of some kind. He listened keenly but he didn't understand.

He inched his way around the door and stood ready to jump into the next room. His heart thumped hard, his eyes unable to focus, and his palms wet, with an uneven deep breath, he braced himself.

This woman was the reason Vivian died.

He wiped the sweat from under his nose and cheek. With quick steps, he hobbled into the room; his pistol aimed center mass at the redhead. "Everybody stop."

The three of them jerked. The redhead recovered first and reached behind her.

"Stop." Nancy stared at her. "Last time I say it."

Inching to his left to a better position, Nancy's eyes never left hers, as he talked to Amy and Mu'izz. "Don't know who you two are but stay put. Got business with Red here. Don't test me. You understand?"

No one replied, so he asked again, his Brooklyn accent like

a whip crack, "Understand?" Their yeses overlapped.

"You were there," he accused the Mistress.

The redhead ignored this and stared like a double-barreled shotgun.

Every nerve and impulse commanded his finger to squeeze the trigger, but long hours of training held it steady. The strain of it made his back ache. His jaw cramped from talking through clenched teeth, "Don't screw with me."

His memory betrayed him. Visions of the two of them played. Viv and the redhead entwined on the bed, flashed through, and vomit burned his throat just as it had that night. "Stand up. Now!" The image of their nakedness and what she was doing to Vivian danced behind his eyes.

"I tried to kill you once before."

The smile that sprang to life on her face dripped disgust as she purred, "I remember ... Mmmm. She tasted yummy. You lunged at the two of us in that position." She looked at him like he was scum. "Who does that?"

His hands shook.

Seeing the trembling, she curled her arms up as if she wrapped them around two legs. "It was you who killed her, not me! I was only sexing her."

The truth of her words turned his whole body cold, and the memory of the lieutenant telling him how much he now owed for fixing the investigation flashed through his mind. "You bitch." He whispered.

With no sudden moves, she turned to face him straight on, her eyes tight with purpose. She raised her right leg, so her foot rested on the couch, like a seductress, but putting her Ka-bar near her hand.

"Don't move at all." He walked in front of her, closer to the other two who were on their feet, his memory of that night overwhelming him.

If I hadn't tried to kill this cooter-robber, Vivian would still be alive.

The Mistress's eyes followed him as he moved in an arc before her. She licked her lips and winked. He growled back as he advanced, his eyes squarely on her.

She attacked, knife in hand. Her weight hit him squarely, her knee shot forward, striking his testicles, pushing them into his body, and forcing him to fall on Mu'izz and then the floor; electric sickness made him grab himself.

She dove for his pistol but as sick as he was, he turned and pulled the trigger. The deafening report stunned her. His shot missed.

She jumped, landing on his chest with her knee, his breath now gone. He shot a second time.

The bullet grazed her shoulder. As she stabbed, sinking to the hilt in his gut. He dropped his pistol. She abandoned her knife and snatched the handgun. Her face inches from Nancy's, she hissed, "A shame you interrupted that day. It was your hand on the knife. You killed her."

Nancy glared fire at her, as he lay gurgling, as Viv's fatal night played through his mind – his lunge, the knife flash toward the redhead as she burrowed between Viv's legs. The bite of the knife on skin, his savage jerk. The blood spurting from Vivian's femoral.

The redhead slapped him to get his attention. "Are you listening?"

He gurgled again; blood leaked from his wound.

She grinned malevolently as she pointed the pistol at him. "You killing her pushed me over the edge, you know. I had a great cum. Too bad about her, though." She grabbed hold of her knife, straining, twisting it. "I only did her to increase my fun. That was the plan – kill her to give me my orgasm. All you did was hurry it along."

"Ahhh!" He rolled with renewed energy, pushed himself to his knees, and scrambled to his feet. Blood poured from his wound. He lurched for his handgun, but she shot him in the face.

He dropped hard.

Sniper rounds hit her apartment, crashing, and popping. She slipped on blood and hit the floor. Before her, Mu'izz's chair was empty.

He hid behind the sofa, trying to escape, ready to dive out of the door.

Pounding from the stairs announced attackers heading their way. Abdul held out his hands and leaned over the couch, "Cut me free, or they will kill me before you do." His eyes pleaded. "Cut me free!"

The Mistress pulled him around the couch, back into the open, and into the blood, making sure he, too, was covered.

He snatched her knife and kicked her away, back onto the sofa. A quick reverse of the knife, and he sliced the zip tie on his legs. She scrambled over the couch, searching for a weapon, anything. Mu'izz dove after her. He stretched hard, fitting his bound wrists over her head, scraping them down her face but she twisted hard and ducked free. She flailed for her pistol. He kicked the handgun away.

The door slammed open.

Mu'izz cut the wrist ties, rolled to the Sig Sauer, scooped it up, and leaped toward the bedroom. Turning in the air, he fired twice at the first blue uniform, dropping the officer. Mu'izz landed on his shoulder and rolled into the darkness of the bedroom.

He fired twice through the door to keep them at bay, then checked the window behind him. Police swarmed everywhere. Red, blue, and white lights flashes filled the night.

"He shot him! Mu'izz shot him." Covered in blood, the redhead screamed as Captain Beaufort ran into the apartment, pistol drawn, and took in carnage – an officer wounded, two more on either side of the other door, and everyone else in concealed positions.

She kept screaming.

He slipped, almost falling on his ass, in a huge pool of blood spreading from under an overstuffed chair, leading to a body shot in the face. "What the hell happened?"

"He was down when we got here."

"Mu'izz?"

"I'm telling you Mu'izz shot him," yelled the redhead.

"Don't know." The senior man winced and answered as he administered first aid to the downed officer. "Mu'izz did shoot her."

Beaufort leaned toward his fallen officer. She'd taken one in the leg and another in the vest.

"Damn it!" screamed the redhead. "They wrestled and Mu'izz killed him."

"Somebody gag her," Beaufort growled it over his shoulder. "Are all of you morons today?" He grabbed his radio mike, "Officer down, and one dead on the scene. Need an ambulance. And hurry."

The redhead wrestled with an officer, still screaming about Mu'izz. Beaufort turned toward her. "Get her outta here."

Two officers grabbed her arms, but she shook herself free. Several others dashed in and pulled her into the hall.

The captain surveyed the rest of the room, paused briefly as his gaze caught the secretary.

He'd forgotten about her. Shit. Can't have her questioned.

He rubbed his chin and then the side of his cheek.

Pointing toward the bedroom door, "All right, everyone. I want three. You, you, and you to stay with me. Everyone else fall back, leave your ARs with us, and take the other woman with you, too. We got this. All but us four, get gone."

The sergeant's expression questioned him. This definitely wasn't protocol.

Beaufort nodded toward the door, "Move. Tell the new lieutenant to go to Plan B. Go on."

"Sir, that's the leader of the ISIS cell."

"I won't say it a third time, Sergeant," barked Beaufort. "Get statements from them and let them go. Take their names and release 'em."

Hope she has sense enough to give a false name.

On the way out, Amy bent down and snatched up a thumb drive that must've dropped from Nancy's pocket.

Beaufort heard the grumbling in the hallway. They didn't bother keeping their voices down.

"What a hot dog."

"–in' for promotio—"

"Crazy."

He smiled to himself. He lowered his voice and tapped the apartment door while talking to the dark room. "Mu'izz? It's Captain Beaufort. I'm in charge." He paused for a reply; when there wasn't one, he continued, "Real fucking big shot now, huh? Whatever your plan is, it ain't gonna work." Working himself up, Beaufort forgot about the three police he commanded to stay.

He tapped louder on the door with each tap.

Beaufort slammed the door and yelled, red-faced. "Goddamn it, Mu'izz. We got your plans, you asshole. Those shitty little papers you left are out here. All you got is your hand in your pants, playin' with that tiny pecker."

"Allahu Akbar!" Mu'izz rushed into the room, firing as he came. Three bullets struck Beaufort in the vest, one in his neck as he fell backward, another entered his orbital socket and passed through the frontal lobe and exited the top of his head.

The Mistress went straight in an ambulance, she had so much blood on her. The EMTs took charge and lay her down, but when the medic turned her back to grab her equipment, the redhead bolted, disabling the male EMT. A burly police officer blocked her escape from the ambulance.

Without slowing, she jabbed the unsuspecting man in the neck, dropping him like a bag of grain. She barreled on through and disappeared into the dark night.

Mu'izz squeezed off another round, killing the closest policeman. Scooping up the AR-15 from the dead man, he squatted behind the easy chair straddling Beaufort's body and tried to calm his breathing. After sucking in as much air as his lungs allowed, he let it out, stood, firing both weapons, and backed into the hallway.

A human wave of blue stormed his way. He ran into the stairwell, bullets zinging off the metal door as he took the stairs two and three at a time going up. Several pairs of boots sounded behind him.

Echoes of ricochets filled the stairwell as the bullets bounced through the air. One round, blew a hole in the wood paneling nearby, sending chips into his face, almost blinding him.

Winded by the second flight up, after the third flight, he had to rest. Footsteps kept coming. He leaned over the rail, fired twice, heard a moan, then ran again.

At the roof, he kicked open the door. Huffing loudly. Where now? He stumbled around.

Lightheaded and barely able to think, He leaned over the fire escape.

Not that way. The mob of cops surged down there. The door slammed open. He fired before they exited.

Return fire whizzed through the air.

Where to go? Too close. Can't be a next time. He sucked in more air and heard them getting ready to rush him.

An idea rocketed through his mind. He shot another two-round salvo and dove the few feet between him and the air conditioner. The noise of their return fire covered his hard landing to their flank.

This side of the building was dark, in shadow. Throwing the

strap of the long gun over his shoulder, he was up and over the small wall, grabbing the rain gutter.

Holding the drainpipe, he slid down, bouncing with his feet. He studied the roof line for chasers as he descended.

The silhouette of a head appeared above, and he stopped, his body tingling, leaning into the wall. His breathing ragged.

Slowly he peered up again; the shadow above disappeared.

He needed to take another chance. Sliding, at the second story, he pushed away. His heart beat a hole in his chest as he fell. His feet stung like hell when he landed, and one ankle hurt badly, but he was down. He stayed motionless, listening.

Everything was quiet. He limped through the dark alley and didn't look back.

CHAPTER THIRTY-SEVEN

Reminiscing with Nancy felt great, at least for those few seconds before he bolted. I would have preferred to spend the day talking, getting an idea of what he knew, but frogs don't have wings, and because of that, they bump their asses when they jump. Know what I mean?

So I was out for a stretch of the legs, so to speak, doing what I was trained to do – a little nighttime reconnoitering. It felt wonderful. It was also a chance for peace and quiet. Sunset happened hours earlier, and as cloudy as it was, without some man-made illumination, I wouldn't be able to see my own hand.

A streetlight stood at the entrance to the alley behind me, about a block away. I hid behind a really ripe dumpster. My memory told me how to find the warehouse, and inspecting it, it didn't strike me as too formidable.

I recalled that I worked pretty well under pressure, and I did have an adrenaline buzz. In fact, my whole body itched while I tried to grow antennae that would sense someone behind me, so I think it qualified.

Mu'izz was missing. According to the newscast I'd seen before I left my newly remembered wife, the cretin had run around yelling, "Allahu Akbar." I knew Mu'izz had been trained by the gurus in ISIS, and whatever anyone thinks about their idiot philosophies, they crank out some spectacular warriors.

Even if he weren't physically here, that expertise would be translated into the defense of his abode. I had to be careful. A serious ass-kicking might grab me like an angry ape if I wasn't on top of the line. I've already had several gorilla beatings and don't want another. I still can't breathe through my nose very well, and I was sure I could double for a raccoon.

All this considered, I used the advice garnered from Sybil. I'd given strict orders to my inner partners not to disturb me unless it was life or death, ours. *Stay in the shadows a few minutes mo—*

Hank!

Of course, at least one inner idiot's idea of life or death is his belief that whatever he wants to say trumps all things and he will die if he doesn't say something.

When I need you, I'll call for you, Hank.

Oy. I'm giving you the benefit of my experience, old boy.

Can it, Hank.

Have to get with him about the way he talks to me. Unfortunately, he was right. The thing about it was that I knew what he wanted to tell me before he started popping off, so I didn't see a *quid pro quo.*

Had to be selective about what senses I used. The place stank of sour garbage. If I'd let myself smell, taste, feel, etcetera, it would've slowed me considerably, because the residual pain from the airplane landing still hadn't left me. I ignored both pain and smell as much as possible.

Ahn wasn't pleased. He was especially partial to them both.

I peered down the narrow back road, through the shadows and tiny streaks of light, to the warehouse. A guard paced near the door, and I saw another hiding behind a dumpster, about twenty feet from that same door.

A regular gauntlet.

I heard Hank's deep chuckle and I had to agree. Hell, we could sneak by a hell of a lot more than that.

Creeping along the edge of the building, I snuck through the long shadow to the next alcove, to an even darker spot. The first guard had his head down, taking a leak, against the wall on the other side. I heard the stream hitting the asphalt an amazing six or seven feet from him.

There was the door. I scooted, mouse-like, past the big, bad cats. The whole trip had been uneventful.

Stupid pussies, snarled Hank.

The worst thing that happened was when I skinned the side

of my little finger, but not even enough to make a three-year-old want a Band-Aid.

The guard strode away, and while he had his back to me, I simply walked through the door and closed it quietly. Nobody challenged me at all. No guard inside the door.

Strange.

The empty building made my testicles retreat to shelter inside, a bad portent at any time. I let Ahn be my early warning system.

It was dark as a sable's den, but Ahn directed me. Between his peripheral vision and nose, he had no trouble navigating. By my figuring, it took a couple of minutes to cross the warehouse floor before finding another door. This one had a knife-edge of light filtering through the doorjamb, and when I opened it, the sudden burst of light killed my eyes.

I blinked furiously and waited for my eyes to adjust. Blood smeared the couch and wrappings of medical supplies lay scattered around. Aside from that, the place was as neat as a spinster's bathroom.

To my surprise, I found a partially hidden safe, open.

What the hell?

I ferreted around and found it empty of papers or money. Damn thing looked to me like someone un-assed in a hurry. But when? Maybe happened last week, or perhaps they scrambled out the back at the same time as I waltzed in the front door.

Oddly, the safe held two switches. I nabbed the one on the right, thinking I'd flip it for shits and giggles and see what it did.

Wait, Stan.

I stopped. It was Sybil. Every orifice I had closed up tighter than a whale's sphincter.

Don't know if she did that or I did, but it doesn't matter.

After that warning, my eyes flicked around the room searching for Mu'izz hiding close by. I told Ahn to listen carefully for anyone else.

Why would two switches be here?

Good question, Sybil. Can you tell me?

I don't know, Stan. Looks to me like he didn't want to do anything with them by accident.

They are in a safe.

Mu'izz's a wanker but seems to me he knows what he's doing. That's a detcord.

You sure, Hank? I know what it is, but I've never seen it.

He gingerly picked up the cord. *That's definitely the goods, Stan.*

I whistled silently to myself. Detcord is a fuze that burns extremely quickly – around 7,500 yards per second, give or take. That's almost a mile and a half per second. So fast, the entire length seems to explode at the same time. Scary shit.

Mmm. Maybe the two switches are like dead-man switches of sorts.

Explain, Hank.

I gave him control of my arms while I watched.

He talked while he checked the area inside the safe with our fingertips to find out where the cord went. *A dead-man switch is something a tosser might keep on hand while he's alive to prevent something from happening, but when and if he dies, he relaxes, the switch relaxes too, undoing the prevention and* ka-boom.

We found two sets of cords tied in a special way to a single line. *Hmm. Knowing ISIS's penchant for wishing to visit their promised land loaded with willing virgins, then maybe they are suicide switches, too. They've used detcord in executions before. But why two?*

I can tell you that, I jumped in. If that's what this is, one is an instant, "Hello Allah and virgins," the other is more of a, "I'm a chickenshit and need time to vamoose." *Hey, hey, mon ami. I would vote for the second switch.*

Good idea, Jacques. I'm with you on that. What, Hank?

Well, chaps, the only way to be sure of what they really are is to follow the leads, see where they go.

I felt an abnormal vibration through the floor. Someone had slammed the outer door.

As we vanished into the bedroom to hide, the apartment door opened and two men walked in, chatting in what sounded Arabic. Near the middle of the room, they both cracked up with uproarious laughter. The one on the right sauntered to the bathroom and the other walked deliberately around the room as if he'd never been there before.

Mister Righty stayed in the can for a while but jabbered in Arabic again and Mister Lefty answered while snooping toward our room. I tried to make myself as unnoticeable as a mouse turd in a dark room; at the last minute, he turned into what I would say functioned as a kitchen.

He foraged and came out with a mouthful of something.

Hank chuckled at me.

Righty finished up in the water closet and strolled back out, thumped Lefty on the side of the head and pushed his shoulder in our direction.

This time, Hank tensed to spring, and I grabbed my Ka-bar. We were ready to slit a throat, or two. Hank leaned forward, almost into the light, and I pulled my arm to the side.

The apartment door burst open, scaring the shit out of me. In ran another guard, yelling and waving his arms, and then pointed beyond the door. In short order, all three cleared out babbling in Arabic, leaving the door open.

I sat as still as Rodin's *Thinker*. After my heart rate fell below one hundred thirty, I ventured back into the room, closing the door to give me a little warning if someone came back.

I went back to the safe. Hank leaned us in closer than before and stuck our right arm in to trace the wires. *Homemade job. The line heads out the back. I'll bet it goes through the wall back there.*

Okay, Hank, let's disconnect them where they join so we don't have any accidental explosions. We need to sashay pronto.

Thirty seconds later, we were again busy snooping through

Mu'izz's lair. We found what appeared to be an armory, with several caches of weapons in which I shopped. After a quarterhour, I came out well-dressed enough to feel fine at a formal killing, but not enough to slow me down.

The detcord meandered around several rooms and ultimately led us to several bricks of C-4. There was a hell of a big bang waiting to happen if someone ever pushed those switches ... again every orifice closed up pretty tightly.

We didn't find anything incriminating, though. Well, that's not quite true. The weapons and plastique were all American-made, even the detcord was domestic, strange for ISIS. I expected most of their weaponry to be old Russian stuff or North Korean, maybe even Iranian. Okay, maybe a few items of captured American shit, but there should have been a mixture of origins. Why all American-made?

I didn't know where Mu'izz was, but at least he wasn't here. He could show up at any time, though, and I was tired of keeping one eye peeled for him.

Hank agreed but asked for an extra second or so.

We've seen enough. Let's get ready and go.

It sounded like a college cheer squad in my head as I dug out several M18 Claymore mines and placed them strategically around the caches. The cheers died in anticipation as I connected them to trip wires.

That'll be a bad day for someone.

On the way out, we revisited the two switches in the safe. Hank made sure they looked hooked-up and still in the same place. I let him do it because he had more experience with that stuff. He did knock them over in the process, but he put them back.

After that, we skedaddled.

The way out of the building was the way in. Using my spectacular hindsight, exiting the same door I entered was probably a mistake.

I squeezed outside and stood as calmly as I knew how,

acutely aware that this was where an ISIS-trained terrorist hung out. The scene hadn't changed; there were at least two guards here, maybe more, and they all appeared as astute as the two morons from before.

I crossed the alleyway but I must've stepped on something, or caused a flicker in the night. The puddle the guard made was still in the middle of the alleyway, and I tried to tiptoe around it. Maybe I splashed in it, dunno, but the nearby guard whirled. He was huge. Quick, too.

In a nanosecond, he had his long gun up and pointed my way.

He gonna shoot!

Damn it, Fox Boy.

Too preoccupied to shush him, I had to dance like a Vegas stripper and do it as quietly as her boobs bouncing.

Now that I'd found my way into guard number one's puddle of piss, I had an epiphany.

The reason I was so good before I lost my memory was because I had myriad voices giving me advice. Hell, that was the reason I called myself Sigma, the symbol of a mathematical sum. I was, and am, the sum of all my parts, or a standard deviation. I don't understand that last thing, but I'll check it out later.

Why the hell then should I want to paralyze myself? Was this what Sybil tried to tell me in that memory?

This personal insight hit me with an internal bolt.

Was this what it meant to be enlightened?

I opened myself as much as possible. I needed to truly be Sigma.

Once Sybil's controls faded, Ahn smelled the guard behind me move closer and Hank chuckled. Quickly I rolled to my left as the man viciously struck at my spine with a rifle-butt. He missed, hitting my shoulder. A jolt of what felt like electricity numbed my shoulder, but I kicked hard with my right foot. I both felt and heard the snap.

Hank finished him with a quick chop of his forearm to the throat. *That'll keep the wanker.*

It made Hank very happy to be included.

The other sentry loomed. I pulled my Ka-bar, flipped and caught it by the blade, again I let Hank throw it. The tang hit that bastard David-Goliath style. He flopped down like a wet cow pie. *Splat.*

Oooh, that was the piss puddle, too.

I rubbernecked, pleased with myself. I had survived, I wasn't hurt, and my testicles were still in their factory settings. That big guy might've done quite a bit of damage with an errant kick.

I sauntered back to retrieve my knife. A few sprinkles of rain fell out of the sky. The notion that I should whistle came over me and "Singing in the Rain" all but burst from my mouth but one of the Inner Group squelched it. As I bent down to grab my knife, a red dot danced around my groin.

Damn.

"Don't move, not even an eyelid."

That wasn't what I wanted to move away from the light.

The voice had come from an old memory, and I knew exactly who'd spoken – Mu'izz. Low, but the obnoxious quality still there regardless of intensity. I followed his voice with my eyes through the shadows. He was too far away for me to wrestle and too close for me to run and hide.

Clever man, Mu'izz.

"Back inside, Sigma." Shit.

CHAPTER THIRTY-EIGHT

Alice stopped the SUV near the crime scene tape and a patrolman leaned down to wave her away. Her only answer was to flash her Homeland Security shield. "Asshole," she mumbled and turned back to the rear of the vehicle, "Need help, Carbonella?"

Carbonella struggled with her leg. "Maybe. Get me the chair."

"I still think this is a shitty ide—"

Carbonella's glare skewered her.

Alice opened the door and Carbonella stretched over to the door handle, pulled, and then slowly maneuvered her stiff leg toward the opening. As Alice retrieved the wheelchair from the trunk of the vehicle.

The doctors had splinted the leg and given her strict orders to stay off it.

She was to relax, for at least a week, but on the way home, Carbonella heard the news and gave orders for Alice to detour here.

"Officer! Yeah, you buddy." She held up her shield as he came around the vehicle. "Help me outta here."

"Yes, ma'am." He grabbed her waving hand, and gently pulled her free of her ride.

"Thank you." She stood on her good leg and smoothed her top, pulling it down over her hips. Alice came around with the wheelchair and Carbonella sat. Then aiming her angel smile at the patrolman, she said, "Thank you again. Who's in charge here now?"

He was quick enough to catch the look in her eyes, and he covered himself in professionalism and stood up straight. "Lieutenant Berry, ma'am. Right over there. The black ma—"

"I don't care if he's black, green, or … never mind. Pull this tape up for me. Alice, park and find me."

Beyond the tape was a nightmare, but it didn't surprise her much. Several cops were dead. Sounds like Nancy, too.

She shuddered at the thought. Threading her way through the mass of police, she hailed him from about ten feet away. "Lieutenant Berry?" She caught a glimpse, "Ronnie? Ronnie!" The lieutenant turned away from what was surely a planning session, saw her and turned back around, "'Scuse me." Walking away from them and toward Carbonella, "Carbonella?

Damn, it's been years."

"Lieutenant now? Good job."

He shrugged. "Thanks. Good to see you too, but why are you here?"

She stopped and straightened her shoulders. "I came originally because one of my people died and the asshole in charge here didn't have the courtesy to give me a heads up. Now I find out that you're the asshole."

"Easy. I must be, because I'm in charge, but I'm sure I won't be for very long. There's terrorism involved."

"I believe the terrorism makes it my crime scene, and Detective Nancy was attached to my task force." She held up her shield, he stopped to gander at it.

Berry's face was impassive. "First of all, ma'am, I had no idea that Detective Nancy was yours."

Carbonella scowled. "How 'bout we cut the ma'am shit. There is enough interagency bullshit without two old friends squabbling. By the way, how's Gary? Still with him?"

"Sure. He's over at the 29th. We didn't want the hassles of working together."

She nodded. They'd been a couple since the Academy. Carbonella leaned past him.

"Who's that?"

Berry rubbernecked around her, "Oh, The good-looking one? Hostage." He lowered his voice, "She's Senator Stonegate's secretary. Said he's on the way. There was another one, some hooker."

"Redhead?"

He nodded.

"Grab her!"

"Can't, Carbonella. We took her to get checked out by an EMT and she bolted."

"Son-of-a-bitch!" Carbonella glared at Berry, good friends or not. "That's the training your people have?"

He held up his hands. "I transferred in last week."

"Well, goddamn. Can we at least search for her?"

"We're on it." He walked back toward the secretary.

"Lieutenant?" The patrolman from the tape called. "There's a woman out here who's looking for someone who may have been involved.

"Victim, or just curious?"

"Says her man was—"

"Listen, sir," a woman's voice came from behind the patrolman. The woman poked her head out.

"Holy crap," uttered Carbonella.

"I need to talk to whoever is in charge."

"Let her in, Ronnie."

He took a deep breath, "What, let her in? She's already …" He gave up and waved her forward.

Carbonella rolled forward. "Doctor MacPherson. Gina Carbonella, Homeland Security."

She held up her badge for a second. "We've been on the lookout for you for a couple of days. Where have you been?"

Doc waved her away. "Listen, since you used my name, I assume I don't need to give any back-story. I heard about this on the television, morning news. Was Stan involved?"

Carbonella rolled closer to the doctor. "I don't know. Give me a minute." She spoke back toward her shoulder, "Berry? Any civilians hurt in there?"

"None that I know of."

The doctor's face was a picture of relief. "This wasn't the

place he talked about before he left."

Carbonella rolled in closer yet, "I've been watching the two of you since before Stan lost his memory. I've been ... never mind. Where did Stan go last night?"

"There is a warehouse about a mile from here. He thought Mu'izz was using it as his headquarters, maybe living there too."

"What?" Berry's ears perked up at the mention of Mu'izz, his cop killer. "Where exactly are you talking about? Better yet, can you take us there?"

I sat for hours in the dark warehouse. The lack of lighting was to intimidate me, but it was more like a chat among friends. Hell, I heard from voices that I rarely had a chance to know.

Mu'izz, on the other hand, ran in and out a few times and three of his goons dragged their knuckles after him, too. About the time the windows lightened up they pulled me into Mu'izz's apartment. I pretended not to know where anything was, hoping that the idiot guards thought maybe I was on the way in when our little fisticuffs demonstration kicked off.

My inner smart-asses spouted off comments about our hosts. I'll have to guess where they got their penchant for being sarcastic. I, however, wasn't in the mood to laugh.

I leaned clumsily against the apartment wall and watched those who belonged. They didn't have to wear the zip ties like me. Those little things acted like a name tag in reverse. At conventions, everyone knows you belong if you wear the tag. Here they knew I didn't belong because of the ties.

Several unshaved cretins wandered through. Apparently, they were new to this little cell of terrorists, but since they didn't wear zip ties, everyone grunted face-to-face and slapped each other's back during a hug. Man, Mu'izz really was connected to Isis.

What would happen if these morons found out he gave not one monkey turd about Jihad and Islamic ideology?

Jacques chuckled gently, and Ahn snorted with a grunt.

Mu'izz and one of the morons ambled in the direction of the refrigerator, I suppose for something to eat. They hung around in there for a while, and then Mu'izz looked for something outside the cooler. He found a napkin and wiped his mouth after his first bite. His cohort lounged against the wall, cheeks bulging. Little chunks cascaded from his lips while he chewed like a cat and tried to catch food with every bite, licking the side of his mouth with every chew.

"Abdul," I called out get Mu'izz's attention. He pivoted and gazed at me, chewing the last morsel arms akimbo. If he was trying to appear to be Superman, it didn't work. "You know that the longer I'm gone, the more likely it is an armed conflict will happen here."

He snorted, rudely scratched himself (or did a little hip-hop dance, don't know which) and turned to leave, only to stop after two steps. "I hadn't realized that you were so all-important, Stan."

"I'm not. In fact, the police captain hates me, thinks I'm an idiot."

"He's dead."

"Who is?" The inner band stilled, cats ready to pounce.

"Captain Beaufort. Killed him when I escaped." He laughed. It wasn't an insane laugh, more like a teenager explaining to his chums about copping his first feel of bare titty. "I shot him and several other cops." He turned to walk off.

"Well, then. They're probably outside right now!" It felt good to yell after him. "You *are* a dumbass. Killing a cop and coming straight home."

His voice trailed in from the bedroom, "Got a plan."

Brother Mick chimed in, *Sounds like he's confessing something.*

Hank took heed, and when he did, something danced down my back again. Not the Stanky Leg this time, though. This was more like a spider tap-dancing while being electrocuted.

Mu'izz walked out of the bedroom fixing his French cuffs with links. "Got a hostage."

I knew what he meant but rubbernecked for the show of it. "Yeah? She pretty? You know you can get more if she's pretty."

A lummox lumbered in, grunted at Mu'izz, and chattered in the mystery language I thought of as Arabic. Mu'izz shot an eyeful at me and left through the apartment doorway. Fully ten seconds later, he came back in, doing his utmost not to look as though he was walking like his ass was slammed.

Hank chuckled and made lewd comments, something about a corn cob. I let him have his fun. "Something wrong, ol' ISIS Guru?"

"Piss off, Stan." He didn't even glance at me when he said it.

That was like farting on a flame. It was a hot time to be had. The noise of laughter inside my head was uncontrollable. That is, until Ol' Abdul yelled at two of the dunces and they stomped over; one of them had a really bad scar and a mangled eye the color of moldy chowder. I think he should have worn an eye patch, but truthfully, he was scarier without one, and if that was the effect he wanted, kudos to him. I mean, his face caused a shrinkage factor of two or three simply by turning in my direction, and I wasn't even close to cold water.

He grabbed my arms and yanked me around until I stood up. Then the two of them highstepped me out of the door and up a stairway, right behind ol' Mu'izz. I hadn't realized how long Mu'izz and I had been verbally fencing, but it was no longer nighttime. It was quite easy to see where we were stepping.

We stopped on a little landing in front of a large, fixed window with a wonderful view of the alley. To a trained eye, the place crawled with SWAT, police, and probably Feds, too. I had to control myself to keep from jumping up and down.

Mister One-Eyed Moose stood behind me and jerked me around, like the snap of a fresh towel. "Stand there so those idiots can see you." His voice had the timbre of a whine mixed with a growl. It was that special sound a dumbass makes.

I eyed him with a bit more respect, but not much. Then I took a quick survey to size things up. Mu'izz had his goons strategically positioned around the warehouse, and true to my recon, they all had wonderful American-made weapons in their possession.

All the orifices from the bottom up, snapped shut. But it traveled like detcord – fast enough it seemed simultaneous.

What do you think, Hank?

Well 'bout time, wanker. Thought you were—

Hank.

We need to work on those ties on your arms.

That's it?

One-Eyed Nimrod shook me again, and the movement ended with him placing a Ka-bar blade against my throat, edge to skin.

I stood still.

Out of the corner of my eye, I noticed someone placing a large piece of poster board next to me. I tried to look-see, but a nasty grunt bubbled out of One-Eye, and feeling his knife hand tightening, changed my mind. We stood there for a few moments, and then he dragged me back to the apartment. There, he shoved me against a blank wall and stood guard at the door, I guess to keep me from escaping.

I suggest patience.

Thanks, Brother Mick, but we need to at least work out a way to wriggle out of this place.

Any other ideas floating around in here?

The silence gave me chills.

Hank's voice interrupted the quiet. *I say, old boy, I might have a spot of an idea.*

CHAPTER THIRTY-NINE

They'd come in quietly, not a single siren had sounded. The tactical squads, stationed within attack parameters, were ready. The Command Post was rough on the outside – an old recreational vehicle parked around the corner from the entrance alley. Carbonella's crew had driven it in after she'd made a call.

Alice sat before her computer checking through her rundown of the equipment. John and Sam both worked their earpieces around their respective heads, checking the volume on their mikes. Both of them horsed around pretending they were Dick Tracy on a case.

Carbonella listened to Sally rambling on about nonsense. The mystery woman's nervous energy was astounding. Add to that, she actively studied all of the equipment and everyone around her, acting like a baby investigating the world.

Carbonella didn't care about the babbling. Her mind centered on Nancy more than anything else, anyway. He hadn't been her partner for long, but he'd been a great guy and certainly didn't deserve what had happened to him.

A sicko with an authentic bloodlust was involved here, and Carbonella had to discipline herself to keep focused. Crazies like this were capable of almost anything, so Carbonella resigned herself to sitting in this cramped RV, confined to her wheelchair while appearing to spend the time with rambling Sally. Her mind whirred, spinning the case facts like a dervish. She kept coming up with the end is near, like some idiot with a sandwich board walking up and down Broadway.

Sam peered over, "Okay, Boss. John and I walked around the street and pretended an argument where we could see down the ally. They have lookouts in several key places."

"Make it march, Sam." Carbonella's face showed boredom deluxe, "I'm not in the mood for drawn out. Concise briefing."

He swallowed quickly and leaned into her, "Sorry, Carbonella. They're set up. No telling what kind of preparations they have in this alley. Hell, anybody with any kind of smarts will tell you that moving down that alley is running down a kill zone."

She dismissed him with a wave, "Now tell me how we're at least as smart because we're federal."

"Okay, Okay." He sighed, "Guess I do it this way too often."

Carbonella glared, and he clamped his mouth shut with a nod.

Sally sat in the corner and chuckled to herself. At least her mind wasn't centered on Stan.

There was some much-needed levity here.

Sam braved it again. "Our people have their IT hookups, and as we speak, we are mounting cameras to give us a view of the warehouse doors and entryways like the alley. Red team has infiltrated through the shops to the east and now stand ready to move from halfway down the alley. Blue team is set for covering watch. We have a helo on the pad ready to move at your go."

Carbonella leaned back into her wheelchair, "Was that hard?" Sam shook his head.

"Okay." She spun her chair to turn her attention to Sally. "We have been tracking you for months. What exactly is your relationship with Stan? You his contact, partner, what the hell are you?"

Sally, too, sat back. She rested her hands on the arms of her chair, "I'm his psychiatrist."

"You're more than that."

Sally nodded and stared at Carbonella, "I am."

"You know Stan has been working for—" "Carbonella?" exclaimed Alice.

Carbonella continued to stare at Sally but answered Alice, "What?"

"You'll want to see this." She turned to Sally. "Both of you."

The two women crowded in to view the monitor in front of

Alice. On it was a picture of the front of the warehouse, and above the door in a window stood two men and a placard.

Carbonella pointed at the window. "Zoom in there. Okay, now enlarge it."

The picture expanded until the men were recognizable: a very big man held a knife to Stan's neck. Stan wasn't pleased. Sally grabbed the back of Alice's chair.

"All right, now move the focus to the left and fix the sign in the center. Enlarge and enhance."

They all stared. What they saw didn't surprise any of them, but it did present some puzzles.

"Okay." Alice thumbed one of the control knobs. "That will take a while."

"Maybe not. Call Ronn— Uh, call Lieutenant Berry on the radio." Alice turned her back while she worked the radio. Carbonella turned to Sally, "How did Stan get up there?"

Doc shrugged. "I'm not really sure. We got into town yesterday, had a confusing reunion with Detective Nancy."

"You talked with Detective Nancy yesterday?" Sally nodded.

"What was that all about?"

"Lieutenant Barry on the radio."

Carbonella grabbed the handset and nodded thanks to Alice. "This secure?"

"It can be on our end, but I'm not sure about theirs."

Carbonella nodded. "Lieutenant Berry, this is Gina Carbonella. "Is the senator's secretary still with you?"

"I think she's grabbing a cup of coffee, but I can have someone get her."

"No, not yet." Carbonella thought for a second. "I'm at the secondary location. It's a warehouse, and we think we have Mu'izz trapped. He's been using this place as a headquarters. It's well fortified, and they have at least one hostage. They've displayed him in a window, a placard next to him with their one demand."

"Which is?"

"They want to talk to Senator Stonegate."

"The one whose secretary is here?"

"Yup."

There was a pause for about a minute. "The same Stonegate that's been touted as a front-runner for the vice-presidential position?"

"He is also the Chair on the Terrorism Committee. There is only one Stonegate.

Charismatic as hell, isn't he? Anyway, that's why I need to talk to his secretary. And you need to zip over here. Put someone else in charge over there. This is the place you want to be. Gonna get crazy as hell."

"Okay." He turned to the officer next to him, "Have someone find the senator's secretary and get her over here."

"Ronnie?"

"Yes."

"Keep things quiet will you?"

"Sure."

CHAPTER FORTY

The pretty blonde fought through the crowd outside the Senate chamber heading for Senator Stonegate. "Senator," her voice pierced the noise but not enough. Several senators turned, but she ignored them, keeping her eyes on Stonegate; they only wanted to lick her with their eyes anyway.

"Senator!" She walked professionally, but firmly through the throng around him. The crush of bodies intense. An anonymous hand brushed against her breast. Asshole. She ignored him too, kept her attention on Stonegate. She tapped his shoulder, two raps before he turned away from his colleagues.

Irritation radiated from him. "Yes." His eyes were sharp and cutting.

"Sir, your secretary is on the line. Says it's important."

"Tell her I'm in the midst of lobbying for the position. I'll call her back." He turned back to the other senators.

He felt her tap again, "What!"

"I'm sorry, sir." Red-faced and close to tears. "She instructed me to say, 'The story is to burn.'"

The senator stared. With all the pandemonium around him, he simply stared at his aide.

Snatching the phone, he strode into one of the side anterooms. "This has to be good, Amy. I'm lobbying for the big VP vote."

"I know you are. But right now, you have a chance to jump way ahead of the pack."

She let a second or two of silence give her words gravitas, but it made him bark, "I'm waiting."

She answered with an edge to her voice herself. "Right now, you are a little flashlight in the middle of the crowd. If you come down here, you will be a beaming lighthouse in a darkened field."

He exhaled, pointedly. "Explain."

She quickly outlined her plan of helping the Terrorism Task Force while on the ground in the midst of a terror attack. "The task force belongs to your committee. You give them personal leadership, your popularity will take off better than Rudy Giuliani during 9/11."

"But I have to leave during the hearings."

"The hearings? That's sinking down into the fray. What I'm telling you is, if we do this right, they can stuff the hearings."

"What?"

"Listen, honey. The Senate confirmed Gerry Ford by *acclamation*. He was the only one they even considered. This move would give you the same notoriety, the same ability to sway the

Senate. Like I said, stuff the hearings. It will be Ford all over again. It won't matter who the president nominates because the Senate won't ratify anyone but you."

The senator pursed his lips and let his eyes roam all over the room. "Hell of a chance, baby."

"Yes, it is. But honey, being in politics is chancy, and this is what the Caucus is all about.

Our sole purpose was to put you in the VP seat. This is the best way I know. Besides, Mu'izz got away."

"What!"

"He ran out, killing Beaufort and yelling 'Allahu Akbar.' He's their prime suspect."

His jaw muscle popped; his mind whirred. A deep breath while blinking slowly, and he nodded, "Okay. Don't let them do a thing until I get there." He hung up, turned toward his aide who now stood right outside the anteroom. "Get me to New York the quickest way possible."

He tossed her the phone. "C'mon. And call the news outlets. Tell them you have a story."

"Hey! What happened to you, you one-eyed big galoot. I'll bet some girl kicked your ass."

Hank laughed, but I heard an *Oh, shit* from somewhere inside. Galoot glared with his good eye at me but said nothing.

Maybe another tactic.

I pushed my back into the wall and stood. Once up, I tried to swagger like a rap star but instead, ended up feeling like an old man in a rest home trying to keep from crapping his pants. I walked closer to him, and he watched carefully.

I bounced around imitating Mohamed Ali. "How about a little Savate, *boxe française,*

French foot fighting?" I let Hank take over, trusting he understood what to do.

Ol' One-Eye smiled like a hungry fox, bounced and bobbed around, too.

Hank grunted convincingly as Mister Cyclops worked his feet, raising his hands to the ready position, good balance and very confident. I'm sure my smile was goofy because I hadn't a clue what was about to happen.

The big man swung with his left and as I pulled away, I saw it as a feint. His right foot lifted in a high roundhouse kick.

Hank was pretty good. The big man's spin underway, Hank slid under with a kick of his own. I'll bet his one good eye bulged and about launched when Hank connected with the big guy's ball-sack. I know his rocks sounded like castanets at a flamenco dance-off, and his coloring dropped to a pale green before he dropped.

Mon dieu! *Well done, Hank.* Jacques led the Inner Audience with his comments. The others overlapped so much it was hard to hear specifics, although I did hear Ahn's double grunt of approval.

While the giant was down, I ran to snatch his weapons. Hank forestalled me. *Wait, Stan. Check his pockets.*

I thought Hank was full of shit but did it anyway. God, I

hated putting my hand in those pockets. I felt something.

Holy shit, was that …

God, he was hung like a donkey. I jerked my hand out.

Fuck!

The other pocket Stan. Another pocket.

Shit.

I really wanted to give Hank the bird or even the evil eye, but it would be like staring at my own hand. I slid my hand into the other pocket.

Be damned! A pocketknife. And a large one too, the kind with a thumb stud.

I started to cut my wrists free.

Stop, Stan. Put that thing in your sock. Yeah, like that. Now grab his pistol. Let them pound on you for a while, Stan.

As he said it, several boneheads rounded the door, and it was as though they had heard Hank telling me what to do.

It hurt like a bitch.

CHAPTER FORTY-ONE

The streetlights stood stately, shining their orange lights on the limo as it passed through the deserted streets. Inside sat the senator with his aide, going over the list of senators he'd yet to schmooze. The radio played softly in the background. A popular talk show host speculated on who the president's choice would be, and when he might submit that name for approval to the Senate.

Stonegate's smile widened each time his name came from the radio, but his brows deepened at the same time. If this works, it'll be like 1973.

He checked himself in his mirror as the limo stopped, making sure he looked his best. The door opened and he stepped out. A quick glance at his surroundings showed him the warehouse district, a tad shabby and inner city, no one in sight except a drug addict tying off his arm and a homeless man building a cardboard house. The only vehicle to be seen sat parked across the way under a streetlamp.

He strode down the street, ignoring the drizzle of rain, with his aide two steps behind. Ahead, a door opened from the parked car and Amy stepped out. He saw her shapely leg first; in her arms she carried a stack of folders, low in front as she walked.

Damn sexy. Those things do bounce when she walks. His eyes tracked them as he waved.

A broadcast van rounded the corner as she approached. Before they parked, yet another entered from the intersection behind her. The block was alive with media.

Amy leaned in close so the crews couldn't see what she said, "Are you sure you want to do this right now, John? Let's at least wait for some news coverage. Right now, nobody actually knows where you are." She shook her head. "Just brush up on this stuff and—"

"I'm doing it. Those vans know. Besides, that little pissant cannot tell me what he will or won't do."

"This isn't your part of the Caucus. We have someone to take care of Mu'izz."

"You mean the little hooker?" His voice echoed back at him from the buildings as he stopped to stare at Amy.

The edge to her voice acid, the set of her jaw stiffened. "I don't care what you think about her. Your job is to become the vice president."

"I told you before. I have the balls to do that. And because I do, I also have the power to do what I want. I will not stand still while this piece of shit tells me what he will and won't do."

He waved her forward. "March on, woman."

She leveled her gaze at him while the corners of her mouth teased upward. Then with a nod to the side, she walked down the alleyway.

The sudden darkness of the urban passage made him blink several times, but it did no good. The three of them walked into the back street, deeper into the stench of rotten garbage. The drizzle was more forceful now but not enough to wash out the smell. Twice he stepped through God knows what, and whatever the second thing was, it stuck on his shoes, probably ruined them. The sound of their footsteps echoing off the buildings didn't help his attitude either.

To his eye, there was a paucity of guards around. He would have had several, but the lack of them did give him reason to relax some. Mu'izz. What a dumbass.

They stopped at a grimy door to a warehouse. Seconds later, it opened. Beyond the door, the air was as black as the darkest part of the alley, but at least musky dankness replaced the reek of rotting refuse. Faint sounds of curt business discussions echoed as he entered, but they weren't close. They filtered from further in the building. The senator guessed it came from beyond the next doorway ahead, where light slivered through the door jamb.

The exterior door shut on him and the two big men beside him. Their body odors hung over him like ghosts while they marched through the lightless room.

Through the door, he stood in fierce light, and a veil of silence surrounded him. The two guards spread out farther and stood at the sides of that door. Stonegate stepped forward, thankfully, free from the body fetor. Somebody swiveled in a chair. His vision resolved and he saw that everyone inside stared at him, and the swiveling was a man turning to face him. Mu'izz. "Senator," Mu'izz spoke softly.

As quiet as it was, Mu'izz's whine grated. Stonegate scowled, this prick is condescending to me?

The large hand of a guard prevented Stonegate from marching to Mu'izz. "I don't know what the hell you think you're doing," his head indicated the thug beside him, "but we all signed on for a specific thing, joining with the rest of us in the Caucus to place me in the White House."

Mu'izz puffed air. "Did what?"

Stonegate shrugged free from the hand and stepped forward. "You know damn well what you signed—"

"I signed up for ISIS at the request of your Caucus. Do you understand exactly what that means? They demand certain things, and loyalty is their coin. They will not tolerate disloyalty. I'm ISIS. you ain't."

Mu'izz stroked his beard with the back of his fingers and grinned to himself, almost as a private joke. "While I'm not a fan of what they do, my association with them was very profitable for us, including you. I intend to disappear and use my money before ISIS comes nosing around." He crossed to his coffee table and picked up his tea for a sip, sitting on his couch as he did.

Stonegate rushed forward, "Hell, no!" The one-eyed guard grabbed him before he reached Mu'izz and held him in a bear hug. Stonegate stared at the Goliath with no effect. "Let go, you moron! I'm a senator of the United States," he hissed. He turned toward Mu'izz. "Are you insane? I'm Berne! Tell your henchman to let go of me." Mu'izz nodded and the big man freed the senator.

"This is bullshit." Carbonella stood up on her good leg, grabbed the table beside her in the RV, and pushed the wheelchair away. "Somebody get me a cane, or crutches, or some goddamned thing I can lean on. I'm done with that four-wheeled scooter." The edge to her voice filled the entire RV. She hopped over to Alice and waited for the girl to raise her head.

It didn't happen. Instead, Alice gazed intently at her computer screen. She glanced up once and back to the screen but didn't acknowledge Carbonella. A full minute of silence passed before she put her hands on her lap and turned to her boss.

Carbonella's eyebrows shot up like a ventriloquist's dummy with the same amount of expression change that it might have. "What is so interesting that you ignored me for so long?"

"Huh?"

"What is so interesting?"

"Media trucks moving into the area."

Carbonella grabbed the monitor and turned it toward her. "This is where Mu'izz is, right? How did they know?" She craned her head, eyes searching for something. "And where's the doctor?"

"Dunno, boss," grunted Sam. "Didn't know we were supposed to guard the doctor.

Thought we were after the bad guys."

John leaned out the door. "Crap. They swarmed in like bees while we were jawing, boss."

"It's Carbonella, not boss. Anyone have something for me to hobble with yet?"

"Yeah, Carbonella, I'll go see if I can find something." John left.

"While he's gone, Sam, find out how the media trucks knew.

And you find me a flippin' cane too!" He shut the door on the way out. Carbonella turned to Alice, "What else happened while we had our eyes closed?"

"Has to do with the senator. I think someone tipped them off."

The door opened and in walked a uniformed officer holding a cane. Carbonella waved,

"Over here. I'm the one in need of a cane. Thanks." She turned to Alice. "Okay, the senator.

Go."

Alice talked, eyes on the screen, "It seems someone from his office tipped off the media that he would be dealing with a terrorist ... hmm. The name Mu'izz surfaced somewhere. It's piecing together. But, what's the deal?"

Carbonella hobbled over to the only other swivel chair in the RV and sat, fingers tapping on the cane. "Is this a huge grandstand for the president's choice to be VP? Or, is this more subtle, shedding Mu'izz like a molting snake?"

"Dunno." Alice fiddled with her keyboard for seconds then peered sideways at her boss and raised her eyebrows. "Maybe Doctor MacPherson might have a clue. Wasn't she around earlier?"

Carbonella turned her head around a like a curious owl. "And again, we're back to what happened to the good doctor? Don't think she's been around for quite some time."

Sam came back in. "A bunch of media vans must have followed the senator like the

Hebrews following Moses. He's in the warehouse now."

"How the hell did he get in there without us knowing?" Sam shrugged without uttering a sound.

"Goddamn it. Are we a federal task force, or simply a bunch of clowns stuffed in an RV?

Don't shrug at me."

Alice stammered and Sam simply stood slack-jawed.

"Yeah, yeah." Carbonella limped to the doorway. "Get

ready. Sometimes I think we are the biggest joke."

CHAPTER FORTY-TWO

The growing darkness made the streetlights dazzle and the view down the alley more shrouded. The entrance to the alley was easily seen, but she paid greater attention to the vans with local TV station logos on them. They parked innocently up and down the street, most without even deploying their Sat-Links, as if locking up for the night as though they doubted that anything newsworthy might be in the offing tonight, but maybe after dawn.

She strolled across the street, head down, hands in jacket pockets, hugging the shadows.

Her hope was that no one would notice a solitary figure.

Turning the corner, she straightened her posture; the farther she walked, the more erect she became. Even her hands came free from the jacket.

She turned down the dark alley connecting to the one she wanted. The fetid stench of fermenting Chinese food filled the air from the nearby dumpster, quite a change from the smells on the day of her decision.

It had been like the other days, recovering from the slaughter. The sun beamed fiercely, turning what remained of the village into a dusty furnace, so bright it hurt the eyes. Clouds of flies swarmed. Concrete, wood, and bricks lay scattered among limbs and body parts of the dead.

A stray dog loped by, dragging a severed forearm, and although people all along the animal's route tried to catch it, the animal scurried quickly this way and that, evading them.

Goddamned jihad.

This was not the first attack she'd seen, but this was different. This was the first in which she'd lost someone. Before,

257

her job had been to render aid. This time, she was considered injured.

Her eyes hurt, not only from the brightness but from weeping too. She was so tired of it.

She'd been crying for days, ever since the attack, and tears would be rolling down her cheeks had she not already depleted her tear ducts.

Scores of people still cried, though, and the sound echoed through the wreckage. Each wail announced yet someone else rending their clothes in mourning, on finding proof of the loved one's death.

The morning breeze had expired hours before and as the windless day progressed, dust clouded the air. The stench of rotting, eviscerated bodies made the day never-ending, constantly reminding those who searched that their task was nearly hopeless.

Because the dusty air was stale and held the fetor from the bodies, many wore *shemagh*s, the scarf that wraps the face and worn in the deep desert to combat harsh conditions — wind, sand, the blaze of the sun.

A disturbance down the way moved the mourners around like sheep, as angry shouting sparked a fight. The voices escalated to screaming, gunshots rang through the air, and people scattered like pellets from a shotgun blast.

They're back? Another attack?

Very little light punched into the alley from the streetlights behind her, and most of that glimmered faintly in the center. Moving along the edges meant the going was much slower, but time wasn't an issue.

There were only two buildings before the corner and she stepped over several tripwires, which dictated an even more sloth-like speed.

She passed the corner, moved to the left, and made out the

warehouse door on the left. She stayed in the darkest part of the passage. Although the guards hid well, she easily evaded them – they were exactly where they were supposed to be, and her mind wandered.

She peered down the village road. The firing moved toward her. Two men at the heart of the fight headed her way, each wore a shemagh on their face. They both fired and moved, yelling at the other in English as they fought, both vowing the death of the other.

The firing came even closer, one slipped into the building she occupied. He ran through her doorway, speeding to the broken window to her right, murder in his eyes.

Her heartbeat ramped up as did the trembling in her arm. With several panting breaths, she steeled herself and pounced on him like a cat, scratching at his eyes, clawing at the shemagh. She wanted to see the bastard who killed her Benji, but her nails were broken, and her fingers only rubbed blood on the covering.

With a push of his arm, he shoved her away, "Move, woman." He didn't even glance back as she fell.

The other fighter lurched through the window, firing as he came. The room exploded with sound, stabbing her ears. She scrambled to safety, and the man she'd attacked fired back, but the attacker knocked him down before he had a good aim. Both pistols clattered away.

The men grappled, writhing together on the floor, punching, kicking. They attacked fully, each drawing blood and grunting, the effort visible.

Sweat poured from the men as they danced for position in the furnace-like room.

The one who'd arrived first took advantage of a split second mistake and charged, knocking his attacker to the ground. He straddled the man, gripped his neck, and squeezed. The second man jerked both arms above his head and rolled, breaking the fierce choke hold, and lurched to his knees.

The man stood, and she heard his strained voice, "Did you kill the couple in their car five months ago?"

They danced for position again.

She heard a labored laugh and then, "They were dogs."

That was what the killer had called her when he attacked her – a dog. He hadn't said

"bitch." It had always been "dog." She remembered the repeated insult as he had pushed her face into the dirt and pumped into her, "You dog. You're a dog ..."

She grabbed a concrete shard with one hand, and wiped her brows with the other. She had to see, but which to kill?

The second man punched hard, doubling the other over. A fast follow-up kick, but he missed. The first man twisted, returning with a terrific blow to the second man's jaw. As they steadied themselves, they both pulled knives, the first man a military blade, the second a *jambiya,* the traditional Arab knife.

They lunged, their knives a swirl of activity as they circled, both drawing blood, but as his blood ran, the second man backed to the window. "We will kill each other here, now, or one will die later." She did not recognize it as the voice as Benji's killer. "I do not wish to die. I will kill you later."

"Go ahead and run. You chickenshit. I'll find you later, asshole."

She recognized the language spoken as American English, same as the killer. Both voices were hoarse. The one she'd attacked had steel-hard, beady eyes; the other's were brown and almond-shaped. One was her son's killer.

That knowledge gave her strength. She would find that man.

She eased open the door and slipped into the even darker interior of the warehouse. Her hand trembled at the anticipation of what would soon come, and she used cleansing breaths to calm herself, but it did no good. She'd waited a long time for this, and her back was cramping from the tension. She had to relax.

Today. I'll finish it today, she reminded herself. Rest easy, Benji.

Voices filtered from the apartment and pulled her toward her targets. The closer she came to the door, the easier it was to identify the voices. Her heart thumped hard in her neck, and like a runner before a race, she shook her hands to relax, and then she stood alone in the dark, listening, waiting to be on point.

They were there. After all the ferreting she'd done, after all the falsehoods, she still did not know which was the killer. She absently fingered her knife. The voices coming through the door gave her strength and she smiled to herself. She knew the sounds.

She'd made up her mind.

Her finger tapped lightly on the knife; there would be no cowering today, as she'd done so long ago. She hardened herself to the task of the day, no matter how painful it could be. The sound of her blood whooshed in her ears with each heartbeat, but she ignored it. This was the day. One way or the other, no matter how painful, she would exact payment today, even if both men had to die. Either Benji's killer would be dead by the end of the day, or she would.

She shrugged. Maybe both

CHAPTER FORTY-THREE

I watched the live-action show featuring Mu'izz, Stonegate, and mister One-Eye. I had to admit, the ol' senator held his own. *Move now, Stan. They're still distracted.*
I shuffled an inch or two toward the door and then stopped.
Not now, Hank. I want to watch a bit longer.
Mu'izz nodded to One-Eye who stuffed a filthy rag into the senator's mouth before picking him up. Stonegate fought rather well for an old man, certainly better than the fight I had with myself to keep from chuckling.

At further direction from Mu'izz, the gorilla dragged the senator to a chair and plopped him into it. Stonegate was fast, but that big bastard was quicker. He jumped behind Stonegate and held the senator's shoulders, pinning him to the chair.

Stonegate made sounds like a moose with its balls caught in a bear trap. I didn't know what color the senator would end up, but right now, he was green and red at the same time. I'm talking pissed.

"Uncomfortable are we, senator?" Mu'izz's grating voice remained calm, almost bored. "To continue, I will take my part of the money and disappear, but since you brought up Berne, there is a little Caucus business we need to go over." The senator appeared ready to detonate.

Mu'izz sat sedately, a king gazing out upon his subjects, which was bullshit. I think everyone in the room would smile as they slipped a knife between his third and fourth rib.

Hell, I knew Stonegate would.

Mu'izz's voice grated even more than before. A cat sharpening its claws on a chalkboard wouldn't have set my teeth anymore on edge. Hell, his every word felt as if a needle scraped my spine.

He walked toward Stonegate. "Let's see, Senator. We have

me, of course, I was there, and we can't forget Stan over there in the corner. Still with us, Stan?"

My lips would have curled on their own had they not been so swollen, so Hank flipped him off, but truthfully it was a race. I tried. He beat me.

Mu'izz chuckled, but I had a whole chorus inside me telling him to fuck off. I wasn't sure, but I thought I heard Sibyl agree too. At any rate, it gave me the kind of peace a Buddhist monk must have. I was at one with my inner world.

The senator's face turned a kind of bruised purple from rage. He tried to stand, again but the One-Eyed Lummox wouldn't let him.

Cocking his head to the side, Mu'izz watched, and then stepped directly before the senator. "I see you are still with us, John. It is John, isn't it? I mean, no one calls you that anymore, perhaps I'll start a new trend." He raised his head, pleased with himself. "Oh, I mustn't forget Amy here. She is truly in the Caucus. And where is … Ah." The redhead stepped free of the shadows.

Those two are ready to kill someone, observed Hank.

Oui. *Someone has crimped their nipples, and they didn't like it at all. Mu'izz had better watch his back.*

I had to admit the boys were right. The women had something stoking their furnaces. I searched anew for escape routes.

The women stepped forward.

Shit. Watch out.

I know, Hank. My eyes followed the redhead. Dressed for combat, complete with a loaded web vest, she had a Ka-bar strapped to her calf. My sphincter slammed shut so hard, I was surprised it didn't scare everyone in the room. Mu'izz is an ass, so I didn't even think about warning him. I should have screamed at Stonegate, but he was an uppity prick. Frankly, I didn't care about him either. So, I tried to crawl closer to the corner to watch Mu'izz get his throat cut.

Except for the combat dress code, Amy was almost a mirror of the redhead. I'd never noticed a resemblance between them before, but it was there now … something about the set of jaws and eyes, and their gaits.

Stonegate calmed down a bit when he saw Amy. One-Eye yanked the rag out of his mouth. "What the hell," screamed Stonegate. "This is bullshit. I am Berne!"

Mu'izz had his back to the two women and openly laughed while rubbing the side of his beard, and Stonegate glared at him to the best of his ability.

The women sauntered forward, both holding weapons. The redhead had her knife and Amy had produced a .32 semi-auto from somewhere. She must've had a thigh holster inside that dress of hers.

They gonna hurt that man.

I know, Fox Boy, be quiet.

Amy jacked the slider on her pistol. "Need some answers, Senator?" leaning on the title.

Mu'izz stepped to the side and Stonegate turned to her.

The redhead openly laughed. "The bastard still thinks he's in charge."

Amy sat on the coffee table and crossed her legs at the knee, "John, you were never in charge. I was Berne, not you."

Stonegate straightened, "Of course I was Berne!"

"You weren't. Who the hell talked on the phone? Who exactly made the decisions?"

"I made the decisions." He stared in silence for three or four seconds before his face contorted with scorn. "You arrogant bitch!"

A dark, sultry laugh bubbled from Amy's throat. "I'm the arrogant one?" She leaned forward and lowered her voice and I too, had to lean forward.

A low moan escaped from him, and she chuckled. "Do you remember the conversation we had about the other woman you knew with *Heterochromia iridium*?"

His face was blank as an ice cube.

"Oh, for God's sake! Two-colored eyes, you idiot."

"Who the hell—"

"—do I think I'm talking to?" Her eyes locked onto his and wouldn't let go. "Do you remember the conversation?"

"Yes, I remember. I told you about the little whore I kne—" She pistol-whipped him.

Hank perked up. *Bugger. That's a hell of a mouse he's got growing.*

I had to chuckle. Think you're wrong, Hank. It's not a mouse, more like a rat.

The swelling was huge. It wrapped around the guy's eye and down his cheek. Hell, his eye gave the impression it might jump out of its socket.

I'll give him credit: Stonegate stared hard at her with his good eye.

Amy leaned in close to him. "Only a prostitute because you made her one!"

The redhead stepped forward brandishing her fighting blade, and her voice sounded as deadly as the blade. "You lived with her until you discovered she was knocked up and then you found someone else. You left her, and your daughter, too." The Mistress lunged perfectly, stabbing him low in his gut, non-lethal but extremely painful. "Hello, Daddy."

I have to believe she missed the diaphragm and heart on purpose because of what happened next. The bullet from Amy's pistol hit him right below the throat. He gagged and thrashed. I thought his good eye was ready to explode.

CHAPTER FORTY-FOUR

"Something important is happening in there." Carbonella withered her crew with her glare, and when no one responded beyond looking at the floor, she took in a breath and eased it out.

"Anyone have a thought about what I said?"

Alice said, "My first thought was, were you talking to yourself? You do, sometimes."

Carbonella snake-eyed her.

Alice wore an "oh, shit" expression on her face and swiveled back around to her equipment. Sam had an aura of constipation about him, and John appeared lost in thought, suspicious in itself.

"Okay, my little morons, let's go from the beginning. We know that Sigma was interested in the Caucus and we suspect who the members are, or were. Go!" She pointed at John.

"The senator, Mu'izz, Captain Beaufort, Sigma himself, and probably, our killer redhead."

Carbonella nodded. "Correct. Sigma never got the chance to tell us if there were any more." She tapped the cane for a few seconds while staring into space, then turned to Alice. "*Now* I'm thinking aloud. Why did Stonegate come down here to meet with Mu'izz? Was he about to fake some grandstand thing to push himself through the vote in the Senate? Thus the media soirée. Or is this a possible Caucus meeting? We know Beaufort is dead, but Mu'izz is in there with the senator. What we don't know is where the redhead is, or what kind of condition Sigma himself is in."

"Maybe they are there for some kind of meeting," ventured Alice.

"Wouldn't Sigma let us know what's goin' on?"

"No, Sam, he wouldn't. He doesn't even know we exist. MacPherson knew about us, but she's gone, disappeared. Have you found her at all? And while we are spitballing, where does MacPherson fit in all of this?"

John leaned against the wall near the door. "She's slippery, Carbonella. Vanished into the dark, toward the other crime scene. I checked with the lieutenant over there, but they haven't seen her at all. Maybe she doubled back. Actually, she's acting more like a pro than a regular shrink. It's too much like she's had training, knows what we're doing."

Carbonella nodded knowingly. "All right. Alice, put the word out to our people watching the warehouse that they need to be on alert for anything and everything unusual. Everyone else to your posts. My gut says something is about to break. Alice, you and I will monitor from here. The last thing that needs to happen is a gimp out there trying to direct things and getting in the fucking way."

She hit the wall with her cane, "Sam!" *sotto voce*-d. "I want you in charge out there.

If you have a problem and have a chance to call, go ahead. If it happens too quickly, punt."

"Gotcha, Carbonella." He ducked out of the door.

Carbonella turned back to Alice. "Make sure we can talk."

"Carbonella, this is Sam." The voice came from the radio.

Carbonella grabbed the desk microphone.

The metallic tint added to Sam's voice. "Getting ready for a radio check, but my men tell me they heard what sounded like a gunshot about the time we broke up the meeting."

"Could they tell direction?"

"—side ... warehouse ... need to ... don't know what ..."

Carbonella clamped her jaw tightly as she watched Alice's hands flying across her keyboard. "Can you get him back?"

Alice's eye funneled her apology to her commander. "Don't know. I do think he can still hear you, but I'm not sure."

Carbonella snatched the microphone, "Sam. Can you hear me?" That was stupid. Even if he can, I can't hear him. "Sam. If you can hear me, get in there. Go."

The speaker crackled, "… you can hear, we're … right now … will report ba … Go. Go!"

"Well, shit." Carbonella grabbed her cane and hobbled to the RV door. "Keep working on getting coms. I can't stand sitting in here, I'm going out on the ground." Exiting through the door wasn't as hard as she thought. Her leg didn't hurt as much as it had. She left the door open and limped down the alley.

Her agents were on top of things. They moved well. Two more steps into the dark alley and she was dazzle-blind from the explosions.

I watched Amy saunter to the senator to inspect. The redhead wiped her knife on Stonegate's jacket, leaned in close, and mumbled something to him. The only thing I made out was her last word, "Asshole." It was fitting.

Stonegate stared. Was the terror on his face because he now knew they meant to kill him, or if it was what the Mistress had said. He had a burst of energy, he writhed, gagging and gurgling.

Amy leaned down, "The Caucus was engineered by Tess and me, strictly to raise your hopes so we could extinguish them. By the way, the woman died."

While everyone's attention was on Stonegate, I snicked open the pocketknife, freed my legs, and then my wrists. I remained in the corner, blending into the wall, but I had to move some. I slowly stretched my legs to test their condition – sore but not crippling.

Amy sat in Stonegate's blood and talked calmly as if speaking to a five-year-old. "I don't know if you can hear me or not, but I don't care." She arranged her dress like a lady, ignoring all the blood. "The woman you left struggled to free herself of that life. It was a tough year. Then she met a black man, a splendid man, and married him. Together they had another daughter. That was me."

Be damned! Sisters.

Shut up, Hank.

"We had a wonderful life, until you started politics. Your face was on the news constantly, reminding her of your life together. Her depression came quickly. She jumped from the top of the building where you turned her into a whore."

A glance confirmed the senator was dead – macabre face, mangled and pale, slack-jawed.

It was obvious.

Amy saw that too. "Come on, Tess. This asshole deserves more, but it won't do any good." She stood, grabbed her sister's hand and they both calmly walked away.

"Oh, don't go yet, you two." Mu'izz's grating voice was low, his fingertips brushing against his beard. "That was quite a performance. But don't leave." Producing a cup of tea from somewhere, he took a sip. He swallowed, his face centering on mine. "We have another member we haven't heard from yet."

This puzzled me. I didn't have anything to say so far, except maybe yippee.

What's popping, old chap?

Don't know, Hank. Something strange for sure. We're in a room full of killers and we're almost moving to parliamentary proceedings.

The door opened, and Sally walked in from the dark room. My heart leaped and then crashed. The Stanky Leg was back, and it made me shiver.

Mon Ami, she doesn't look at you at all. Her face is set, determined.

Jacques was right, and it had me scratching my head.

"Puzzled, Stan?"

"Shut up, Mu'izz." I watched my wife saunter into the room. Dressed all in dark clothes, clearly she'd snuck through the night to get here.

Mu'izz didn't let it go. "Who was it that told us where you were in Zermatt, Stan?" The bastard chuckled.

"I'll bet she told you later that she was trying to protect you.

But how about when you were trapped by the sisters here? Who showed up to rescue you, and when you left, negotiated a truce? Even better, stayed with you until we arrived."

Hank hawk-eyed Sally with our eyes as she continued to the couch. Her eyes still avoided mine.

I tucked the knife in close. I hadn't a clue what she was doing, but I had to be ready for whatever. My hand teased the edge of it.

Wait, Stan. Don't move yet. You don't want to hear this, but—

Can it, Hank.

There was something wrong. Sally appeared at ease walking around the three killers, as though they were equals. Her demeanor … Was that a glare?

Mu'izz continued, "Sally, why don't you fill your husband in?" He leaned on my title.

"Sure, Abdul." Her full-bodied voice filled me with both expectation and dread. She turned, her eyes were remote as Stonegate's expression.

Holy shit. Watch out, Stan. The way she's standing.

Hank.

But, Stan she turned you in to the police, and—

Han—

I've had a bad feeling about her since—

Goddamn it, Hank. Shut. Up!

My ass cramped so much, it hurt.

This is bullshit.

I studied Sally, but I didn't like what I was seeing.

Was Hank right?

She was talking again.

"… to worm my way into the group, and Stan here was an easy way to do that." It burned when her gaze wiped over me, and I quickly gagged Hank before he twisted a knife into me with his tongue.

She stood, discernably weighing chances across the room. "I

needed something that the group had."

She squatted to adjust her boots and a glint flashed in her right hand. Her eyes cauterized everything they brushed as she stood.

Mu'izz chuckled and ignored her. "Have you figured it out yet, Stan? You were only a pawn, something she used. She didn't care about you at all."

He irritated the shit out of me, but I had no idea whether he was telling the truth or spinning another lie.

I checked her out again. Her eyes didn't soften at all; they were more controlled and determined, as if they could incinerate everything instead of simply cauterize.

Mu'izz chortled, "What did she tell you? She was hunting for someone?" The sound he made turned into a sardonic laugh.

That's what she said.

Shut up, Hank.

"Didn't you ever wonder what she was doing?" He shrugged, "She came to talk with me, wanted to join up. Said she had violence in her but didn't know how to use it. Wanted me to teach her. Even paid me to do it." He took a leisurely sip of his tea; I watched Sally glower and the corners of his mouth lifted up for a nanosecond. "Even interviewed me. Hell, I had to tell her my whole history, all the training I'd had."

Again, he laughed, a hateful sound.

A micro-moment later Sally erupted into action.

I pulled my knife.

Explosions rocked the building. It vibrated first through my shoes, my ears a nanosecond behind, followed by violent shaking. Crap fell from the walls and ceiling alike.

Doc was as agile, like a gazelle, and her eyes focused on me. Her expression of disgust made me shrivel, everywhere.

Is that indecision there? How, when there was clearly so much purpose there?

I didn't get an answer. The whole damn thing surprised me. But let's face it, I have an abundance of smartass in me.

Gunfire erupted beyond the apartment door. Sally snapped her head away from me and ran on, knife at the ready, for Mu'izz. At first, I thought she intended to rally with him and his morons against the attack that burgeoned. She ran straight at him. Then – unbelievably – she yelled, "Benji," ran into him, knocking them both off-balance, and then she stabbed hard catching him near the hip.

Good stab.

I had to admit Hank was right.

Mu'izz was intent on getting into the safe when she cut him.

Amy yelled, "Did you bring those idiots outside?"

I looked around to see who she was yelling at. Decided it must be me. She would be mean as a bull with a nut-cinch on tight.

I tried to think of something extremely witty. "No."

Her hand held the pistol she'd lately killed with, leveled in my direction. If she were closer, I'd be looking right down her barrel.

Another explosion rocked the building and I fell against the wall.

Amy fired, barely missing me. The round sent concrete fragments from the wall in every direction. She had the visage of Lucifer incarnate as she aimed again. The Mistress pushed Amy aside and smiled in my direction like an archfiend, and quick as a striking snake, she threw her Ka-bar.

Hank straightened us to full height and slapped the knife away as it flew point first. I was stunned.

Mercy fuck! That thing almost … then it stuck in the wall. Damn Hank. That was a hell of a show.

Move, Stan!

I fell to the floor as Amy fired again. I grabbed my own knife and high-crawled across the floor.

Gunfire blazed outside. Rounds slugged into and through the door, shattering the wood, blowing it open. Mu'izz and Sally faced off, both as mean as rabid badgers. Mu'izz dragged his left leg, blood streaming into his shoe. He had a knife in one hand and held a phone to his ear with his other, his words inaudible because of all the gunfire. But if his eyes reflected his thoughts, he called for murdering a town full of disabled mothers while nursing their babies.

He dropped his phone and dragged his leg toward the wall, swinging his knife at Sally.

She feinted at his bad leg and stabbed Mu'izz in the other. He lurched for his safe. His knife hand dropped, slicing her shoulder as she stabbed again as he scrambled.

Battle sounds raged. The distinct booms of three or four flash-bang grenades rumbled through, followed immediately by several three-round bursts. Muffled moaning and the smell of carnage filled the air – blood, feces, gunpowder smoke.

Ahn loved smelling the cordite. He didn't say much about the other stuff, though. Those things must be normal about battle for him. The cordite was new. He positively frothed.

Both legs bleeding, Mu'izz opened the safe, and I chuckled, delighted I'd broken the connection between the switches.

Stan.

Not now, Hank. I want to see Mu'izz's face when things don't blow.

Stan!

Not now, Hank. I'm trying to see—

Stan, I put one of them back!

Another explosion rocked the outer warehouse.

What?

The detcord. I reattached one of the detonators when you let me put them back in the safe. You were busy with something else. You know I keep telling you to watch everything.

My head jerked toward the safe.

Not the time for jokes, Hank.

Another shot ricocheted off the wall. It was way too close. The Mistress. She aimed again.

I dropped to the floor as she pulled the trigger. The round

creased my shoulders, burning as it flew by.

That bitch has to die.

Hank didn't even answer. He knew it was true.

Adrenaline set me on fire, hiding my wounds from me. I leaped after her into the warehouse battlefield. The only light came from the muzzle flash of rounds fired. Between bursts, I tripped over a dead terrorist, his weapons clattering across the floor. I followed the sound after them but fighting broke out again and battle noise drowned out everything. I searched my memory for the direction of the weapon I'd heard skidding across the floor.

There!

Thanks, Ahn. I leaped toward it and was attacked from the shadows by the big man grabbing my throat. I rolled hard, breaking his hold, and snatching a knife, as I stood. It was my turn to lunge. I stabbed him quick and hard, sinking the blade into him just below his good eye. The effect was immediate, almost dropping on top of me. I danced backward as he plopped to the floor. Tucked in at his waist was a sidearm. I checked the magazine, saw the glint of brass, charged, and locked the round, safety off.

My eyes adjusted, between the next set of flashes, I saw the Mistress run around a corner.

I took off after my foe but kicked something else. The long gun I was after before! With a careful sweep of my feet, I kicked it again. An AR15. I checked the magazine, full, locked and loaded, and stuck the pistol in my belt.

At the corner, I slowed, clicked the AR15 safety off and flipped around the corner.

CHAPTER FORTY-FIVE

The blast didn't knock Carbonella down, but the shockwave made her stumble; her cane steadied her. The moaning of her people filled the air even before her dazzle-blindness faded.

Claymores. Must've been claymores.

With her sidearm drawn, she moved deeper into the alley, to the cover of a dumpster.

A man's scream of pain erupted from deeper in the alley, a woman's low moan not far away. Several shots banged from the abutting alley, close enough to demand more caution.

The alleyway was nasty and filthy, but she knew she had to crawl. She held her cane in one hand and dragged both her leg and cane to the side. Through the smell of sulfur in the scorched gunpowder, her nose pinched from the rotten stench of the garbage, but as she crawled, the stink of human excrement became stronger. She was several feet away when the man's moaning became breathy, then disappeared. At first sight of the man, she stopped. Most of his face was gone, the remaining eye glazed, and his viscera splayed.

My God. Sam. I sent him out … five minutes later, he's mangled and dead.

Her tears rolled. Her stomach heaved, and a quick jerk of her head sent the vomit away from the body.

Carbonella rose behind Sam's body to view the woman, but had trouble zeroing in on a direction. The moans were slight now, the firefight creeping closer, she took a chance and raised onto all fours and grabbed a look-see.

Carbonella was already nose-blind to the bowel remains, and now the sharp tang of blood hovered over everything. A woman lay sprawled in front of the dumpster, one leg at an impossible angle, fractured and bent mid-thigh, blood spurting from a horrific gash.

Oh, shit.

Carbonella crawled as fast as she was able around the dumpster, pulled her belt from her pants, and tied a tourniquet on the lacerated leg, high toward the hip. The tourniquet tightened,

Carbonella moved toward the other alley.

The cracking of bullets increased. Several bursts fired from different directions simultaneously, loud and frequent. A number of impacting rounds thumping the concrete near her, sparking as they did, as she crawled her way to the fight.

Bullets buzzed through the air like warring hornets. Combatants ran, crawled, all fighting and focused on one idea – the enemy's destruction.

Through the carnage, her ears picked out a familiar voice: Sam giving direction, "Ready! Move!"

He's alive!

Tears streamed down her cheeks.

Order came to the confusion.

At Sam's command, agents fired from overwatch. Others burst from the shadows, each firing of their own volition. Again, smoke from the gunfire filled the air. Three forward agents reached the warehouse, one opened the door, the other two threw stun grenades. The agent at the door fell, a mortal explosion in his chest. Scant seconds later, dazzling brilliance flashed through the door and windows. Carbonella reeled from the shock wave.

Warehouse firing stopped momentarily, and Carbonella took advantage. She struggled forward as quickly as her cane allowed, firing twice on the go. Others assaulted the warehouse, slipping through the door in force.

Inside, a shadow moved and fired – missed.

A machine gun fired from a stairway overhead, strafing the warehouse floor, concrete shards zipped everywhere. Agents fanned out. She stopped, took aim, and fired twice. The machine-gunning stopped.

Light filtered from several open doors and Carbonella's eyes adjusted. A door burst open, letting more light into the large warehouse.

The Mistress ran through.

Carbonella fired. Missed. As she paused to reload, Stan raced out behind the redhead, giving chase. She let them go. The real prize was getting the senator out, and she bet he was in that room.

The firing around her slowed.

"Sam. Sam!" she yelled through growing silence between gun bursts.

"That you, Carbonella?" His voice was in front of her, barely this side of the opening. He was using the door as concealment. Just on the other side, more terrorists had taken up positions, and the gunfire slacked off while they reoriented.

Carbonella hobble-skipped forward for cover next to the door, her shoulder against the cinder block wall, pistol at the ready. "Take this room."

Automatic fire burst from the room, hitting an agent and dropping her to the concrete.

The firing stopped, but every time an agent moved, the gun rattled again. They were pinned.

Stabbing Mu'izz galvanized Sally. Nothing in her life had felt that good.

The explosions outside had startled her, though, and the bastard got away. "Don't run from me," she growled. He'd only gone to a wall safe, and she dove after him, blade still in hand.

A vicious kick caught her in the ribs, knocking the wind from her. Her knife sliced his calf. He dropped the leg too quickly for it to immobilize him. He moved with a limp.

She had to rest for a couple of breaths to recover.

She watched him do something in the safe, and then do a double-take around him. He picked up a green cord, stared at it for a second, and then shrugged, reached in again, Then loped away again.

She forced herself after him. This was what she'd trained for: he was one of the two men in Israel. They were both here, and today she would see the Benji's murderer die. She ran again.

He'd ducked into the weapons store.

She sped up. If he came back out, he'd do so firing. Rounding the door frame, she saw the rifle and dove to the floor.

The gun burst all but ruptured her ears. The bullets struck altogether too close. As soon as the three-round burst stopped, she rolled back to the couch for cover.

Several of Mu'izz's men ran to the apartment door, shooting into the warehouse proper. One had an M60 machine gun on the floor, its barrage deafening. Seconds later, the machine gunner flopped to the ground. The others stopped firing for a second to watch.

Screams filtered in from the warehouse, and the men at the door set up a chant of "Allahu Akbar." At first, simply to bolster their nerves.

But the chant grew, "Allahu Akbar."

Each time louder, "Allahu Akbar. Allahu Akbar! Allahu Akbar!" An assault on the apartment, the firing stepped up.

Working herself to her feet, she ran into the other room only to trip on a huge stockpile of weapons.

She scrambled up again, and saw him. Mu'izz was ready for her. Pistol in hand, he aimed at her chest.

She stood motionless as he stared into her eyes. The memory of Benjamin tugged at her.

This is a man she'd trained so hard to kill. She stared back.

In books and movies, the bad guys always seem to kill the daughters. But this wasn't a story. This had been her life, her baby, her Benji, who'd had his life cut short with a sweep of a knife and thrown at her feet. For years, she'd acknowledged that the two men hadn't recognized her.

That mistake would kill this one.

Sally dove to the weapons pile and grabbed a pistol. She racked the slide as the killer aimed. She pulled the trigger twice, just as that piece-of-shit killer had taught her. One bullet hit his arm, dislodging his aim. The second hit his leg and he stumbled backward.

Springing to her feet, she fired again, twice. They both hit his hips, crippling him and forcing him back. He tripped over a wire!

A huge detonation blew Mu'izz into the opposite wall. Pellets peppered the cinder block and most of the weapons on the other side of the room, zinging like flaming meteorites. The noise deafened her, the cloud of blue smoke suffocating.

The force blew her back too. Her hearing faded; her head rang. She coughed and retched.

Standing still until her dizziness settled, she walked over to gaze at Mu'izz. She wanted to spit on him, but she didn't. Nor did she give in to the temptation of kicking the body. She crawled up next to his bleeding body.

"You don't remember me." She thought of her baby, her husband. "I watched you two fight that day in Israel, and one of you killed my family, my baby."

"You ..." He mumbled and gurgled.

She watched him fight to keep his eyes filled with anger, and like lightning, her hand grasped the knife handle. Then she ran the edge across his neck as hard and slowly as possible.

"You killed my Benji." As she uttered the name, she stabbed him in the chest. Again and again, she stabbed, working her way down his stomach and back up to his magnificently mangled throat.

She stood up straight and watched him die.

Throwing the knife across the room, she picked up a pistol, racked the slide, and slid out of the door, ready to fire. Most of the fighting was over, at least in the apartment, but now she had to find the other man.

CHAPTER FORTY-SIX

They'd found Stonegate. Carbonella leaned over the body, joined by several of her agents.

Sam stood on her left, peering at the body. Sounds of the battle echoed through the apartment. "Carbonella, we need to vamoose." He pushed her gently toward the door.

Carbonella pushed back. "Sam, a sitting senator is dead, and we knew he came in here."

Sam glanced again and gave a curt nod. "I gotcha, boss. I understand, but it doesn't matter at all right now. We have to get the hell out of here." He spoke into his radio. "Need to get the bomb squad in here."

Carbonella pulled her attention away from Stonegate and focused on him. "What do you know?"

He pointed around the room. "There is detcord wound around almost all of the walls and columns."

Her eyes widened for a split second.

"Yeah, boss. We have to un-ass this place. No joke."

Carbonella straightened and canvassed the room. It wasn't protocol, but she had to leave the senator's body behind. "All right. Everyone out." She raised her voice, "You heard me. Up, out. Sam, get out too. No, wait. You called Emergency Bomb Disposal. Got to get them here ASAP. Next, secure a two-block perimeter. Don't let anyone inside that line. Except EBD. Go on!"

As they all left her with the senator, she leaned against the couch.

What the hell have I gotten into now? Goddamn it, Carbonella.

The inspiration struck. She took her phone from her hip pocket and took pictures of the senator from every conceivable angle.

She hobbled to the apartment door. "Hey! I need two or three people in here ASAP. Got to drag this body out of here."

I ducked behind a crate as the bullet thumped into the wood, not far from my head.

This bitch is seriously good, Stan.

Now, Hank? Let me get through this.

I studied the area around me. There were more weapons, mostly in crates, but some lay haphazardly around, a few handguns, sniper rifles, odds and ends. The light from a far room cast beams across the area alongside long shadows. I crawled to those shadows.

Stan, we need to make this quick. Don't forget the detcord.

Shit. I had.

Firing, I ran closer to the Mistress, but from off to my side, someone else fired, the bullet hit the wall next to me.

Amy! Goddamn, I forgot about her, too.

Quite diddling yourself, mate. Mind your business, and don't forget we're on a short fuse.

I didn't tell Hank to shut it. He was right. Instead, I returned Amy's fire and found cover behind a stack of crates. Time was indeed ticking, and I had no idea how long the timer was on the detcord. In truth, I only had Hank's suggestion that there was a time involved; he was an insufferable prick.

If Mu'izz actually did trip it, and he actually had put it on a timer. Maybe, maybe—

Quit screwing around, Stan.

The redhead fired a couple more times. To me, that meant that she was trying to keep my head down.

Getting ready to run?

I took a chance and poked up my head.

I was right. I glimpsed her backside as it turned beyond the next opening.

Damn it.

The feel of the muzzle on my occipital bone made me freeze. I'd forgotten about the sister. Of course, that also meant that she was too close, especially to someone hyped on everything my adrenal glands put out. Plus, she didn't know about Hank.

He twisted hard, raising our arm, dislodging her completely. The move dropped her on her ass. Her pistol fired and I kicked her between her legs, hard, like kicking a door in. It didn't get the same response as kicking a man, but it doubled her over. Hell, she may have even puked.

I picked up her weapon from where she dropped it and fired. I should have killed her, but she'd given me a break a moment ago by not killing me, so I took deadly aim and waited for her writhing and gagging to stop.

Things had quieted down, suspiciously so.

I think everyone knows about the detcord, old boy—

"Put the gun down." The damn redhead's voice came from a place other than where I saw her leave.

I did as directed, even backed away from it.

Amy stood. "Kill me, but don't ever kick me like that."

"Save the crap. Either shoot or let me go, doesn't matter because the whole place is about to blow. Want to live? We need to get the hell out of here." *Tell them you re-wired, Stan.*

Not now, Hank. They wouldn't believe me anyway.

"Because of Abdul's wiring?" The Mistress laughed, and Amy snickered too. "Walk away, sis." The redhead indicated with an upward nod what she'd said.

"I re-wired."

Amy smiled big, leaned in to me with a kiss, and whispered, "Good luck." Her eyes were deadpan as she turned and waddled a step away.

The sound of a shot echoed off the walls and Amy dropped.

I hit the floor. The redhead too, only she wiggled around like a wounded snake as she tried to find the shooter.

My head snapped around to zero-in on the sound.

In the process, I caught a glimpse of Amy. The bullet had

traveled through the upper right corner of her forehead. It was completely gone. Brains spilled everywhere.

The Mistress fired back twice then turned to me, "Get up, you bastard. Up and move!"

She jabbed her pistol into my side. "Move."

Reluctantly, I did.

Mon Dieu, *Stan, that was Doc.*

What?

He said Doc shot her. Probably aiming for you, old chap.

I turned my head like an owl, didn't really have time to chat, but thought I'd have a look.

Sally had been acting strange, and Hank always suspected her as a traitor.

The Mistress goosed me with her pistol and pushed me toward the door, interrupting my thoughts. She high-stepped me all the way out of the warehouse. Amazing what happens when there is a loaded pistol pressed against your ball-sack.

It was dark outside, well dusky; several lights had come on, streetlights, a few neon business signs, and some windows shone with the beginnings of nighttime glare. The big thing though, was the downpour. Within two or three steps, I was soaked.

She prodded inappropriately for maybe a half block, then the ground shook and a tremendous flash illuminated everything. A split second later, a huge explosion sent shards, concrete blocks, and dust that turned to airborne mud in all directions. The concussive force launched both of us about three feet into the air. I dropped flat on my face in a huge puddle.

My head hurt, and everything spun when I woke. I vaguely remembered running from something but hadn't a clue from what. All I knew now was that I wanted to get away.

Things stopped spinning. I saw the Mistress lying nearby, and clarification happened quickly. She'd captured me and—

The sound of gunshots echoed and the concrete next to me sparked even though the concrete was soaked. The Mistress moved at the sound. I rolled to my feet.

I ran before I'd even chosen a direction; besides, Sibyl was whispering to me, which irritated the hell out of me.

What do you think is happening, Stan?

Now?

It was her calmness that really pissed me off. I didn't have time to be calm and have a chat. Someone was shooting. Luckily, I had chosen a direction away from the shooter.

I'd snatched the Mistress's handgun and was out in front of her by about ten meters.

More gunshots.

I turned the corner, sprinted down a deserted street, and found an open warehouse entrance. I ducked in and hid behind the door. The place was deserted, but enough reflected glare from the burning warehouse for me to see. I gulped huge sums of air to control my breathing.

The white sound of rain destroyed any sense of direction my hearing might offer.

Seconds later, the door crashed into my shoulder, and in ran the Mistress. I let her go past, into another room, and then followed. Even though the air had smoke and crap from the demolished warehouse, I breathed without making noise, moving in the dark and flickering of the fires.

I slipped into the silent room. It was silent. No one breathing hard.

Ahn suggested she was to our right, hiding in the deepest shadows of the room. I didn't know how he could distinguish anything with all the shit floating in the air, but I trusted him and headed that way, pistol pointed ahead of me. Ahn gave me updates of her positioning as she moved around. Each time he modified it, I pointed in that direction.

Finally, I stopped. "Come out, or I'll fire." Ahn told me to track left.

"I will shoot on three. One … two … th—"

"I'm coming." A shadow stepped forward from exactly where I'd been aiming.

I moved to the side and let her move past, into the next room for more light. As she stepped into the light, she morphed from the shadow into the redhead. I told her to stop.

She turned. I maintained level aim. Although her face was hidden by shadow, I heard a chuckle in her voice, "So you think I'm the enemy?"

Everything inside of me fell so quiet, that even my tinnitus disappeared.

"Meaning?"

She openly laughed. "Who the hell do you think all those bullets were for? Me?"

The silence inside gave me more willies than her words. The length of my back had ticks square dancing on it.

Gradually she turned toward me and stepped forward, pressing the warmth of her body as it pressed into mine. "That crazy doctor is aiming at you. Mu'izz tried to tell you." I didn't hear any of my horde. Could Doc be firing at me? I backed away.

She laughed, low and sinister. "You know, I think we would fit together nicely." She reached out toward me.

From the corner of my eye, I saw a shadow leap from nowhere.

The gunshot was almost in my ear, and shit sprayed from the other side of the Mistress's head, as she plopped to the ground.

I pivoted and raised my pistol at the shadow. The gleam of a .9mm showed me where it was aimed – my heart. My pistol was aimed at the person's nose. My eyes had adjusted by now,

but I didn't need to see who it was. Doc stood half in shadows, half out.

Shoot! Stan, shoot her. She's a nutter—

Shut up, Hank.

Her weapon didn't falter. "Put your weapon up, Stan. You don't need it with me. I'm your wife."

I started to lower it, but Hank hit ballistic.

Are you crazy? She's been trying to kill you for a couple of hours now.

Let me think, Hank.

I started to lower it again.

Damn it, Stan. Think all you want but don't lower that thing. At least give me control while your brain works on this stupid shit.

I lowered it again.

Staaan.

His growl really irritated me.

Okay. I gave him control of the pistol.

Her eyes weren't friendly at all, the weapon still leveled at me. "Still won't trust me,

Stan? I've been with you since near the beginning."

"Why were you shooting at me?"

"Wasn't. I was shooting at the women."

Mate, that would mean she's a spectacular shot.

I blinked at her a couple of times. Didn't know if she was able to see them or not.

"Mu'izz made a butt load of sense."

"You mean about me betraying you?"

"Yeah, I mean that. You also never told me what you were doing."

"I saw you and Mu'izz in Israel the day you two fought. I knew one of you killed my family, so I decided to kill you both."

"But."

"Haven't. And won't. I married you. Doesn't that count?"

I was acutely aware that her weapon pointed at my heart, and I needed to shoot. But my weapon had lowered to her chest. I loved that chest. Hell, I loved her. "You shot in my direction several ti—"

Can I shoot her, Stan?

Her eyes hardened.

Stan!

The aim was perfect.

CHAPTER FORTY-SEVEN

Only the Mother provided a perfect night like this. Stars blinked randomly above, and I stood with arms raised as the cool breeze flowed around my naked body, in complete oneness with nature. The elders of the villages stood in the fields surrounding me, each as bare-skinned as I in the way of the Mother.

The ring of torches flickered behind us, giving the elders better light. Each was here to witness their Sybil officially pass from the old to the young – me.

She lay on the ground before us, her face relaxed, hair draped gracefully about, and limbs splayed into the five-point star of the Mother. The smell of burning cedar from the ritual fire filled the air. Above, the blessed moon beamed her light onto her servant, turning the green grasses around us a smoky blue. The sight of the Old One lying in the silver light gave my spirit peace.

I would remember forever what she showed me in the last moments of her life – the strings of life and how they connect all our lives. It was so vivid that the memory almost sucked me back into the dream state, but I resisted. I needed that dream state only to know more. Those dreams were the mark of the Sibyl, and that dreamy trance was how she knew the innermost secrets of the Universe, how she guided the elders.

A gust whipped through us, tossed my hair behind me and brought me back to the ritual. I thought the torches would blow out, but they didn't. The moonlight bathed me, and I tingled everywhere.

Slowly, and with much care, I allowed the dream trance to fill me, and as it did, I vibrated in harmony with life, the bliss of knowledge bubbling through me. I moved the old Sibyl's arms from the five-point star, crossed them over her chest, and moved her legs together to close her cauldron of life.

She had passed from *The Giver of Life* to *The One Who*

Cares for the Dead. She now lay in his care, resting for the next life.

The shining moonlight made me glow on the inside, and I understood even more than before. There was no *now*, no *then*, in which things happened. There is only an instant and all of us happened in that little speck. I saw my other lives, all of them, living and dying, killing and loving.

I talked with them and traveled with them, most of all I experienced all that they did.

Some things I understood, others not at all. What I didn't understand was how only one of these other lives could conceive of what I now knew – that life was never destroyed, it simply changed. Each of my lives had to be grasped in its entirety to master what was reaped by living.

Why was there only that one life in particular that figured it out? All of us continually live and yet continually lie dead. No matter what, our personalities belong to a larger spirit, and when that spirit is played, it's a plucked string beating in harmony with another – we beat in sympathy together.

They are not the same, each with a different personality, but they are always part of the whole that never changes. It matters naught whether they believe in each other.

I took a deep breath. The air smelled different and I liked it, refreshing. The odor of the sea, slightly fishy, salt in the air, and don't forget the human smells of *pommes frits* cooking from the vendor on the street. I loved this place.

My open second-floor window along the Grand Canal let in all those sights and sounds.

There was magic out there too. For such an old city, it smelled fresh and new, and I reveled in it.

I'd spent that whole day thinking, I traveled to Amsterdam, so why not go there anyway?

Money wasn't an issue.

I'd remembered my personal account was in Switzerland. It was how Sally had afforded everything she did. We were married after all.

There was one thing that bothered me about what I remembered, though.

Hank?

Yeah, mate?

What were you thinking? You didn't even shoot her. You deliberately aimed away.

Yeah. His chuckle irritated the shit out of me, but I let it go. *You loved her, mate, and I thought I'd take the chance. Nothing to lose.*

Nothing to lose? The hell we didn't! She could've killed me.

True. But I'm already dead. Like I said, nothing to lose.

God! I tried to choke him but still haven't found the way.

"Stan, what are you thinking?" Her voice floated over me.

I rolled onto my side and gazed at Sally's beautiful face. Truthfully, I did a lazy slide with my eyes, stopping at choice spots on her along the way. "Nothing. Pissed at Hank. He's an asshole." I shrugged.

Her deep, bubbly laughter was short but effective. I too smiled. God, but she was gorgeous. She rested her hand on my arm. "Yes, I agree." Her voice was so sexy. "I've thought all along that's what he was. But does it matter?"

She lay on her side, same as me, and I couldn't keep my eyes from photographing her breasts. Even on her side, they dipped only slightly toward the bed, and her nipples pointed directly at me like those mystifying masterpieces that always stare at you no matter where you are in the room. "Are you going to be Doc again? Why can't you be Sally, and let it go?"

"Because I will always be both."

The answer sent me falling in a well of thought. It was precisely what my dream had been about, or my memory, hard to tell the difference anymore. I found myself back in the night at the funeral, with flickering flames giving the only light.

"Sybil," I mumbled the name.

"What, Stan?"

"Huh?" I zipped back to my room with Sally so fast that vertigo made my head hurt. The meaning of what I'd remembered was clear, it sparked something else that had bothered me for a while now, "What does Sigma mean, Sally?"

"That's a hell of a jump."

"What does it mean?"

She sat up, wrapping the sheet around her breasts. "There are several meanings to Sigma.

It's the eighteenth letter of the Greek alphabet."

"Not that. In math." I scooted around to use her thigh as a pillow.

She tickled my chest lightly with her nails. "The uppercase Sigma is used to indicate a sum of a field in an algebraic equation. But you already know this. It's what your code name was."

"I know, but if I recollect rightly, there is also another meaning."

"The lower case sigma? Why would you need that?"

"Please."

"It refers to standard deviation, a standard measure of distance from the center line of a group."

"That's the one I want. That's what life is. My true self is really a small sigma away from the rest of us living in here."

Whatever that means. Now that we have that out of the way, old chap, can we perhaps caress those wonderfu—

Shut up, Hank.

"One other thing." I stared into her eyes, "Why were you shooting at them instead of me?"

That sweet smile again. "They were kissing you, rubbing on you."

"No, I mean, earlier you explained that you meant to kill both Mu'izz and me for the death of your boy. How did you know it was Mu'izz you needed to kill?"

"I fell in love with you."

We all pondered that, but it still had something missing. "Maybe, but the woman I now know would have finished what she started anyway. It would have hurt her tremendously, but she would have killed me."

Her face hardened in the blink of an eye. "Okay. When I leaned in close to watch him die, watch his blood dribble out of him in several places ... he called me a dog of a whore. That's what he called me before."

I sat quietly, envisioning what had happened that day.

She brightened as quickly as she had toughened, "I shot those girls because they were kissing and rubbing you. They're dead now, no more rubbing. That's my job." Mon Dieu. *Can we get to rubbing?*

Damn it, Jacques.

I gazed up at her, "You know they are all in here. I can't get them to leave no matter what we're doing."

She chuckled a deep throaty laugh and waved me to come closer. "Do they cheer for you? I mean we have to get your blood flowing correctly."

"I think it's already there." A dirty little smile spoiled my face, and my eyebrows shot up and down a couple of times as I zeroed in on her lips. They tasted light and airy; the way morning glories smell when sunlight first caresses them.

God, I love this woman

ALSO, BY -- JW Bell

The Great Zero-Sum

THE DAU
THE SIGMA CODE CRONICLES
BOOK TWO
J W Bell

Chapter One

Colonel Noh San-jun tapped his swagger stick on his left hand as he strode down the trail of The Residence. He'd just gotten off the phone with his long-time friend Kim Jong-un, the Chairman of the Workers' Party and Supreme Leader, and headed to the tunnel works to visit the prisoner.

His eyes took an inventory of weapons caches that Kim and he had insisted upon as he marched. Good. Done, all of them. He grunted approval to himself. He reminded himself to try out the digital locks on them. The combinations were all set to Kim's birthday. They were easy to remember that way.

He approached a line of soldiers, and they snapped-to, presenting arms. He held his stick up to return the salute and gave a curt nod. Chosen for their girth, his two aides marched behind him in match step. They looked like trim Sumo wrestlers and were much stronger than he, the two were impressive. Noh chose them for their prowess, appreciated their obedience, but loved their sadism.

The building before him disappeared into the nearby hill. One aide broke formation, double-timed to the heavy door, and pulled on it. The door creaked. Colonel Noh acknowledged nothing and no one as he'd strutted through. A minute later, the big door boomed shut behind him.

The three marched down dingy hallways so bare they

appeared just as they were, concrete tunnels. Clear incandescent bulbs hung from lone wires and illuminated the way just enough to display what a crude dung-heap the prison was.

There were access doors to the central tunnel system that connected most buildings on The Residence; it was an underground passage for defense. Noh had just passed one such entry.

Its appearance was similar to a deep cell, the door of iron crosshatched bars.

The sound of their footsteps clacked on the concrete and reverberated through the tunnel. Noh's nose wrinkled from the smell of rot issuing from a cell as he walked by, and the itch of mildew in the air gave him the urge to rub on his nose. He stopped mid-reach and continued onwards. There were more important things to think of than relieving an itch.

He halted before a door indistinguishable from any other in the building – laced with bars of rusty iron. His hands caressed the stick behind his back, and he stared through the metal crosshatching at Hahn. The aides remained a couple of meters behind him and stood at attention.

Hahn Kang-min's mind was still slow from waking in his cell if he could call it waking. The rest he should have gotten during the night had never come, only fitful dread. His arms continued to tremble the way they had when he'd crawled onto his mat to sleep.

The involuntary shaking wasn't from the cold, although the air was crisp. It was warm for early spring.

They will know soon. The thought woke Hahn often during the night and had been the reason for his restlessness.

The investigators are merciless.

Disgusted, he spat close to the hole in the floor designed for his bodily wastes. They won't stop until they find evidence, some sort of discrepancies. Once they begin, they find, always. No matter what you did, they knew.

He grimaced with an internal shrug. Even if they find it, they won't know what it is, or how they should use the information. He almost laughed and would have except for the welling feeling of eumyang approaching, the changing of fortune. There was never an escape from that.

The universe flowed like the tones of harmony, each moment relating to every other like the twists of a melody, and the overtone vibrations that resounded through everything must, and will, eventually balance.

He'd been here a week, maybe two, and his feet had been numb since the first night. They would be useless soon, even if they let him out. The first meal had been pathetic, stale rice, no Kimchi. All the food was bland and close to rancid. He hadn't eaten this poorly since he'd gone to science school. The difference was that here the fare never improved.

This prison cared nothing about vermin – neither that the creatures ate part of every meal, nor that they left feces in it. By now, and because of the vermin, parasites infested Hahn, and if the investigators didn't kill him, the little beasts within him would.

The only thing left for him now was to make sure he protected his family.

Both the clang of the main door echoed down the hallway, and the hobnail boots stomping alerted him. Someone came. His trembling increased.

The approaching sounds grew, and his eyes automatically flicked about his small cell, an unconscious attempt at searching for a place to hide. He'd done it countless times since being locked up. Always the same results too.

There's not even a blanket for cover. Why would I find something to hide behind now?

He knelt on the cold concrete, closed his eyes for another few seconds, and willed some kind of plan into existence.

The universe flows with harmony—

The steps echoed louder. His eyes shot to the openings between the iron bars. Boots appeared first. Then there was Colonel Noh, glaring. Noh's appearance screamed the Supreme Leader's involvement. This situation is a disaster.

In an instant, a second thought formed. Should I have the missile fly as designed? Was hindsight in this sharp and clear?

His bowels almost let loose. He concentrated hard and held them but not the urine. It soaked his pants as he reminded himself of how unimportant he was.

Hahn's eyes would not move from the terror before him. He tried blinking rapid-fire to push his brain into high speed, and his teeth teased his upper lip. But no new plan developed.

Stick to it, Kang-min. The plan. The family depends on the plan.

Noh snorted. "You are so stupid, Hahn."

Simply Hahn? Not even basic politeness — Mister Hahn? Nothing. Hahn felt as if someone stood on his chest. His head spun, and he struggled to pull enough air in to steady it.

"Did you think our intelligence wouldn't know?"

The twang in Noh's voice hurt Hahn's ears, and for the first time, he thought he detected a hint of a Chinese accent. He perked his ears.

The loathing filled Noh's eyes. "You would do this to our glorious missile program?"

He stuck his swagger stick through one of the openings between bars and ran the leather cap of it around the square opening. "You risked everything, your country, yourself, your family.

There are only two things you can save now – one will be the country."

My family! Save the family. Hahn started a mantra – my family, my wife, the twins. My family, my wife, the twins ...

"You will tell us what you did. You will also tell me how to undo those things."

Mustn't talk yet. My family, my wife, the twins ...

5

"I did nothing, Colonel." Hahn bowed correctly to Noh, but as he did, his rectum opened.

He blinked several times, swallowed, and tightened his ass as hard as he could.

The chuckle bounced off the cell walls. "Shit yourself, did you? You fucking moron."

Noh pulled the keys from his pocket, shook them, and jingled them against the bars.

Noh's brows touched above his nose, and he motioned with his head. It was not a nod and carried no respect. Instead, it was a direction for his aides.

The two soldiers took up positions behind him, mirror images of propaganda posters, mean as hell. They could smile after eating horse shit, maybe even the food here. No, he shook his head, and his mouth formed a crooked smile — horse shit, perhaps pig puke, not this food.

"You are laughing now, Hahn?" Noh unlocked the door and stepped back as it screeched open.

The two soldiers stared at Hahn as if he was a chicken; they were to twist the head from its neck.

Their boots sounded like one as they stepped forward.

Defiance formed on Hahn's face, but his eyes betrayed him, and more feces dribbled.

The two dragged him past Noh and down the tunnel, letting his bare feet scrape the concrete.

After only a meter away from his cage, Hahn's mouth watered after smelling kimchi the fermented cabbage, his captors had dined on last evening. The soldier grabbing his left arm chuckled and nodded at Hahn, "So terrified, smells like shit." The other laughed.

My family, my wife, the twins ...

At the big entrance, they paused. "Open by order of the Supreme Leader." The right one kicked a resounding frontal kick. The sound of it boomed like a dull gong in Hahn's ears.

"Open!"

Seconds later, the door creaked, and the dreary sunlight filled the air, too bright for Hahn.

They dragged him down the road to the target range. All of his senses peaked.

Hahn's nose smelled everything – the almost frozen ground, hickory smoke from a fire not far away, even boiling ramen that a nearby soldier stirred for breakfast; the garlic and cabbage in it filled his nose. The tree leaves were only budding, but he detected their nutty aroma, heard the scrape of leaves against each other.

Noh pointed at a large wooden frame erected before a massive earthen berm that showed craters and rocks half blown apart. "Place the traitor there." He turned, pulled on gloves, and placed both his hands and the swagger stick behind himself. Once positioned, he leaned fore and then back.

My family, my wife, the twins ... He labored for breath. My family, my wife, the twins ...

A cloud of steam came from Hahn's mouth with each struggle of breath, and he couldn't stop trembling and shivering.

Shackled at both wrists and ankles, they spread him like a bat in flight. The cold metal bit into his skin, and if the temperature dropped a few more degrees, the things would freeze to him.

He watched Noh stand before him – the winter cap perched on his head, the baton held by gloved hands, and wearing the quilted jacked all bespoke winter. Noh turned to face him, his eyes aglare, but entertainment also showed.

My family, my wife, the twins ... My family, my wife, the twins ...

The guards marched closer to Noh, who stood by a bench. With cruel insight, Hahn knew the seat was a weapons drawer of the kind that dotted The Residence.

Hahn's heart almost pounded a hole through his chest. This time his bowels emptied all together. A gun range. This place is a gun range! All the rumors flooded through his memory — the stories of executions.

My family, my wife, the twins ... The mantra came back stronger, faster. My family, my wife, the twins ...

With a swagger, Noh closed the distance to him. "Hahn. Do you see that small building there, on the side of the little mountain?"

Hahn blinked in the direction Noh pointed. The shack wasn't hard to see, although it was a great distance away. It had no vegetation around it; the land was bare. Everything had died. "I will take your family to that building."

"My family?" My wife, the twins ...

The deadly set to Noh's eyes branded the inside of Hahn and feeling that burning chilled him even more.

"What did you do?"

"I–"

"That shack over there is our chemical building, where we test weapons. Tell me what you did, or your family goes in. The current test is anthrax, a new strain that produces symptoms in minutes yet makes death agonizing."

"No! I will tell–"

"Yes, you will." Noh waved towards the small mountain, and Hahn could see movement around the building. "That is your wife and children. As my guest, they will watch your execution, or they will test anthrax next."

The two aides pulled a camouflage net down, unveiling an enormous anti-aircraft gun.

They tilted the aircraft killer skyward and fired three times.

The sound pounded his ears, his chest felt the shockwave of it, and he shat himself again.

ABOUT THE AUTHOR

J.W. Bell's life reads like an adventure story. He was a Field Artillery Officer in the Army for ten years, is well-versed in long-range and large-caliber weapons, and is an expert with small arms — handguns, rifles, machine guns. Oh yes, he trained in explosives and is excellent with hand grenades. His military thrillers use actual terminology and weaponry. The military courtesy and discipline portrayed is accurate. He traveled extensively throughout Europe, Asia, and the U.S., living in Hawaii for several years. He coached gymnastics for a time and worked for years as a roughneck in the oilfields of Oklahoma. He became a teacher and still holds a lifetime teaching license to teach music and drama. He composed his first symphony and now has a good start on his second. Currently, he lives in Arkansas on a small acreage with ten of his twleve children, five boys ages six to eighteen and five girls ages six years to sixteen. He has two older daughters who live in Little Rock with their own families. The family of twelve has four dogs and cats, two horses, one pony, and two pet pigs on the acreage. Additionally, there are four cows and one sheep in an attempt to become self-sufficient. In keeping with that theme, the last inhabitants of the property are the goats; they are prolific, so it is hard to give solid numbers for them, somewhere over ten and not quite fifty.

There is always something happening around the house, as the children are home-schooled, everyone has chores, and J.W. carves out time to write.

J.W. BELL

ABOUT THE PUBLISHER
Indies United Publishing House

Indies United is a co-op of like-minded authors, working together to showcase our books and our diversity as writers that embrace over a dozen different genres. We openly encourage and support both new and established authors in their pursuit of finding their audience while bringing to you books worth reading.

To find out more about Indies United, please visit our website at *www.indiesunited.net